SUSPENDED IN DUSK II

CURATED AND EDITED BY

SIMON DEWAR

SUSPENDED IN DUSK: VOLUME TWO
ISBN-13: 978-1-940658-97-1
ISBN-10: 1-940658-97-7
Grey Matter Press First Electronic Edition - July 2018

Anthology Copyright © 2018 Simon Dewar
Volume Copyright © 2018 Grey Matter Press
Design Copyright © 2018 Grey Matter Press
Cover Artwork © 2018 Dean Samed
Assistant Editor, Anthony Rivera

GREY MATTER
P R E S S

CHICAGO

Grey Matter Press
greymatterpress.com

Grey Matter Press on Facebook
facebook.com/greymatterpress

IN MEMORY OF DALLAS MAYR:
MASTER STORYTELLER, TEACHER, ICON, FRIEND

TABLE OF CONTENTS

EDITOR'S FOREWORD
SIMON DEWAR

I'M HAPPY AND HUMBLED AGAIN to be providing a new collection of stories to readers, in part two of the Suspended in Dusk anthology series, this time released by Grey Matter Press (GMP).

A very thoughtful interviewer recently asked me what about the time of dusk appealed to me to choose it as a theme for the anthologies. My response was this:

Life is change, and change is either for better or worse. Change, one way or the other, is taking you into the light or the dark. This time of dusk—the time *between* times—is the time between the light and the dark. This grey area that we all find ourselves in from time to time is the fulcrum, the tipping point. This tipping point is the penultimate moment of change—where things either come good, or go badly, badly wrong. This is a fantastic place for great stories to be found, written and collected, I think.

Suspended in Dusk 2 is the product of a mix of men and women, of new and established writers, of people whose first language is not English, people who speak multiple languages, people of colour, people from at least four continents, people of different sexual persuasions, people who are of a religion, people who are of no religion. I'd say it's impossible to achieve a perfect mix, but having said that, this book ain't just the usual who's who either. There's diversity in this book and it adds to the flavour and the depth of work within these pages. I'm incredibly proud and honoured to be bringing these authors together and sharing their stories with you.

Some brief acknowledgments: Many, many thanks to Anthony Rivera and GMP for taking a chance on this book when it was between publishers and looking for a new home. Thanks to Angela Slatter for her lovely introduction and wisdom, and to the authors for putting up with the rollercoaster ride. Thanks to my family who put up with my creative obsessions.

Lastly, dear reader, thank *you* for picking up this book. I hope you enjoy reading *Suspended in Dusk 2* as much as I enjoyed collecting and editing it.

Simon Dewar
Canberra, Australia
11 December 2017

INTRODUCTION
Angela Slatter

MANY YEARS AGO at the Brisbane Writers Festival I sat in on a panel which featured John Ajvide Lindqvist, author of the superb modern vampire novel, *Let the Right One In*. He made an observation that has stuck with me ever since: humans are the only creatures on the planet who go out of their way to scare themselves. You don't see other creatures swimming close to sharks—apex predators that will eat them—just for a frisson of fear.

I hadn't ever thought about it in such a fashion, but he was absolutely right. We do go out of our way to scare ourselves. We drive too fast. We stand too close to the edges of cliffs. We ride rollercoasters. We squeal our way through haunted houses at shows and fairs. We hang out in cemeteries after dark to see if anything might appear. We watch movies that run the gamut from psychological terrors like *The Others* or *The Awakening* to slasher flicks like *Halloween*, *Friday the 13th* and, the-even-more-terrifying-because-it's-almost-real, *Wolf Creek*. We read books by Caitlín R. Kiernan, Stephen King, Clive Barker, Kathe Koja, and Shirley Jackson that have us hiding under our covers.

In our reading, many of us actively pursue the rush of adrenaline, the thudding heartbeat that shakes the rest of our body, the shortness of breath that feels like an oncoming heart attack and the certainty (for however brief a time) that we are prey. Whether we continue with it or not, almost everyone's story-time experiences start with horror. What else are fairy and folk tales but our first horror stories? Two appalling cases of boogie fever: a queen forced to dance in red-hot iron shoes and a little girl whose feet must ultimately be amputated because the red shoes just won't let her stop dancing. A woman who'll throw her own sister over the sea brim to drown in an effort to win the princely husband competition

= worst sibling rivalry ever. Mothers who happily desert their children in forests, and fathers who decide that marrying their own daughters is the Best Idea. Sure, the forest contains dangers but the true horror lies not in being eaten by wolves and/or bears—while it's not the optimal outcome, at least they're following their natural instincts—but in the things other humans do to us. We hear these stories when we're very small and, even if we turn away from them sooner rather than later, their messages about death and fear and dreadful things have already been embedded in our child's heart and mind. They lie there waiting, lurking and, I suspect, stealing one sock of every pair.

Horror is a genre named specifically for the effect it's meant to have: to make us feel dread, terror, and not a little bit of awe at the spectacle of our inevitable mortality. We all know we're going to die…we just don't really think it will happen to us, or at least not quite yet. It's a far off place. It's the October Country. One of my grandfathers was fond of saying he didn't mind dying, he didn't want to be there when it happened. He wasn't a horror fan, preferred Westerns in fact, but I still carry those words around with me. With horror maybe we get to have a preview, a try-be-fore-you-buy kind of thing without the commitment to actual death. Just maybe coming close to the edge reminds us we're alive.

Horror pushes the button on our fight-or-flight mechanism. We seek it out to add a bit of spice to the day, read or watch it for pretend scares, manageable fear in bite-sized chunks. We tell ourselves that it can be put away when we close the book, turn off the television, leave the cinema. We kid ourselves that we're safe in our boring lives, we tell ourselves that we're in charge. We can quit any time we want. That when the pages are closed the monsters, be they supernatural or fiends in human suits, can't climb out again…but remember what I said about fairy and folk tales and their messages stuck deep in our subconscious?

Yeah. Still there. You can't wash them away.

The night may well be dark and full of terrors as Melisandre says, but bad things happen in the daylight too. Serial killers appear to be the world's largest growth industry. When we step outside we're in danger; when we're at home that often doesn't change, whether we lock the doors or not. And we still don't know what keeps going bump in the night.

Horror literature is, to me at least, the history of sharing nightmares. Just as misery loves company, so too does fear. Past masters such as M.R. James, Bram Stoker, Joseph Sheridan Le Fanu, Barbara Baynton, Arthur Machen, Mary Shelley, Edgar Allen Poe, all knew that a terror shared was a terror doubled…and tripled…and quadrupled. They also knew they didn't need to outrun their monsters, they needed to pass them on to you. In this grand tradition of sharing and scaring, we've seen some incredible horror anthology series over the years, from the classics to the new kids on the block: Stephen Jones' Mammoth Books of New Horror, Robert Aickman's Fontana Books of Great Ghost Stories, Mark Morris' Spectral Book of Horror Stories, and now Suspended in Dusk looks set to continue in this vein.

In this collection you'll find work to make you shiver and shudder, quake and quail. You'll partake of the terrors that Stephen Graham Jones, Damien Angelica Walters, Alan Baxter, Sarah Read, Nerine Dorman, J.C. Michael, Benjamin Knox, Paul Tremblay, Ramsey Campbell, Letitia Trent, Paul Michael Anderson, Gwendolyn Kiste, Bracken Macleod, Dan Rabarts, Annie Neugebauer, and Karen Runge all have in store for you. But you won't put the book down, or not for long anyway.

Reading on the couch, you'll wrap yourself tightly in a blanket because that's the kind of protection which is second only to ensuring that all your limbs are not hanging over the edge of the mattress at night. Periodically, you'll get up and check the locks on the doors and windows. You'll keep reading and you'll tell yourself that you're safe. That your loved ones are safe. That no one will burst through that carefully locked door or, worse still, sneak in through the tightly latched windows as you sleep. That you're just enjoying an *amuse-bouche* of death and destruction, nothing serious, nothing permanent. That you're neither hunted nor haunted, that it's all in your imagination, that it's just a book. That you're in control.

Tell yourself that enough times and maybe you'll believe it.

Maybe.

Angela Slatter
Brisbane, Australia
04 October 2017

ABOUT ANGELA SLATTER

ANGELA SLATTER is the author of the urban fantasy novels *Vigil* (2016) and *Corpselight* (2017), as well as eight short story collections, including *The Girl with No Hands and Other Tales*, *Sourdough and Other Stories*, *The Bitterwood Bible and Other Recountings*, and *A Feast of Sorrows: Stories*. The third novel in the Verity Fassbinder series, *Restoration*, will be released in 2018 by Jo Fletcher Books (Hachette International).

She has won a World Fantasy Award, a British Fantasy Award, a Ditmar, and six Aurealis Awards.

Angela's short stories have appeared in Australian, UK and US Best Of anthologies such *The Mammoth Book of New Horror*, *The Year's Best Dark Fantasy and Horror*, *The Best Horror of the Year*, *The Year's Best Australian Fantasy and Horror*, and *The Year's Best YA Speculative Fiction*. Her work has been translated into Bulgarian, Russian, Spanish, Japanese, Polish, and Romanian. Victoria Madden of Sweet Potato Films (*The Kettering Incident*) has optioned the film rights to one of her short stories.

She has an MA and a PhD in Creative Writing, is a graduate of Clarion South 2009 and the Tin House Summer Writers Workshop 2006, and in 2013 she was awarded one of the inaugural Queensland Writers Fellowships. In 2016 Angela was the Established Writer-in-Residence at the Katharine Susannah Prichard Writers Centre in Perth.

Her novellas, *Of Sorrow and Such* (from Tor.com), and *Ripper* (in the Stephen Jones anthology *Horrorology*, from Jo Fletcher Books) were released in October 2015.

Contact her at www.angelaslatter.com

ANGELINE

Karen Runge

I'T'S NOT LIKE HE WAS MY REAL FATHER OR ANYTHING. Still, I sometimes think my final memory of him is the only thing I really see clear. It returns to me, stinging-bright, electric, every time a man pulls me into his arms. He can smell of days-old sweat infused with booze, or the musky-male tones of aftershave, the fresh bite of toothpaste. He can smell like motor oil and greasy hair, garlic and cheese, leather and suede. It doesn't matter. He'll pull me close at the waist, I'll wrap my arms around his neck, and the moment I close my eyes, there I'll be. Four years old again, folded tight in my father's arms as he carries me down the street. I see the late afternoon sun washing gold down on us. I feel the lurch of his steps, his heart beating against mine. The sweat on his palms, bleeding heat into the thin fabric of my dress. I feel him trembling. I tighten my grip. I hold my breath. Sometimes when this memory hits, I don't quite catch myself in time and I say the word out loud: *Daddy*. Whispered in a stranger's ear. And some men like that. But most don't.

I don't know that I have any other memories of him. Sometimes I think I do, but they're sketchy, stiff. Like something printed on cardboard, bent and battered, the edges feathered. They're a little too bright too, like an image of heaven—something I've imagined instead of actually seen. I know he was very tall, and very thin. He smoked unfiltered Marlboros, and to this day I love the smell of cigarette smoke in a man's clothes and hair, the yellow stains between his fingers, nutty-sweet against my tongue. I know he used to tuck me in, and maybe he told me stories, or sang me songs. I'm not sure. Maybe not. I know he used to take me to the swing park down the block, that spare catch of yellow grass and red dust strewn with trash. I remember it because I remember swinging. And I think it was him, because the hand that pushed me was strong and firm, and not small and thin like my mother's. I remember laughing. Weightless, dizzy, high above the ground. Maybe I remember that, most of all.

It's not like he was my real father or anything. Still, when I look back on my childhood, all I see is him, and me. His arms around me, and mine around him. My breath caught in my throat as he carries me down the street.

***

The motel where I lived and worked was called Sunny Blue, and my room was on the second floor. It had a bed and a television set, a small bathroom attached. There was a bookshelf by the bed where I kept my kettle, an iron, a hair dryer. A battered hardcover copy of *Senseless*, stolen from the library (though not by me), which I read over and over again. When I first took the room there used to be an armchair by the bed too, but it smelled so bad I threw it out. A stink in the upholstery like fried fish and spoiled blood that gave me strange dreams. There was a parking lot out front of the motel (mostly empty), and a swimming pool behind (always green). It wasn't a bad motel; it was good enough for families passing through to stay the night with their kids. It wasn't a great motel either though, because I was there of course. I wasn't the only long-stay resident, but I was the only one with this kind of living. I paid for the room in cash every week, and Saul took it without question. He was a big guy, balding, who didn't talk a lot. His eyes were the colour of weak coffee, he had a scar across his chin, and I sometimes thought he sort of liked me. He called me Angie-Lee, which was wrong, but I didn't correct him. Keeping Saul on my side was important to me. I used to fantasise about things going wrong, and Saul being the one who came to the rescue. Breaking the door down, bellowing, a look in his eyes like outrage broken on hurt. Gathering me up, safe in his arms. Holding me.

I had a regular roster of twelve clients. Five were married, six were over fifty, and one of them was barely eighteen. I loved all the men who came to see me. Their frailty, their fragility. I loved them for their need, and the ways they tried to hide it. Little boys masquerading—hard-mouthed smiles, vulnerable eyes. They needed me as much as I needed them. But of the twelve, there were four I held onto tightest. They were precious to me beyond the cash value they ascribed me. Precious to me in all the ways that cut a little deeper, count a little dearer. Precious because, each in their own way, they reminded me of my father.

***

Baxter came on Tuesdays, mostly. Of my four lovers, he was the one I'd been seeing the longest. Three years to the end, I think. He was dying. He never told me this in so many words, but it was clear just by looking at him. When I first met him he was tall and thin, with that stooped-scarecrow look that reminds me so much of my father. Bony shoulders, slit smile. But his stooped-scarecrow frame devolved to a brittle skeleton wrapped in loose skin. Waxy texture, clammy sweat. When he sneezed or coughed, he left blood spots on the tissues. A fine mist, more pink than red, churned from the depths of his lungs. Expelling a little more of his essence every time. His eyes sank deeper into his skull over the final year, and mostly when he came to see me then he didn't have the energy to really do anything. We lay down together on the bed, his arms around my waist, my arms around his neck. I nestled against him and breathed in the smells of tainted sweat and slow sickness. He kissed my forehead with his thin, paper-dry lips. In those moments, I loved him more than any of the others. He sensed that, I think. He breathed a little faster, held me a little tighter. I would turn him over to rub his shoulders. I kissed the sunken flesh that slipped around his spine and ribs in finely wrinkled folds. And I closed my teeth on the word: *Daddy*.

He usually stayed an hour, sometimes two. Before he left, I made him peppermint tea. I sat cross-legged on the bed and watched him sip it. The delicate, clean aroma of the tea trickled up the walls and along the floor. It highlighted, instead of hid, the dirty chemical taint that flowed off of him. The smell of his disease.

In the final weeks, every time before he left I'd catch myself wondering if I'd ever see him again. I kept the tears behind my eyes as I helped him dress, helped him stand, took his money. I walked him out the door and along the open corridor to the stairs. His steps were slow. My eyes stung.

Saul watched us from the front office as we passed. More than once he stopped me on my way back up.

"Christ, Angie-Lee, what the hell could you possibly be doing with that creature?" he said.

"I don't kiss and tell, Saul," I said and smiled. Words like this come out my mouth sometimes, in moods and tones not really my own. And Saul stared at me, thinking, biting back the questions he knew I wouldn't answer anyway.

Back in my room, I cried for the dying, and for the dead. I buried my face in the pillow he'd just lain on. I wrapped myself in the sheets still spiced with his scent. The smells of death, and not of lust. I tried to recall an image of my father. But in moments like that, I can't see him anymore.

***

Usually after one of Baxter's visits, I'd dry my eyes and head back out. Flip-flops on my feet, my hand full of coins. I'd slap down the stairs, wave to Saul, and cross the parking lot out to the street. There's a payphone there. Box-shaped, battered door, the damp stench of old urine and rusted metal trapped inside.

I dropped the coins into the slot. I dialled. I listened to the electronic buzz of the phone, ringing on the other side. *Here-here. Here-here. Here—*

When she picked up, she always knew it was me. I don't know how, an intuition, a sense, whatever still existed between us. She waited for me to speak.

"Hi, Mom."

"Angeline." Sometimes she said my name with happiness, bright and high, and I'd know she'd been drinking. Sometimes she said it with dread, low and slow. Or anger, fast and biting. I didn't care. It's rare to hear someone say my real name. Say my name right. Maybe she knew that, too.

"Why did you always tell me daddy was sick?"

She sighed.

"He wasn't really sick though, was he? Not really. Was he?" And usually, when I asked this question too many times, she'd hang up.

***

Hank drove an old caramel-coloured Bentley. He wouldn't change the paint job because he said that particular shade helped to hide the rust. The thing's engine was train-wreck loud, blasting black exhaust fumes behind it. It gave me good warning when he was pulling into the parking lot. He wore a black leather jacket like my father did, and he smoked menthol cigarettes with the filters snapped off. Mint and tar swirling in his mouth, tainting his saliva, spread across my skin.

Of all the men I loved, Hank was the one I most hated. Hours before he came round, I'd already be dreading it. Dreading him. When he arrived, he'd layer a section of the floor with paper towels. I went down on my knees, and he handed me a litre bottle of iced tea— peach or lemon, store-bought. He made me chug it empty in front of him. Then he crouched down, eye to eye with me. He cupped my jaw with the gentlest touch. He licked my lips, the tip of his tongue just touching my teeth. Then he rammed his fingers down my throat until I brought the tea back up. Bile and sugary water pooled at his feet, splattered over his hand, his shoes. He couldn't get excited any way else. He said it was something about watching the spasm, the expulsion. The relief in my face when it was over. Sometimes I think I almost understood. I wouldn't have allowed this from anyone else, except he always did the cleaning up, and he always said he was sorry.

"Sorry, Angel." Slow and sweet, like he meant it. He put his fingers in my mouth again, gentler, so that I could taste the cigarettes he'd smoked.

And with my mouth thick with his touch, his taste, I couldn't say the word I most wanted to say.

Daddy.

***

On slow days, lazy days, usually Mondays, I went down to the office and talked to Saul. I sat beside him, his feet up on the desk, my legs crossed underneath, and we passed a bottle of bourbon back and forth. Sometimes we did this without talking—I kept my eyes fixed out the wide front windows when I felt his glance jumping to and away from me. I tried not to flinch at that furtive touch. Saul never touched me. Not once in his life. And he looked and talked nothing like my father did. But he was a father. And I'm a daughter. And that's all I need.

When his eyelids puffed up like tiny soft pillows and his tongue moved a little slower in his mouth, I knew it was safe to ask him about her. His daughter. The one he lost.

"She had curly dark hair, something like yours, only yours is a little straighter."

My hair is ash blonde and pencil-straight, but I never reminded him of this.

"Her name was Amy. She liked to ride her bike up and down the street. She had a boy's laugh, bony knees. I took her on a flight with me once and she decided then and there that she wanted to be an air hostess. She thought the ladies were so pretty." He smiled at this, fading away from me, lost in a memory I couldn't touch.

"What did she used to call you?" I asked. I asked this every time.

"Pop."

"Not Daddy?"

"No," he sighed. "Not *Daddy*."

And he'd hand the bottle back to me then, because he had a way of understanding things, I think.

***

Glen wasn't a father. I think it's something he craved. To have a little girl to treasure, to dote on, to dress. He bought all the clothes he wanted me to wear. The dresses were baby pink, lilac-blue, sunshine yellow. They had lace and frills and cap sleeves. They drew my figure ironing-board straight, and pressed my breasts flat. The skirts flounced at the hips; they fell to just above the knee. The panties were hideous, like something a Victorian child might wear. Loose elastic, boxer-shaped, lace trim. He didn't like me to wear make-up, only lip gloss, palest pink. He called me *honey*, he called me *darling*. He combed my hair, he sang me songs. He gave me lollipops to suck, and watched me with delight. Then he sat me on his lap and bounced me up and down with his arms closed around my waist. This was the part I loved him for: the part that made me feel like a child, treasured, safe in her father's arms. And when I called him *Daddy*, he didn't mind at all. Later he would switch from gentle to rough with a suddenness that stunned me. He left bruises on my wrists and the taste of metal on my tongue. But I treasured every mark.

There was something a little tortured in him, I think. A look in his eyes like a million battles broken on self-restraint. The world against him; him against him. Rage and inner torment, just barely suppressed. This was why I loved him, for that look alone. I saw it in my father's face, too. On that day, that final day, when he bent to pick me up. When he carried me down the street away from home, my mother calling out behind us. The only moment I really remember of him.

***

My mother lived in a small brownstone house in the suburbs, and she didn't know what I did. Probably she had her suspicions, but she never asked. My visits to her were sporadic, painful, and bitter. Sometimes I saw her as little as just twice a year. She made me dinner while I sat in her kitchen, tapping my bare feet on the exquisitely clean linoleum. Crossing and uncrossing my legs. Wrapping my hair around my wrist.

"Why can't you ever sit *still*?" she said. She said this every time. And she'd look me in the eyes, and I'd see a fleeting touch of rage in her face. Behind that: agony, pure and biting.

I know she dreaded my visits probably as much as I dreaded making them. What she didn't know was how much I hated her. The closest I ever came to confessing this was when she asked me to bring dessert, and I arrived with a raspberry tart neatly wrapped in cellophane. Ginger crust, dusted white with icing sugar. I felt something like pride when I bought it. I tried to imagine what she might do with my gift. Throw it against a wall? Stomp on it? Weep over it? She certainly wouldn't have eaten it.

She took it in silence. She set it down on the sideboard. She didn't look at it again. For dessert she cut up two peaches and drizzled them with cream and honey. I ate mine with gusto, staring at the tart the whole while.

"You're not funny, Angeline," she said right before I left. The closest I got to an acknowledgement. She didn't hug me. She hasn't held me close to her once since I was a little girl.

"I'm not trying to be," I said, and turned away.

It was days before I felt bad.

***

The third man I loved was newest to me, and I fell for him the fastest. I fell for him almost on sight. His name was Brian, which had been my father's name, I think. He smoked Marlboros and wore a leather jacket. His jacket was brown, not black, and his cigarettes were filtered. But I forgave him for that. He was scarecrow-thin, and very tall. He had a look in his eyes like sadness swirled through fury, and it's a look that scared me. But there was helplessness there too. A vulnerability that melted me. *These are my father's eyes*, I thought when I looked at him. But I didn't say that word, at first.

Daddy.

I didn't meet him the regular way. I was walking back from the late-night convenience store, dressed in shorts and flip-flops, a loose T-shirt. My hair was twisted up off my neck, and the plastic bag filled with my purchases brushed against my leg. Rustling at each step. The streets were semi-lit, the air was warm. I was thinking about untying my hair, of feeling its weight down my back. I'd bought a roll of paper towels, a bag of cheese-flavoured popcorn, a bar of soap. I'd gone there for the soap really, and milk—but the popcorn caught me, so I'd forgotten this last item. It was just as I remembered this—*the milk!*—when his car slowed alongside me.

"Need a lift?"

I turned, saw a blue Ford, a haggard driver looking at me from an open window. The streetlights were too far away to catch his eyes. "No," I smiled. "Thanks."

"What's your name?"

"Angeline."

He sped the car up ahead of me, pulled up against the curb. By the time I reached him he'd cut the engine and opened the door. He sat half-way out in faded denim jeans, one hand held out to me. "Can I carry that bag for you?"

Carry. And when I looked at him again, I saw him anew.

I stopped in front of him. "That's where I live," I said, pointing with my free hand to the sign that blinked SUNNY BLUE MOTEL.

His smile widened. Yellow teeth, soft eyes. Shining pale grey under the lights. "Angeline. Let me carry that bag up for you."

And I knew he knew me, really knew me. Because aside from all the other things I recognised in that clear gaze, he'd also said my true name.

I let him take the bag.

That first night, he held me tighter than I'd ever been held. The power of him, overwhelming me. For days after, my ribs were tender, my lower lip stung, the insides of my thighs were dappled with bruises.

"I'm an old man," he told me in the calm clasp that always follows. "I'm older than you think, and I'm dying. There are so many things I've wanted to do, but never quite dared. I'm a coward, a dying coward, and I'm running out of time. Every sunset, to me, is a melting clock. Ticking me down." He said this as he stroked my hair. Soft fingers, a father's touch.

Love, I knew. *This is love.* And I didn't ask him to pay, but he left some money on the bedside table for me anyway. Crisp bills, neatly clipped together. More than I would've asked for. Along with it, a note:

SWEET DREAMS, ANGELINE.

The very words I think my father would have used.

***

Sitting in the office with Saul the next day, he asked me, "Who was that new guy I saw you go by with last night?"

"His name's Brian. He's a wonderful man."

Saul's gaze touched me, then left. To and away. "Where's your mother, Angie-Lee?"

"I don't have one."

"Your father?"

"He left. He tried to take me with him, but my mother wouldn't let him. I wish he had."

And we sat in silence for a few minutes. Then he passed the bottle back to me.

***

The next time Brian came to me, he surprised me with flowers. Lilies, big ones with waxy, white-coiled petals and long, lime-green stems. After we were done, I surprised him with a slice of raspberry tart I'd bought that morning. Ginger crust, dusted with icing sugar.

I sat cross-legged on the bed and watched him eat.

"One of my favourites," he said, spooning it up. "How did you know?"

"I've known you always," I said. "My mother used to make this for my father. For… *Daddy*. She made it every Sunday. She was making it on the day he left." And I smiled, even though it reopened the new cut on the inside of my lower lip, and I had to lick back blood.

His own mouth red with berries, he looked back at me and smiled.

***

I don't know why, but I called my mother after that. My second call in less than a week, unusual for me. Still, she knew it was me calling and not someone else.

"Angeline." Her voice was tired, heavy, drained. Groggy and only half-conscious. I'm not sure if that was because she'd been drinking, or if it was because it was past two in the morning and she'd probably been asleep.

"Mom, can you teach me to make raspberry tart next time I come?"

"Please stop." And her voice was brittle, sharp. Scrap-metal rusted by rain and sun. "You know the thought of that turns my stomach. Your stepfather—"

"He loved me."

"Did he, Angeline? More than me? Sometimes I think you don't remember him right."

"I remember him just fine," I lied. And for a reason even I don't understand, I laughed.

"Don't be perverse, my girl," she said.

And I hung up.

***

The next time I met Brian, he was sicker than before. Pale, trembling, with bags under his eyes. This poor man. This poor, beautiful, broken man. But there was something stronger about him, too: a light in his eyes like dazzle, like vulnerability broken on love. A special kind of excitement that lit me right up.

"Hi, Daddy!" I said when I opened the door to him. He was wearing his leather jacket. There was a cigarette behind his ear.

"Hi, Angeline."

Thrilling me with the sound of my name. My true name, and not some fantasy version. Not some proof of me being misunderstood. And I knew that with Brian, I wouldn't have to wear any frilly dresses. And if he put his fingers in my mouth, it would be out of love, and not to force anything out of me.

He stepped inside, stepped past me. Even as I turned my back to him to close the door, he had his hands on my hips, his mouth on my neck. Tongue and teeth, a soft touch that bit.

"Hey, you don't want to talk?" I said. Because I'd been hoping for that. Some memory-swapping, sweet or bitter, but either way something real. Taking our clothes off even as we spoke. His shirt, my bra. Lying down beside each other, stripped. Whispering in each other's ears. His arms around me, and mine around him. The smell of him sweeping over me.

But it didn't happen like that.

"Come here," he said, and closed his grip. He lifted me, the balls of my feet no longer touching the floor. And I was weightless, dizzy, high above the ground. Laughing. He threw me down on my bed, a collision of springs. A gravity-smack.

"There are rules," I said. I said it by rote, spitting a strand of hair out my mouth. "You can't manhandle me without us discussing it first. If you want to—"

"Shut up."

I laughed. I don't know why. "What do you want, then?"

"What I've dreamed of all my life."

"Which is?"

"To stare into a whore's eyes as she dies."

I didn't understand. My laugh came out half-gasp. I said the word without thinking. "Daddy."

"Say that again," he smiled.

"Daddy."

"Take your clothes off."

I did. And as I did it, he softened. He sat on the edge of the bed and watched me wrestle with straps, elastics. He smiled and I smiled back. The air brightened, tension softened.

"Daddy, I love you."

"I know you do."

"Do you love me?"

He smiled. Yellow teeth, pale grey eyes. He still wore his leather jacket, it squeaked when he moved his arms. A sound I remembered. He smelled of cigarettes. That smell I knew so well. He leaned forward, he climbed on top of me. He put his fingers in my mouth for me, and I tasted it. Grit, salt, nicotine. Spice and sweetness. Lust, not death. He took his hand away, touching me. Rubbing his hands over my shoulders. My heart thrummed. And I said it again, in my mind at least.

Daddy.

I had just enough time to scream when his hands slid to my neck. Knowing, though I don't know how I knew, that this was going to hurt me. My scream came out in a high-pitched squeal that sounded a little like laughter, cut off when he pressed his thumbs into my throat. There was a sudden, cracking bolt of agony, like I'd swallowed two burning hot stones. I tried to gasp, but the air hit the wall made by his hands. My chest spasmed, my face filled with blood—too tight against my skin. My cheeks throbbed, my eyes bulged.

"Say it again," he said.

But I couldn't speak.

A burst of blue and black shattered across my vision. Against my pulse, I heard my hands thumping on the mattress. *Here-here-here-here-here—*

I might've clawed him, and I almost did. But I didn't want to hurt him. Not him. *Not him.*

I didn't see the door break open. I heard it through a thundercloud of pounding blood and desperation. The wall in my throat collapsed, I tore in air. The blue-black dizzied down to a static swirl, and Saul was there, ripping my lover off of me. A look in his eyes like outrage broken on hurt.

***

Sometimes I think that memory of him is the only thing I see clearly. The look in my Daddy's eyes as he turned from me, kicked Saul away, and fumbled the switchblade out of his pocket. I saw Saul recover, I heard the crash as they collided. I heard a crisp, sharp popping sound as the blade punched into Saul's chest. My daddy, he was wide-eyed, snarling. A look in his eyes like vulnerability broken on rage. And Saul—I remember him too, of course. Screaming with tears in his eyes, stumbling back, landing on the floor and for a moment just sitting there, his hand wrapped around the blade's handle. There was very little blood, just a slowly blooming circle of red, staining his shirt where the knife went in. The look in his face was of frailty, fragility. Hard-mouthed grimace, vulnerable eyes. Little-boy hurt. Because it must've hurt. I know.

The truth is I don't remember much after that. I know I made it out my room, and I ran down the stairs. I ran across the parking lot. Running hurt because I couldn't breathe right, my throat was swelling up. Brian's fingers, hot stones, cracking every time I tried to take in air. Pressing.

Daddy.

An angel had left a few coins scattered on the floor by the payphone. Without them I might've tried calling anyway, I think. Listening to the dull buzz of the dial tone—impotent, useless, wasted—as I punched in numbers. Until it gave up on me and responded with those sharp, brutal beats.

No. No. No. No.

But I saw the coins. I picked them up. I dropped them into the slot, my hands barely steady, but steady enough. I called my mother. And she knew it was me.

"Angeline."

I tried to talk but my throat hurt too much. My voice came out rasped and ragged. It came out in torn sobs.

"M-M—"

"Angeline, baby."

I stood in the stall and tried to breathe as my mother said my name, my names, all the names she ever had for me.

Angie. Angel. Darling. Honey.

And I remembered that she'd made me wear those dresses. Her touch. I remembered her fingers jammed down my throat. Her thin hands, hard fingers, and the bruises they left on my skin. Even as she called me *Angeline. Honey. Darling. Baby.*

I remembered that Sunday afternoon, my father picking me up, wrapping his arms around me. His voice in my ear, "You're coming with me."

The smell of raspberry tart, ginger crust, burning in the oven. That smell following us down the street, that street bright in liquid light. The sun in my eyes so I couldn't see, but I heard her—my mother—calling after us.

"Angeline, baby…"

I wanted to answer her. But I couldn't speak. I slid to the floor with the phone pressed to my ear. Bare against the filth, I breathed in the smells of old urine and rusted metal. I listened to my mother's voice as I tried to cry, as I tried to get air in past the knots tangled in my throat. Pain, pulsing. The tastes of blood and nicotine. But no matter how I fought to clear it all and catch my breath, I couldn't say the word I most needed to say. And I knew, but didn't really know, which word it was I most wanted to speak.

Mommy. Daddy. Mommy. Daddy.

ABOUT KAREN RUNGE

KAREN RUNGE is an author and visual artist based in Johannesburg, South Africa. She is the author of the short story collection *Seven Sins* (Concorde ePress, 2016), and the novel *Seeing Double* (Grey Matter Press, 2017). Her fiction has been published in such magazines as *Shock Totem, Something Wicked* and *Pseudopod*, and anthologies such as *Double Barrel Horror Vol. 2* (Pint Bottle Press), *Death's Realm* (Grey Matter Press) and *Suspended in Dusk: Volume One.*

THE SUNDOWNERS

DAMIEN ANGELICA WALTERS

T HERE'S A FACE AT THE WINDOW, someone on the other side of the glass, peeking in. Too-big eyes, too-pale skin, mouth slack.

"William, is that you?" Margaret calls out.

He doesn't answer, and the face is still there. It's angry and awful and *hungry*. Its mouth opens and closes, as though it already has her in its jaws. She cries out in wordless alarm and twists her hands, too afraid to draw close.

A woman Margaret doesn't know comes into the room, and her face is all teeth. Where is William? He was just here. Why would he leave her alone like this?

"It's okay, Miss Margaret. Let's shut the curtains, yes? It's getting dark outside."

"Where's William? Is he outside?"

"Everything's fine," the woman says as she tugs the curtains closed, hiding the face.

No, everything isn't fine. If William is outside, the woman should let him in, not shut him out. He must be at the store; he said he was going to the store, didn't he? Why is he taking so long? He should be here by now.

"Who are you?"

"I'm Jae. I come here to help take care of you."

"I don't need anyone to take care of me."

"But sometimes it's nice to have a little help, isn't it? Come now," the woman says, "dinner is ready."

"I don't want dinner. I want William. *He* takes care of me." She steps back from the window on unsteady legs. The curtains are wrong. They're ugly dark things, and *her* curtains have flowers.

"Who changed the curtains?"

The woman frowns. "The curtains?"

"Yes, they're wrong. Who put them there?"

"I guess the other ones are in the wash right now. Maybe we can look for them after dinner."

"Why are you trying to trick me? Where is William?" The woman reaches for her arm, but Margaret smacks her away. "Don't you touch me." Why is this woman here? Margaret doesn't need any help. She isn't a child.

The woman rubs her arm and shows all her teeth again. "Oh, you're a feisty one today, aren't you? Come on, now. There's no trick, just dinner. Chicken and mashed potatoes and peas, all with a little pepper the way you like it."

Margaret lets the woman help her into the kitchen and into one of the chairs.

"Is William here yet? He hasn't had dinner either."

The woman smiles, this time with no teeth. "He must be running late, honey."

Margaret presses her lips tight and narrows her eyes. She hates when people call her honey. Only William is allowed to call her that.

***

Margaret picks up the phone and dials, but all she gets is a busy signal. She's dialing the right number, so why won't William answer?

"What you doing, honey?"

The woman smiles, but she has too many teeth and Margaret doesn't like it. Not one bit. When people have too many teeth, their smiles are usually lies, and she hates liars. Gripping the phone tight enough to make her knuckles ache, she says, "I'm trying to call William. He should be here by now."

"Okay."

"Don't take the phone away from me."

"No, I won't, but it's time to take your medicine."

The woman holds out a plastic case, the lid open, and a glass of water.

"What are those for?"

"Let's see. One is for your blood pressure, one is for your stomach, so you can drink milk without getting an upset tummy, one is so you won't worry too much, and the last one is to help you remember things."

"I remember things just fine."

"I know. I know you do, but this is for just in case. Dr. Mitchell wants you to take them and we don't want to make her upset, do we?"

Margaret shakes her head, hangs up the phone, and takes the pills one by one, sipping from the glass in between.

"Now it's time to wash your hair."

"Why?"

"Because we need to make sure it's clean, that's why. Don't you want it to be clean?"

"I want to call William."

"Okay, you go ahead and give him a call and *then* we'll wash your hair."

Turning so the woman can't watch her, Margaret dials the number, holding the handset away from her ear when a busy signal starts. She hangs up, dials again. Again, a busy signal. Maybe someone changed the number and didn't tell her. They wouldn't do that to her, would they? She watches the woman in her kitchen as she rinses out a glass. She better be careful and not break it. If she does, William will make her buy a new one.

★★★

There's a face at the window, someone on the other side of the glass, peeking in. Too-big eyes, too-pale skin, mouth slack.

"William," Margaret calls out. "William, there's someone here."

He doesn't answer, doesn't come in, but a woman does, a woman with bright red curly hair, like Margaret had when she was a little girl.

"What's wrong?" the woman says, wiping wet hands on a crumpled paper towel.

Margaret points toward the window. "She's out there."

The woman looks out and shakes her head, making her curls bounce. "No one's there," she says, starting to close the curtain.

Margaret stands, hands fisted at her sides. What sort of game is this woman playing? Does she think Margaret a fool? "She's right outside. I know you can see her. Why are you lying to me?"

The woman's eyes shine and she blinks a few times, reminding Margaret of an owl she once saw on her daughter's field trip to the zoo.

"After dinner, why don't you and I put together a puzzle?" the woman says. "That would be fun, right?"

"I don't like puzzles," Margaret says.

The woman points to a stack of boxes atop a table. "But those are all yours."

Margaret pounds her fists against her upper thighs. "Stop it. Stop lying to me. I don't understand why everyone lies to me all the time. You think I don't know what I like? I don't like puzzles. I've never liked puzzles. Please call William. Please call him and tell him to come home right now."

The woman puts her hands up, palms facing out. "Okay, okay, I'll call him. But maybe you should eat something while we wait, okay? Are you hungry? I've made dinner."

"No, I'm not hungry. William and I ate already. He made grilled cheese sandwiches and tomato soup. Those are my favorite. He knows *all* my favorites."

"I know. You used to make them all the time when I was little."

"When you were little?" Margaret cocks her head to the side. Now that she thinks about it, the woman does look familiar. "Jenna, is that you?"

"No, Mom, it's Gracie, your other daughter. Jenna will be here tomorrow night."

"I haven't seen you in a long time. I know you're busy with school, but you should visit more. Your father likes it when you do. William," she calls out, "Jenna's here!" When he doesn't answer, she says, "I think he's in the garage working on his car. He loves that car. You should go out and talk to him. He'd like that."

"Okay, I'll do that a little later."

"Do you want me to fix you something to eat while you're here?" Margaret asks, trying to recall if William bought milk today or not. She can't drink it, but he uses it in his coffee, and Jenna likes it in hers, too.

"Let me take care of it instead, Mom. Maybe we can even have a little chocolate cake after."

"That would be lovely, but I only want a small piece." Margaret pats her belly. "I don't want to gain too much weight."

"Okay. Let me go and get things ready."

Margaret watches her walk away. A phone rings once, but it isn't hers because the ring is wrong. The woman starts talking softly to someone else. Maybe William is in the kitchen with her. She hopes he remembered to buy milk for his coffee.

She gazes at the window and, through a small opening in the curtain panels, sees a face.

"William?" she whispers.

From the other room, she hears a voice. Has her daughter come to visit? Margaret hasn't seen Gracie in a long time. She gets up to check, but the curtains catch her eye. They're wrong somehow. They're supposed to have flowers on them. Did someone wash out the flowers? The sofa seems fine, though, but there's a blanket on the arm she doesn't recognize. She doesn't like it when people are in her house. They change things, and they think she won't notice, but she does. She folds the blanket so it will fit on the shelf in the linen closet.

"She's very agitated at night lately... The doctor calls it Sundowners. It's common, unfortunately... No, shadows, reflections, that sort of thing. They can make it worse. Closing all the curtains and turning on all the lights helps a little... I know, I just hate seeing her this way."

Margaret isn't sure who they're talking about, but she shivers. The Sundowners must be the people who change things around. She wishes they'd go away. She doesn't need things to be changed. She likes it when they're the same way. She looks down at the blanket in her hands, not sure where it's supposed to go. She shakes it open and drapes it around herself, pinching the ends together so the Sundowners can't see her.

***

When the woman with all the teeth goes into the bathroom, Margaret gathers up her things, tucking them in her purse. But she can't find her car keys, even though they should be on the hook next to the front door. William's keys are gone, too, but he took his car to the shop to get it fixed. The brakes, she thinks. He always has trouble with the brakes.

"Where you off to, Miss Margaret?"

"It's time for me to go. I have to get to work. I'm a teacher, and I have to be there on time."

"Oh, yes, I know, but you don't need to worry about that because school is closed today. Come, look at the calendar."

Margaret follows the woman into the kitchen where she points to a calendar hanging on the wall, the boxes marked with careful red Xs.

"See? It's Saturday," the woman says. "No school today, but Jenna's coming over today. Won't that be nice?"

There are too many Xs on the calendar. Someone's been marking them off when Margaret isn't looking. She takes the pen clipped to the top of the page and slips it into her pocket. Now no one can make the Xs except for her.

***

Margaret adjusts the throw pillow and sits straighter on the sofa, a half-finished puzzle spread out on the coffee table before her. She doesn't like the women in the other room. She thinks they're teachers, too, but all they do is gossip. If the principal hears them, he'll fire them, and it will be their own fault, no matter what they say otherwise. Margaret hates gossips. She always has.

"She managed to get out to the garage again. I told her the car was in the shop, and she didn't get mad this time, so we went for a drive in mine. She liked that a lot so you might want to try it the next time she gets upset."

"Is she still asking about my Dad?"

"Almost every day."

Margaret takes out another puzzle piece but she can't make it fit. She doesn't really want to work on the puzzle, but William isn't back yet and a puzzle is better than sitting still and doing nothing. The women keep talking, though, making too much noise. Margaret prefers the quiet. Everyone knows that.

"I almost wish she'd forget about him completely. Does that make me a terrible person?"

"Oh no, honey, it doesn't. This disease is a terrible thing."

"Maybe I should take her to the cemetery. Do you think that would help?"

"It might just confuse her, make her upset all over again."

Margaret doesn't want to listen to the women anymore. Why are they in her house? Why won't they leave? She wants them to go, but they won't listen to her. They never listen. And they're talking about her. They think she doesn't know, but she *does* know. They're talking about her and lying.

The medicine they give her makes her forget things like where she put her keys, how to put together a puzzle, and sometimes even words. She won't take it anymore and if they try to force her to, she'll scream until someone comes to help.

"I guess, in one way, I'm glad she doesn't know. I mean, it would be awful if she did. Sometimes I look in her eyes and she looks scared, but that's just the disease, right?"

They want Margaret to think she's losing her mind, but they're wrong. Her mind is perfectly fine. She's been teaching for a long time. They wouldn't let her do that if she wasn't fine.

"My sister said she hit her the other night. I thought the meds Dr. Mitchell prescribed were supposed to help with that."

Margaret scratches her temple. Maybe they aren't talking about her after all. She and William don't have any children. Not yet. She's too busy with her job. They both are. She isn't even sure she wants children.

There's a face at the window, someone on the other side of the glass, peeking in. Too-big eyes, too-pale skin, mouth slack. An old woman, like a witch from a fairy tale. A *Sundowner*.

"Go away," Margaret says, but the woman doesn't leave. She keeps staring in, watching her. "You can't come in. You're not allowed in here."

The Sundowner keeps staring in, watching her. Margaret knows what they want. They want to take her away, take her far away so William can't find her. But he won't let that happen. When he gets here, he'll make everyone leave. She tries to stack the throw pillows so the Sundowner can't see her, but they won't stay in place.

"Mom, do you need help?"

Margaret blinks in surprise. She didn't know her sister was stopping by. "Emily, what are you doing here? Why didn't you tell me you were coming over?"

"No, it's me, Jenna."

"My sister's name isn't Jenna. She's Emily."

"I'm your daughter."

"I don't have a daughter."

The woman makes a funny sort of sound and gives Margaret her back, but she closes the curtains. When she leaves the room, Margaret peeks quickly behind the fabric, and the Sundowner is still there.

"Leave me alone," she says.

The Sundowner opens and closes its mouth like a dying fish, and Margaret hears the faint whisper of its voice although she can't quite make out the words. A woman she doesn't recognize—maybe one of the neighbors?—comes into the room, and she lets the curtain fall back into place.

***

The woman with the teeth offers her a plastic case. "Miss Margaret, it's time for your medicine."

The pills resemble tiny pearls—Margaret wore pearls at her wedding, her mother's pearls, which belonged to *her* mother—but they aren't jewelry. They aren't medicine either, and they'll make her sick, not better, if she takes them. They all want her to stay sick so they can treat her like a child and talk to her like a child, so they can take care of her, but she doesn't need them to take care of her. She isn't a child, she isn't sick, and she doesn't want them in her house anymore.

"I want William."

"I know that, but you have to take your medicine to keep you well."

She smacks the case from the woman's hand and pills scatter across the floor with a hundred tiny tapping sounds. "I won't take them. I won't! You're trying to poison me. Don't think I don't know what you're doing. You're all trying to poison me."

"Honey, now that isn't—"

"No! You talk about me and talk about me, and you think I don't hear you, but I do. I know what you're trying to do. You're trying to make me think I'm losing my mind, but I'm not." Margaret's voice gets louder and louder, but she doesn't care. She's tired of the strangers in her house. She wants William. "Where is he? Why are you hiding him from me?"

"It's okay, honey. It's okay," the woman says.

Margaret pulls back from the woman's touch. It isn't okay. Nothing's okay. No one will tell her the truth. There's something wrong, she knows there is. She just doesn't know what it is, and she's so tired of being afraid.

***

Margaret wakes from her nap and pads into the living room. A woman with red hair is asleep on the sofa, so Margaret walks very quietly. The front door makes a little creak when it opens, and she holds her breath, but no one comes. She knows if they do, they won't let her look for William.

He's late, but it isn't his fault. No one wants her to know, but the Sundowners have him. They're keeping him from her, but she's smart; she's been a teacher for a long time. She'll find them, and she'll make them give him back, then all the strangers will have to leave her house. William won't let them give her medicine anymore. He won't let them stay.

The car isn't in the garage anymore. The Sundowners took it so she'd think William was running an errand, but she knows better. They can't trick her that way. They move things around in the house and change things to confuse her, but she's smarter than they are. They think she can't remember, but she can. The curtains should have flowers, her keys should hang on the hook beside the door, and her sister always calls first before she comes to visit.

She sets off on the path toward the street and once there, makes a right and keeps going, staying close to the curb. Her shoes are comfortable, so if she has to walk a long time, it'll be okay. She'll find William before it gets too late. Their daughter is coming to visit, and he'll want to see her, too.

Behind her, someone calls out, but it isn't anyone she knows. It isn't anyone at all. Its face is angry, its mouth open and full of teeth that want to bite and take pieces of her away. That's why the curtains are wrong. That's why *everything* is wrong.

There's a bigger road up ahead, with lots of stores and other buildings where she can hide. Someone will have a phone she can use to call William. She walks as fast as she can, but not fast enough because it grabs her arm.

"Mom, please stop," it says. "You're going to get hurt."

Margaret tries to pull free, but it's clinging too tight. It's pretending to be her daughter, but its face is wrong. She knows what her daughter looks like. She remembers. It's only trying to trick her. They're all trying to trick her!

"William," she screams. "Help me! You have to help me! Please, William, please!"

She keeps screaming, as loud as she can, but William's too far to hear. No one will come to help her. The Sundowner yanks her arm, but Margaret twists away and keeps running until she reaches the street. Cars rush by in a blur and there, William's car. She'd recognize it anywhere: four doors, dark blue paint, a dent in the bumper where he hit a cart in the parking lot of the grocery store. She waves her arms and shrieks his name. Why isn't he stopping? Can't he see her? She steps down from the curb, waving her arms faster.

"Stop, stop!" the Sundowner shouts.

It gets so close Margaret can feel its breath on her neck and she whirls around, grabbing its arms. "You can't have me," she yells, pushing with all her might as a bright silver car approaches. The Sundowner pinwheels its arms and falls onto the car, bouncing off into the street. And then it isn't moving anymore.

There's so much noise—horns blaring and brakes squealing and people shouting, but Margaret smiles. Now the Sundowner can't hurt her. It can't hurt her ever again.

ABOUT DAMIEN ANGELICA WALTERS

DAMIEN ANGELICA WALTERS is the author of *Cry Your Way Home*, *Paper Tigers*, and *Sing Me Your Scars*, winner of the *This is Horror* Award for Short Story Collection of the Year. Her work has been nominated twice for a Bram Stoker Award®, reprinted in *The Year's Best Dark Fantasy & Horror* and *The Year's Best Weird Fiction*, and published in various anthologies and magazines, including the Shirley Jackson Award Finalists *Autumn Cthulhu* and *The Madness of Dr. Caligari*, World Fantasy Award Finalist *Cassilda's Song*, *Nightmare Magazine*, *Black Static*, and *Apex Magazine*. She lives in Maryland with her husband and two rescued pit bulls. Find her on Twitter @DamienAWalters or on the web at damienangelicawalters.com.

CRYING DEMON

ALAN BAXTER

CLAUDE STOOD WITH HIS BACK to the rough brick wall, trapped. Would it be another beating, or just a merciless verbal barrage? Big Tim was there, a giant among year 10s with a brain inversely proportional to his mass, so fairly safe to assume fists would fly. Claude had nearly made it home, only one block away, but the bicycles skidded up, cut him off, encircled him. Now the old drama would play out again.

"What's up, Claauuude?" Tim drew the name out as an insult.

"Just want to go home." Claude's voice was barely above a whisper.

"What's that, gayboy?" A heavy slap whipped Claude's face to one side and he tasted blood inside his cheek. "You made me look like a fool in chemistry."

"It's not my fault you're too dumb to know—" Another slap prevented him finishing the sentence.

Pointless to even engage, he raised his arms to cover his head and braced for the onslaught.

"Not gonna talk any more, fag?" Tim asked.

"Just slap him," another one said, but Claude had his eyes closed and didn't know who. It didn't matter, they were all basically the same person who thought being gay was the worst insult, even though Claude wasn't gay, who needed to assert themselves physically because they were so insecure, because they were beaten at home and abusers learned to pass that horror on. They were the broken ones and Claude needed to just walk away, tell an adult, rise above it. It had been repeatedly explained and was fucking worthless. He couldn't walk away when they surrounded him. He had told adults, so many times, and they had repeatedly punished the bastards, but that just made them come back harder, meaner, more carefully out of sight. All such bullshit.

Claude even tried being the bully himself once, passing it on to another kid, but that only triggered a week of physical sickness and shame. Guilt still burned his cheeks at the thought of it.

And then the fists started to fall. Claude cried out, tears fell, his face and body flinched and throbbed with the assault. He fell and they started kicking, gravel scraped his cheek, a tuft of dry grass poked his cornea, his elbow whined as it struck the wall, and then silence. Fading laughter and the whirr of bicycle tyres. He opened his eyes, one swollen almost shut already from well-placed knuckles, and he was alone on the quiet street, bruised, bleeding, among the dirt and grass and tattered chip wrappers. Reduced to nothing once more.

Wincing against a dozen or more hurts, he picked himself up and limped home.

He called out a hello to his mum as he entered the house but hurried upstairs before she could emerge to greet him.

"Good day, love?" she sang after him.

"Yeah, fine." What was the point in telling her any different? "I've got homework."

"Okay, love."

He went into the bathroom to clean up. It didn't look as bad as it felt. After he'd washed and pressed a flannel soaked in cold water to his bruises, the attack was almost unnoticeable. Except for the swollen eye, already darkening. He'd have to think of a way to explain that.

Buzzing in his pocket distracted him and he pulled out his phone. A message from Aaron.

u ok?

At least he had one true friend who cared. He tapped a reply.

Who told u?...

...big tim boasted to camille and she told my sister

Bloody fast. i only just got home...

...so you ok?

Yeah i'll be fine...

...get online want to show you something

Claude went into his room and pulled his laptop from his bag, plugged it in. He booted up an app so they could chat by voice and Aaron answered right away.

"Sure you're okay?"

"Yeah, it's just pain. Who cares, right?"

"I do. Your mum and dad do."

"But no one can do anything. Tim's had his fill for a while. Might leave me alone for a few days. He'll drop out at the end of the year anyway, be selling us fries by Christmas. What do you want to show me?"

"Check it out."

A jJpg file popped into the window and Claude opened it. He sat back in shock at the sight of a boy, no older than himself, lying on a concrete floor, naked. His chest flayed open, ribs on display like a white cage smeared with blood. "The fuck, man?"

"You think it's real?" Aaron asked.

"How the fuck do I know? Why are you sending me this?"

"It's from a game."

A kind of relief leaked through Claude's shock. "So it's not real then."

"Well, that's the thing. Apparently it is. It's a game on the Dark Web, but you have to finish it."

"What do you mean?" Claude leaned closer to the screen, half-turning his face away even as he did so, trying to decide how authentic the image was.

"If you don't finish, you become part of the game. Like this kid."

Claude laughed softly. "That's some real urban myth bullshit, man."

"Remember Clare Bailey? Went missing a couple of months ago, we had school counselling and everything?"

"Yeah."

"Apparently she played. That's how I know about it. My sister heard the rumour, but didn't follow it up. I did."

A chill tickled through Claude's bruised stomach. "So don't play, I guess. Why would you anyway?"

"If you complete it there's a serious reward."

"Like what?"

"Dunno. Still trying to find out. But I need to dive the Dark Web deeper to learn more."

"Isn't that dangerous?"

"Nah, I use Tor to route through to some message boards. There's no risk, people are paranoid. I use a fake email, of course. And VPN as well as Tor. Here's another."

A second file popped into the feed, an animated GIF.

"I don't want to see more!" Claude said.

"This one's different."

Grimacing, Claude opened the image. It was a young girl, maybe seven or eight, standing in a dark corridor, shifting rapidly, uncannily, like she stood on undulating ground but everything was sped up. She wore a stained and tattered nightdress, her long, black hair greasy and hanging over her shoulders. Her face was a blur, the features somehow smudged as she vibrated, the GIF repeating over and over. Her head quivered side to side, the dark smear of her mouth stretching and closing, stretching and closing.

"Shit." Claude clicked the image away. "That's disturbing."

"Right?"

"You should be careful."

Aaron laughed. "I will. But I have an idea. We find the game and send it anonymously to Tim."

Claude paused, thoughts tumbling together for a moment. Then he smiled slightly, winced as his split lip stung with the movement. "Just to fuck with him?"

"Sure."

The sick feeling leeched back into Claude's stomach, a visceral clenching. "Nah. I don't want to be like them. I want to be better."

"We're *not* like them. This is revenge. You know a turd like Tim would never be able to finish a game like that. It's a kind of puzzler RPG apparently."

"Yeah, but it's not real. How can it be?"

"Who knows, man?"

Claude's mum called up the stairs, time for him to walk the dog and feed the chickens before dinner.

"I heard that," Aaron said. "Go do your chores. I'll let you know what happens."

"Be careful."

Claude signed out and headed down, deciding a wayward cricket ball during sports that afternoon would be his explanation for the black eye.

***

At school the following day Tim was suitably mellow. He grinned crookedly at Claude once or twice, clearly admiring his handiwork in Claude's swollen eye, deep black now and already yellowing around the edges.

Claude wished just once someone would beat the shit out of the big idiot, but he was smart enough to know it would be short-term enjoyment and ultimately unsatisfying. He'd rather just be left alone to his science fiction and role-playing games and love of physics without being attacked and called gay because of it. It really didn't seem like too much to ask.

At lunch, Aaron caught up with him. "You gotta come over after school. I was up half the night, you won't believe what I found."

"Really?"

"Yeah, I have to go to the library and do the homework I ignored last night. But come over later! You can have dinner at mine, I okayed it with Mum."

"All right." Claude sent his mother a message and she replied that he call her to pick him up no later than nine o'clock. A fair deal for a school night.

***

They sat in Aaron's room with the door shut, huddled close together at his desk. The laptop screen was solid black, but for a single white pentacle upside down in the centre. They'd been staring at it for several seconds.

"I'm gonna click it," Aaron said eventually.

Claude frowned. "I dunno, man. The forum said you have to finish the puzzle or the code will wipe your drive."

"It also said the puzzle was easy, you can have as many tries as you like. And it would give up the link for Crying Demon."

It had taken Aaron most of the previous night to find his way through the mire of data, but only a few minutes to explain the results. Crying Demon was, apparently, a game created by someone possessed by the Devil. At least, that was the most common story. Others had it that it was made by a victim of child abuse, or created by an abuser. Others still that it wasn't actually made by anyone, but existed of its own volition. It seemed largely irrelevant. The game allegedly contained a maze and puzzles, and if you got lost or stuck you became physically trapped inside. If you beat it, you got access codes to a stash of digital currency, easy to use on the Deep or Dark Web for all kinds of nefarious transactions. Or perfectly legal ones, simply remaining anonymous.

"It's all bullshit," Claude said. "Has to be. How can you be actually trapped in a game?"

Aaron clicked the pentacle. A hissing erupted from the speakers and slowly turned into a distant scream, a voice from a closed basement, a cry of agonising pain. The pentacle broke apart into pixels and drifted away to nothing. A white spot appeared in the centre of the screen and expanded into a monochromatic corridor. Whether it was poor-resolution graphics or heavily filtered video they couldn't tell. The screaming continued and another voice rose under it, repeating a phrase in reversed speech, staccato and echoing.

The boys glanced at each other, half-smiling. Claude's stomach rippled with nerves.

"W, A, S, D?" Aaron asked.

Claude shrugged.

Aaron put his fingers on the keyboard and pressed W. The vision moved forward along the corridor and the screaming faded to near-silence, but the backwards speech continued.

Aaron stopped and the scream surged back. He hit W again and the vision moved on, wailing fading. He used the mouse to look around, but the flickering, poorly resolved environment was unchanging. "Keep going?" he asked.

"What else is there to do?"

After several minutes of walking the corridor, they came to a solid wall. Dead end.

"What the hell?" Aaron said quietly.

He pressed D to rotate the view one-eighty and the vibrating, smudge-faced girl from the GIF of the night before stood right behind them. She launched forward with a screech that made their ears sing, and both boys leapt back from the desk. Aaron's chair went over and he went with it, but Claude saw the girl's mouth stretch impossibly wide as she lunged and the screen went black. After a few seconds, the white pentacle returned.

"Jesus fuck and shit," Aaron said, picking up his chair.

Claude's heart slammed against his ribs. He took a few deep breaths, shook his head. They both broke into nervous laughter.

"How was that a puzzle?" Aaron asked. "One corridor and a jump scare."

"It's all a myth," Claude said. "Crying Demon doesn't exist. It's trolls fucking with people."

"Nah, the stuff I read last night, the screengrabs I saw. There's more than just that." Aaron clicked the pentacle and began walking the passage again. This time he scanned around more as he went, checking above as well as to either side. The passage was open to a night sky, as poorly resolved as the rest, pixelated birds or bats flitting by periodically. Then a kind of awning appeared, a white inverted pentacle flickering beneath it.

"Mouse click for jump?" Claude said.

Aaron left-clicked and nothing happened. He right-clicked and their point of view sprang upwards. The scream returned, intensified, became an ululating wail and the screen spread into bright white. The boys sat back squinting. The white resolved into a room with three doors, old banded wood like a medieval castle. Each door had a set of Roman numerals above it, VII, XIX and VI VI VI.

"Seven, nineteen and six-six-six," Claude said.

Aaron grinned. "Six-six-six is the number of the beast. My dad loves Iron Maiden, that old metal band. Plays that shit all the time."

"Guess that's the one then."

Aaron clicked at the door and the screen went to black with a single line of white text, a URL, across the centre. As Aaron hovered the mouse it became a hand to activate the link. He clicked.

Blood poured down the screen, catching on unseen areas to spell out the words "Crying Demon" in a broken, crabbed variety of fonts, each letter a different typeface, some capitals, some lower case. Laughter bubbled up again, the strange, backwards speech babbled beneath it, repeating a single phrase over and over and over. A glittering START button resolved at the centre of the screen.

"Don't!" Claude said.

Aaron grinned. He hit the back button on the browser and the screen returned to nothing but the link. He highlighted and copied it.

"What are you doing?" Claude asked.

"I set this up earlier, fake profile." He opened another chat app. His profile pic showed a pretty blonde leaning forward to display a deep cleavage, the username read: *iSwallo451*.

"Who's that?" Claude asked.

"Some random off an image search. I friended Tim with it last night, the dick accepted right away." He connected to a username, *LordTim69*, and typed "Amazing!" then pasted the Crying Demon link.

"Wait!" Claude said, but Aaron hit SEND.

"Fuck that guy. You seen your eye lately? Let's give him a scare."

A response from Tim popped up.

…whats this?

Aaron grinned at Claude, then wrote.

youll love it…

They sat waiting for a response, but nothing happened. After a few minutes Aaron shrugged. "Oh well. Guess we'll see."

Claude swallowed rising nausea. "Hopefully he'll ignore it."

"You're too forgiving. Let's finish those character sheets for Friday's game session. Kate and Mohammed have said they're in."

"Okay."

***

The following morning at assembly the mood was sombre. The teachers sat on stage, faces serious, downcast. Once everyone had filed in, the headmaster stepped up to the lectern and cleared his throat.

"Ladies and gentlemen, we have some concerning news. One of our students, Tim Howell, has gone missing."

White heat flooded Claude. Aaron's gasp beside him seemed to come from far away.

"If any of you spoke to Tim yesterday after school," the headmaster continued, "in person or online or anything else, please come directly to my office. Even the most insignificant detail could be helpful. That's all for this morning. Off to your classes, please."

The hall erupted into hundreds of hushed conversations.

"What the fuck?" Claude said, eyes wide.

Aaron was pale, his lips trembled. "Is it really possible?"

"Should we go to the Head?"

"And tell him what? That a fucking Dark Web game ate Tim? That's insane, right?"

***

The rest of the day was a trial of guilt and fear for Claude. He and Aaron walked home from school together and not much conversation passed between them at first.

Eventually, Claude said, "Did we kill him?"

Aaron shook his head. "It can't be real."

"I didn't think so, but is there another explanation?"

"I've been thinking about it," Aaron said. "I reckon this whole thing is set up by some child molesters or some shit. Right? Like a trap. They scare kids into going somewhere, sneaking off, then they come and collect them. Maybe Tim ended up in a white van last night, you know?"

Claude nodded slowly, turning the idea over in his mind. "Yeah, maybe," he conceded eventually. He looked up. "In which case, we have to do something! Tell someone. We could play the game, find out what the trap is, and tell the police."

Aaron shook his head, staring at his shoes. "No way. I'm not chancing it. Tim was a prick, I fucking hate him. So should you. Look what he did to you just recently, let alone all the times before. Too bad for him, it's done."

Aaron strode away.

"Wait!" Claude called. "How does that make us any better than him? Now we're worse!"

Aaron yelled back without turning around. "No! Fuck him! I'll see you tomorrow, Claude."

***

Claude sat at his desk, the message app open in front of him, *iSwallo451* typed into the username box, but the password field was blank. He'd tried quite a few, but no luck. His phone buzzed and a message came through from Aaron. He opened it, hoping his friend had changed his mind.

…Mohammed can't make Friday after all. You ok to play Saturday?

Claude sighed, replied *yeah*, and turned back to his laptop. His eyes narrowed. The message gave him a clue. He typed the name of Aaron's dark elf assassin into the password field and the app opened up. The last two messages were right there.

…whats this?

You'll love it…

And above those, the link for Crying Demon. *Amazing!*

Claude's hands were trembling as he stared at the lines of text. He'd meant what he said to Aaron, couldn't allow himself to be like Tim. And he couldn't condemn even a dick like Tim to child molesters. He had to be better than that. Should never have let this happen.

He clicked the link. The page poured down, the START button emerged, and Claude clicked before he could think more about it.

His screen crumbled into a swirling mass of pixels that slowly resolved into a corridor. It appeared to be video, gloomy like the place was lit with low-wattage bulbs. Or maybe he was trapped in some perpetual dusk, right before a night that would never fall. His fingers found the keyboard and he began to move forwards. The corridor moved under him, monochromatic, jagged in resolution. There were many turns this time, lefts and rights that made little sense. But Claude was a role-player. He dragged over a pad and pencil and sketched as he went, mapping as accurately as he could. Backwards gibberish and distant moans and screams leaked thickly from the speakers and he wanted to turn them off, but feared he would miss some essential sound component of the game if he did. Though it wasn't much of a game, just seemingly endless corridors. A pointless maze.

He emerged into a room, geometric patterns on the walls, fuzzy in low res. Across the space was a young child, standing with her arms hanging limply at her sides, rocking back and forth on her feet. Her head rose to observe Claude, but her swaying didn't cease. The only exit was a door directly behind her.

Claude moved to the wall and slid along it, never letting her out of his sight, then turned quickly through the door. He hurried down the next corridor, this time the dusky sky purpled with approaching night, a few stars starting to come out. He jumped as a still image flashed onto the screen along with an echoing gun shot. A naked man, clearly resolved in a high-definition photo, erection in hand, grinning widely. A small, naked boy lay curled on the ground behind him.

"Fucking hell," Claude moaned.

Another gunshot and the image was gone. The corridor continued.

The screaming rose as his movement ceased, so he carried on, mapping as he went, another room, two slowly swaying kids this time, a boy and a girl, heads down. Two exits and he chose the one on the left for no particular reason, marking the other door on his map.

The corridor devolved into stark black-and-white, badly rendered, the white blowing out occasionally. Another flash frame photograph, a woman in a hooded white robe atop a cliff, leaning forward arms outstretched, well beyond tipping point. The corridor returned and Claude kept going. More turns, more rooms, more ghostly undulating children with black eyes staring or heads hung. He checked corners and walls, looking for anything a bit different to the endless wandering. More flash frames of the gross and the grotesque. The backwards phrase repeated again and again, drilling into his brain.

Another figure stood in front of Claude, blocking the way. A stocky young man this time, swaying and staring at the ground. The figure was like the others: low res, blocky, too bright in the highlights, almost black in the shadows. As Claude approached, his breath caught. It was Tim, toes pointing slightly in towards each other, knees a little bent, head hanging, arms limp at his sides. He wavered like seaweed in a lazy current.

Then Tim looked up sharply, raised one arm. At first, Claude thought the bully was reaching for him, then realised he was pointing back the way Claude had come.

Heart racing, Claude turned and the girl with smudged features rushed up behind him, hands clawing forward. Her mouth stretched open and she began to wail, but not a human sound. Electronic, an old modem scream trying to reach a dial-up connection it would never find. It grew louder and louder, pinging and screeching, and Claude pressed hands over his ears, but the wail became a squeal and it was inside his head, forcing out against his ears, pressing into the backs of his eyes, and he sobbed. This was it. The end and it was going to hurt. He realised he wasn't in his chair any more, but in the pixelated corridor, standing in the cold air, the dusky sky high above, the concrete hard beneath his feet. The backwards speech rose in volume, began repeating more rapidly until it warped into words he could understand.

"Never leave, eternal dusk, crying demon. Never leave, eternal dusk, crying demon."

Claude screamed as the girl's icy cold fingers wrapped over his shoulders, hard like bone.

"Never leave, eternal dusk, crying demon."

Then another noise. "Claude!"

A different weight on his shoulder. A slap. "You right, buddy?"

***

Claude fluttered his eyes open, in his chair, at his desk. His computer screen was blank, the laptop gone to sleep. Aaron stood looking down at him, eyes concerned.

"Dude," Aaron said, almost a whisper. "When I came in, for a moment I thought I could see right through you."

"Through me?"

"Like you were a ghost. Had to touch you to make sure I wasn't tripping out."

Claude blew out a slow breath. "Thank fuck you did."

"What do you mean?"

Claude paused, wondering how much he should let on. Deciding to share nothing for the moment, he forced a laugh. "Wouldn't want to be a ghost!"

That swaying, flaccid figure of Tim, pixelated and monochrome... He fought back the urge to vomit.

"I wanted to say sorry," Aaron said. "Then you weren't answering texts for so long, so I came over. I lost my temper, but it's not your fault. You're right. We fucked up. *I* fucked up."

Claude checked the time. He'd been home over two hours, though it felt like less than thirty minutes. How long had he been in the game? *Had he been in the game?*

"I fucked up," Aaron said again. "What are we going to do?"

A sense of finality settled over Claude. He pointed to the map sketched on his pad. "This is the game," he said. He told Aaron everything.

"Are you serious? You were in there?"

Claude shrugged. "You said you could see through me. Another few seconds and I'd be done. She had me."

"Far out…"

"I have to go back."

Aaron looked up sharply. "What?"

"I've got a map to Tim. I've got to go back for him."

"And do what?"

"Bring him out. Save him. You have to watch me play. Don't watch the game, have your back to the screen and watch *me*. I'll go in and go to Tim. I reckon maybe it's timed. You don't find the way out before a certain amount of time passes and she gets you. I'll go to Tim. When I start to feel like the game's got me, I'll grab him. When you see me fading, slap me like before, bring me out. Maybe I can bring him with me."

Aaron stared silently for a moment. Then, "You think that'll work?"

"Fuck knows, but I have to try. We have to do something."

"Do we?"

"If we don't, we're worse than he ever was. I can't live with that. If it doesn't work we go to the Head tomorrow and tell him everything."

Aaron took a shuddering breath. "Okay."

A few minutes later they were set up. Aaron sat beside the desk, where he couldn't see the screen, watching Claude. Claude wore headphones and flexed his fingers a couple of times, then reached for the mouse. "Let me start to fade," he said. "But you hit me hard before I go too far, right?"

Aaron nodded, fear stretched white across his face.

Claude clicked the link. The sounds were a hundred times worse in headphones, the screams and reversed speech worming directly into his brain. He tried to ignore everything as he navigated the corridors following his map. He avoided the rippling ghost children, ignored the flash screens as best he could. They were all different this time, randomly generated, scenes of child molestation, gore, surgical procedures, suicide. He pushed on along the final corridor to where he had last found Tim.

The unfortunate bully stood there like before, eyes downcast, swaying. Claude moved around him, looked back and forth along the corridor. Nothing. He was still in his chair, still in his room. Aaron sat wide-eyed in his peripheral vision, staring. Claude clicked for action against Tim, but nothing happened. He moved forward, tried to walk through him, but was prevented until he manoeuvred around.

"Not enough time," he muttered to himself, realisation dawning. Previously he had been cautious, moving slowly, looking everywhere. This time he had followed his map directly. He estimated he had several minutes before the clock began to run down. Maybe he could find a way out, finish the game. Would that still give him a chance to save Tim? Could he maybe save Tim and score the digital currency reward?

He moved away from Tim, further along the corridor than he'd been before. A T-junction at the end offered him left and right. He chose left, moved along as the screaming and backwards talking increased in volume.

-flash- *A young man holding a dog over the flames of a bonfire.*

More corridor, another junction up ahead.

-flash- *A naked man crouched over the corpse of a woman, reaching into her eviscerated mid-section, eating her organs. His head snapped around and blood poured from his mouth.*

Claude cried out as the image blinked away and he was back in the corridor. Mist drifted from his mouth as he yelled, the air so cold. Hard concrete pressed against his feet. He looked around frantically, his room gone, Aaron gone. He was in the game.

The grating whine and pings of an old modem pushed through the background noise. Spinning around, he saw the smudge-faced girl bearing down on him. He screamed and ran, hammering back along the passage. He tasted blood on the icy air, smelled vomit and shit and stale piss. The corridor seemed endless. He'd only made one turn, he needed a corridor on the right, that's where Tim was.

Hard, frozen fingers raked his back and Claude wailed and tried to double his pace. His lungs burned with the effort even as they sucked in so much frozen, fetid air. A dark gap appeared on his right and he turned, skidded and stumbled. The cold hands grabbed at him again and the backwards speech rolled forward.

"Never leave, eternal dusk, crying demon. Never leave, eternal dusk, crying demon."

Claude yelled incoherently, tears streamed his cheeks, his stomach felt like water, his legs like seaweed. He drove himself on, saw Tim's back up ahead. The modem scream intensified, battling with the chant in volume.

"Never leave, eternal dusk, crying demon."

Claude leaped forward and wrapped his arms around Tim as the girl's frigid hands closed over his shoulders like metal clamps. They squeezed, blackness swam at the edges of his vision and then repeated strikes around his back and neck, Aaron yelling his name.

The world cracked and fractured. Pixels and video streaked and swarmed through his eyes and he was falling, a massive weight in his arms, then an impact took the wind out of him.

He heard Aaron first, sobbing loudly and repeating, "Fuck me, fuck me, fuck me."

Claude rolled over on the floor of his room and pressed into something hard and cold. He leapt up, head swimming. Aaron was backed against the door, hands over his mouth.

On the floor at Claude's feet was Tim, face down, motionless. Claude crouched and tipped him over. Tim flopped onto his back. He was cold like he'd been in the fridge, his skin grey blue and dull, his eyes wide, staring, pupils dilated so far only a tiny band of colour remained. He was long dead.

Claude's scream joined Aaron's as he heard the pounding of feet on the stairs, and then his father yelling his name and rattling the door.

ABOUT ALAN BAXTER

ALAN BAXTER is a multi-award-winning British-Australian author who writes supernatural thrillers and urban horror, rides a motorcycle and loves his dogs. He also teaches Kung Fu. He lives among dairy paddocks on the beautiful south coast of NSW, Australia, with his wife, son, dogs and cat. He is the author of the dark supernatural thriller trilogy, *Bound*, *Obsidian* and *Abduction* (The Alex Caine Series) published by Harper-Voyager Australia and Gryphonwood Press in the US, and the dark supernatural duology, *RealmShift* and *MageSign* (The Balance 1 and 2) from Gryphonwood Press. His latest book is the horror noir novella, *The Book Club*.

As well as novels, Alan has had more than 70 short fiction publications in journals and anthologies in Australia, the US, the UK and France. His short fiction has appeared in *The Magazine of Fantasy & Science Fiction*, *Beneath Ceaseless Skies*, *Daily Science Fiction*, *Postscripts*, and *Midnight Echo*, among many others, and more than twenty anthologies, including the *Year's Best Australian Fantasy & Horror* on several occasions. His award-winning first collected volume of short fiction, *Crow Shine*, is out now.

At times, Alan collaborates with US action/adventure author David Wood. Together they have co-authored the horror novella *Dark Rite*, the action thrillers *Blood Codex* and *Anubis Key* (Jake Crowley Adventures Books 1 and 2), and the giant monster thriller novel *Primordial*.

Read extracts from his novels, a novella and short stories at his website—www.warriorscribe.com—or find him on Twitter @AlanBaxter and Facebook, and feel free to tell him what you think. About anything.

STILL LIFE WITH NATALIE

SARAH READ

I T'S NOT A GRAVEYARD, IT'S AN ECOSYSTEM. I mean, yeah, there are graves, all tilting across a ragged lawn, and that's all most people see: death, stones like rows of dry teeth. And in some graveyards, that's all they want you to see: marble stark against a blank slate of manicured grass. And yeah, the light's better in that sort of place, where the trees are tamed into shape and let the sun through. But the flowers are better here.

To paint flowers, you need an old cemetery. A century of mourner's offerings gone to seed, taken root. The best kind of garden gone feral. And wild, native things carried on the wind that feed on all the richness under the soil.

It's impossible to get my easel level on the lumpy ground. All my paintings are askew, slanted. I like it that way, now. It's a whole new perspective—a new way to look at graves, at flowers.

We don't have cemeteries like this back home. The water table is too high. All the bodies get stacked in stone huts, or burned and stored in a field that's paved like a parking lot of corpses. And nothing grows but infernal moss. You know how to paint moss? It's a wash of green. It takes less skill than finger painting.

I add a bit of blue to the petal of a tiny violet.

At home, all that heat and wet makes the lifecycle swift. Accelerated decomposition. Sprouts splitting their seed cases right in front of your eyes. Plants die in layers, black and sticky, each generation insulating the last.

It's cold here. Things move slow. It's only September, but the tips of my fingers ache. The cold soaks in, and everything smells like ice weeks

STILL LIFE WITH NATALIE

before the snow arrives. The light has changed, and I realize I've been here for hours. Only a few small blossoms finished. My models will shrink overnight, close up, maybe get nipped with frost.

I swish my brushes in my canteen, toss them in a stained wood box. I lay the wet canvas carefully in the trunk, nestled between the easel and spare tire.

I look back at the wild violets peeking out of the shadow of the stone. Their heads are already lowered, as if praying over the grave. A few of these blossoms will live forever, though, on canvas.

The picture will never be finished, now. None of them ever are. Life moves too fast in the graveyard: the light shifts, and death comes too soon.

***

"You're going to fail that class, Colin. Are you going to tell your mother? Or shall I?" My mother's cousin—her doppelganger running twenty years behind—thumbs threateningly at her cell phone, scrolling through the texted chronicle of reports she's made on my progress.

"I paint better than the professor."

"Not if you count finished pieces." Natalie stretches across the couch like she wants me to paint her. I've told her I don't do portraits. I do still life. "Still Alives"—the flowers of the dead. They're the memories: the last remaining thoughts of those that feed the roots. Clear minds grow pretty things. Dark thoughts grow weeds and poisons. I'm not just painting flowers, I'm painting echoes: the last story the dead have to tell.

I can see in Natalie's eyes that her grave would grow thistle and nightshade. I've warned her to see to her thoughts, lest she sleep eternal in a weed patch. But I think she likes it. I think she'd finger paint dandelions.

"So what are you going to do for your first New England winter? What are you going to paint?" She cracks her back and folds an arm behind her head.

"I took some photos. I guess I'll paint from them." She must see me shudder. Knows I hate the thought. Knows it's not the same.

"Are you still going to call them 'Still Alives' if the flowers are dead under three feet of snow?"

My teeth hurt. My whole face does. It must be the cold.

***

They call the largest model a conservatory. It has a heavy-duty composite frame and panels made to withstand heavy snowfall. Best of all, they're opaque, and the light inside is milky, ambient. Deep troughs of rich earth line the long walls. The aisle is just wide enough for my easel.

Natalie squeezes a lump of dirt in her hand, crumbling it. "What are you going to plant?"

I'll need a lock for the door. "Nothing. Just going to see what grows."

She furrows her brow as best she can against the stiffening effects of Botox. "Things don't just grow, Colin, you need seeds."

"There are seeds in there already. I just don't know what. Violets, probably. Definitely roses, lilies, carnations. Dandelions, probably. Weeds."

Natalie's face falls. She shakes her head and scrubs her dirty palm against her pants. "Colin, you didn't."

"I can't give up my theme, Natalie, that's half the beauty of the painting."

"You took the grave dirt?"

"Just the top layer. I put the sod back down. No one ever goes there. No one will ever know."

The greenhouse door slams. Fiberglass panels rattle like dull drums. She'll be calling my mother. Condensation dribbles down the frosted fiberglass. Sweat runs down my back. The heat, the dampness, it feels like home. But the grave soil is pure New England. It smells of promise. Of stolen summer. Of art.

***

"You're grinding your teeth."

"What?"

"That's why your jaw hurts." Natalie pulls my hand from my jaw and wipes at the mess my fingers have left behind. Dirt. No paint. There hasn't been paint for weeks.

"It's not worth the stress, Colin. Just drop the class. Take an incomplete and register again in the spring, when the flowers are back."

"I can't fail, Natalie. That's not an option."

"Waiting for the right time isn't failing. Your theme is important to you. Great. Your professor will understand. But you're not going to get daffodils in October. Not here. Not unless you plant them yourself. That's not how nature works."

She's right. Her words are skunk cabbage and nettle, but they aren't wrong. I said it myself—it's an ecosystem. You need the whole cycle to make life.

I miss my classes. I tell the professor I need the time to work, need the light. It's not a lie. I head back to the graveyard where the flower stalks have turned to dry sticks and the grass stabs at my knees and palms like little sabers, like an army guarding the treasure under the soil.

The New England winter earth is hard, hoarfrost crackles under my spade as I pry at the layers of dirt. A lattice of ice holding everything together.

I lay the lumpy bag carefully in the trunk, nestled between the shovel and spare tire. Haul my harvest back to the long conservatory.

Finger bones rattle in terra cotta pots like dice in a cup, casting my fortunes. I drop fistfuls of rich earth over them, the same dirt they've known for thirty years. Long leg bones stretch along the flowerbeds. The oil at their core no longer shines, but it's still there, a matte stain on dry meat. I can smell the life left there through the dust. Like iron and old fruit. I seed my ground with these forgotten dreams, and see what grows. Pleasure or poison, it's all art, either way.

I'm tired and my back aches too much to bend over my canvas. And I need time. Patience, while the roots find their source.

***

I never thought I'd be so glad to see moss. I wash green across the canvas, feel the texture of the woven fibers against my roughened fingertips, callouses grating, my skin cells becoming a part of the piece. The smell of it comes in waves as intoxicating as the color, chlorophyll sweat clinging to my face like dew. My breath comes so quick it dries the paint in front of me before I've finished spreading it. I dip my hand back in the paint and smear it across the canvas. A few more days of warm wet and filtered winter sunlight, and there will be flowers. Flowers always follow the green, and the green always comes first.

***

The stalks bend under the weight of shrinking blooms. Petals drop to the dirt without ever growing vibrant. The paintings look as if viewed through smoke. I dab more brown along the edge of a leaf.

"Are you ever coming inside?" Natalie only speaks in oily ivy now. She casts so much darkness that I swear the plants are starved for light.

"I need to turn something in tomorrow. At least show some progress." I rub my arm along my upper lip, wiping away the drops shaken loose by speech. Her glasses are fogged, but I feel her look. Like my mother peering out of her eyes.

"It doesn't look like the flowers are doing very well." She touches the tip of a finger to a limp petal and it falls.

"God damn it, Natalie!"

She turns on me, leans into her shout. "They're not 'Still Alives', Colin. They're dead. You're letting them die. Flowers need to be nurtured." She turns away so fast that the breeze in her wake knocks another petal free.

She's right, though. About the nurturing. Flowers need to be fed. Not just once, but over and over. I need to complete the ecosystem. I'm going to miss class again.

***

All my nails are split and my palms are a mess of blisters, but I can hold a brush.

I never noticed how many colors there are in dirt. It isn't just brown. It's a thousand browns, gold, green, even blue like Natalie's hard eyes.

And ants are not just black, but are mahogany anywhere the light shines off their beaded bodies.

Spiders the color of dirty glass, inside a dark rainbow of organs.

Worms the color of salmon and skin, and worms the color of bone.

The dirt is alive. Still alive. Long after the flowers die. Long before new seedlings split their casing and take root, punch tendrils through the earth to the richness waiting there.

Nothing grows in dirt that isn't moving, churning, recycling itself in the long throat of worms.

Life comes from life, or what life leaves behind, hidden in the dark center of bones. And hollow bones hold only echoes.

The liquid pooling in the sunken eyes is mustard-seed yellow, almost ochre, but a color I've never mixed before. My hand shakes as I dip the brush, gather pigment from around brittle lashes, and spread it along the edge of a daffodil. The perfect color for where the shadow of a headstone falls across the buttery petal.

There are flowers, now. It's early spring in my little garden. But there aren't enough blooms to fill a gallery.

I lower the head of Albert Vernon 1926–1999 into the pot at my feet. Scalp slides from bone and teeth tumble from leathery lips as his cheek-bone comes to rest against the pottery.

"Show me a pretty story, Albert," I whisper to him. The smell of him sticks to my tongue, stink turning to flavor, and it's ochre, too. "Your wife was all wild morning glory and bluebells. I bet she covered you with roses."

I pour dirt over him. Gather water from the condensation troughs and saturate the soil. I need more blossoms, and fast. I still haven't finished a painting.

***

Natalie brings me a package. She walks right into the greenhouse. Doesn't knock. I still need a lock.

The package is wrapped in red paper, green ribbon tied around it. Already? I'm running out of time.

I don't want to set my brush down, but I do it. Get it over with. If she argues, I'll just be distracted longer.

"Merry Early Christmas. I thought you could use this now. Didn't want to make you wait." She smiles. It's a nice smile. It's a shame I don't do portraits.

Then her face wrinkles. "Ugh! It stinks in here."

I scan the beds. Everything planted, nothing visible except the flowers. Little pops of color bobbing over buried secrets.

"I got a weird fungus. Can't get the stink out." I smile back, take the package, snap the ribbon, rip the paper. Inside the box, resting on a pillow of tissue, is a pair of wool fingerless gloves. The stitches are strained in places, loose in others.

"A lady at work showed me how to knit them. I thought they might help you paint outside in the winter."

She'd sewn roughly cut suede patches to the palms.

"And maybe your hands won't get so beat up gardening."

Her thoughts are all buttercups and forget-me-nots, morning glory vines twisting around my heart.

"Thank you," I say. I've forgotten how to say anything else.

She smiles. Sunflowers—Black-eyed Susans. Colors I haven't seen for months. Hues that have gone dry in my paint box. Colors I need.

The composition of her thoughts is stretched across the canvas of her face, and it's more than I can resist.

***

The secret of Still Alives is that they are portraits. Not of faces, but of minds. A moment of heart frozen in time, like a bulb wintering in the cold earth before the right gardener calls it up from the soil. Not everyone gets a portrait of their best moment. Only kings and queens, and Natalie.

The earth in my flowerbed dances with life. And from its shifting soil, a thousand blossoms unfurl.

It reminds me of home.

ABOUT SARAH READ

SARAH READ is a dark fiction writer and freelance editor recently relocated from the foothills of Colorado to the frozen north of Wisconsin. Her short stories can be found in *Gamut, Black Static,* and other places, and in various anthologies including *Exigencies, Suspended in Dusk: Volume One,* and *BEHOLD! Oddities Curiosities and Undefinable Wonders.* She also writes numerous articles about crocheting and fountain pens. She is the Editor in Chief at *Pantheon Magazine* and an active member of the Horror Writer's Association. When she's not staring into the abyss, she knits. You can find her online on Instagram or Twitter @inkwellmonster or on her site at www.inkwellmonster.wordpress.com.

LOVE IS A CAVITY
I CAN'T STOP TOUCHING

STEPHEN GRAHAM JONES

WHEN I WAS FOURTEEN, I ate a cooked piece of thigh meat off my girlfriend Sherry Wilkes. Back then she was "Shari" with an "i," with a heart for the dot when she could get away with it. Now she's Sherry with a "y" again, nearly twenty years later. I can still see the girl she was at fourteen, though. It's the eyes. All the women in her family have the same look.

I ate a piece from her, she ate a piece from me.

We never had sex, either. Maybe because we didn't have to, after that? It was like we'd gone out of order, skipped the tenderness, gone straight to the part where we consume each other.

We didn't make it long after that Thursday night, both our legs gauzed and bleeding. Not because of shame or regret, and it wasn't that awkwardness that follows the kind of intimacy we'd shared, either.

I think it was that we could see the dim shape of the next step, the next stage. The one that would leave us dead in our separate rooms, our suicides planned down to the minute, our bodies abandoned, like to prove we were meeting somewhere else, screw this town.

My leg turned up infected later that week.

Sherry's leg never got infected.

That's because she went first, probably.

We loved each other, see.

Not like I love my wife Alice. How I love Alice, that'll last until we're old and grey. It's already taken us through lost jobs and late nights, and it'll take us through hospitals and alcoholism and whatever else it needs to. Because it's a love that's corded with muscle, a love built to last. How I loved Sherry, though—Shari with the "i"—that was white-hot. Some nights, alone in my room in ninth grade, I thought it was going to burn me up, leave nothing but a pile of ash on my sheets for my mom to find.

When we whispered "forever" to each other, it wasn't a promise, it was a dare.

Now I know we weren't good for each other, of course. Like, healthy. The rational part of me knows that if we'd somehow managed to stay together in spite of ourselves, then, even at our age, there'd be domestic disturbance calls once or twice a month. And that would just be the part of our relationship making it into the public eye. Behind closed doors—I don't know.

We would eat each other up.

I guess it's as simple as that.

It's better we stopped where we did. I can't deny that.

But I also can't deny that one night two fourteen-year-olds locked in a type of one-upmanship love that neither would ever feel again, that they did something they could never take back. That they would never want to take back. It started with a lie about the Thursday night junior varsity basketball game, the one they were each going to with different friends. Not with each other.

Instead of that game, they walked out into the woods with a knife, with a coat hanger. With a roll of gauze. To play a different game.

They weren't holding hands. They weren't smiling. Love, it can be grim. It can be so grim it hurts.

They walked out just past where any headlights would cut through the trees, and then they set down their implements and caught each other's eyes, like to see who would blink first.

Neither of us did.

Sherry had worn shorts. She's always been smart like that.

Because it's what the doctor did for vaccinations, I rubbed the spot on her thigh she'd already traced with a ball-point pen.

"You were supposed to bring rubbing alcohol," she said.

"My mom would have noticed," I said.

She was sitting down, and I was sitting lower, taking a knee like Coach always said.

This is how people propose, and get proposed to.

When she nodded yes, the collar of her shirt pulled up into her teeth, to bite, I blew on the pale skin of her thigh, then I carved into it.

The same way when you're eating watermelon with a spoon, you go in a little then scoop that red meat back up?

My scoop was more ragged, but, before the blood rushed in, it left the same kind of crater.

And Sherry, she screamed—I would too—but it was through her teeth, it was through how hard she was biting into her shirt.

She had the gauze balled in her hand and pressed down right when I was done, pressed down like trying to squash the pain away.

The bite of her thigh I had in my palm was deep red, and the muscle had striation to it, and one side had her skin still, and some peach fuzz on it. Just enough.

I held it in my hand while she carved on me, my pants pulled down to my ankles. Right before the blade went into my muscle, that was what I was worried about—how stupid I must look, standing there in my underwear.

Because she was a more delicate eater, she ran the fine edge of the blade up and down before cutting, to shave the few long hairs off.

We were both crying by the time it was done. This is how you know it's love.

The next part was easy.

We just skewered the two bites onto the coat hanger, roasted them under her lighter, taking turns because it kept heating up, burning our thumbs. We laughed because it was stupid that thumbs could matter, after what we'd done to our legs.

I didn't want it to, but the peach fuzz on the bite of her thigh, it curled up and smoked away.

Next, just like we'd planned, we slid the meat off, and we fed it to each other.

I took the bite she offered all at once, to show how little hesitation I was having about this whole thing, but Sherry had been raised better. She took one bite, her incisors just brushing the pads of my thumb.

The meat was still red in the center.

She swallowed, then took my wrist in her hand, guided the rest of the bite in, her eyes locked on me the whole while.

When we limped out of those trees, we were different people than we'd been. It was nighttime now. Everybody was at the basketball game, watching the JV team lose again. There was no one to witness our transformation, no headlights to throw our shadows tall against the trees. No deer or raccoon considered us, then scurried away. The mosquitoes didn't make a tunnel for us to walk down.

The reason I was the one to get infected, I figure, was that Sherry's blood was on that blade.

I couldn't have cleaned it with the lighter, though. You don't clean the blade if you love someone.

And I didn't throw that piece of her up, either.

I've never thrown it up.

One dusk, I walked into the mystery and the muscle of love, and I came back from that darkness holding a girl's hand, and I kissed her lightly on the lips before we parted ways, my fingertips to her hip, and I was aware of her musculature in a completely new way.

The divot is still in my leg. The cavity. The well the tip of my middle finger knows so, so well.

Sitting at my desk, I can rub my finger into it through my pants.

Alice says it looks like a weakness in the muscle.

I don't let her run her finger down into it, of course.

Sherry doesn't know about it all, I don't think.

Because our town is small, I still see her once every couple of weeks. More in the summer.

As near as I can tell, she doesn't wear shorts short enough to show her scar, and I never see her at the pool. And I stay until dark, some nights.

There's a couple of girls there, though.

One's named Claire. The other's Clarissa.

Girls with names like "Shari" with an "i," they do things like name their daughters with the same letter up front.

Their eyes are just like their mother's.

When they break the surface of the water after a dive, it's like Sherry's rising all over again, in slow motion.

And their thighs, high up on their thighs, dusted with golden hair— some days I have to close my eyes. And some days, when the pool closes because night is sifting in, some days I collect my towel and my lotion and

I turn left after walking out the pool gate, left, not right, which would be towards my house.

There's two girls jumping from line to line of the sidewalk in front of me. They're walking into the darkness. The older one's eight, the younger one six.

I'm just following them to keep them safe, I tell myself.

And my mouth, it's not watering.

That would be wrong.

Like love knows the difference.

ABOUT STEPHEN GRAHAM JONES

STEPHEN GRAHAM JONES is the author of sixteen novels, six story collections and more than 250 stories. His werewolf novel *Mongrels* was published by William Morrowin 2017. Stephen's been the recipient of an NEA Fellowship in Fiction, the Texas Institute of Letters Jesse Jones Award for Fiction, the Independent Publishers Awards for Multicultural Fiction, three *This is Horror* awards, and he's made *Bloody Disgusting*'s Top Ten Novels of the Year. Stephen teaches in the MFA programs at University of Colorado at Boulder and University of California Riverside-Palm Desert. He lives in Boulder, Colorado, with his wife, two children and too many old trucks. Visit him on Twitter @SGJ72.

THERE'S NO LIGHT BETWEEN FLOORS

PAUL TREMBLAY

M Y HEAD IS A BOX FULL OF WET COTTON and it won't hold anything else. Her voice is dust falling into my ear. She says, "There's no light between floors."

I blink. Minutes or hours pass. There is nothing to see. We're blind, but our bodies are close and we form a yin and yang, although I don't know who is which. She says the between floors stuff again. She speaks to my feet. They don't listen. Her feet are next to my head. I touch the bare skin of her ankle, of what I imagine to be her ankle, and it is warm and I want to leave my hand there.

She's telling me that we're trapped between floors. I add, "I think we're in the rubble of a giant building. It was thousands of miles tall. The building was big enough to go to the moon where it had a second foundation, but most people agreed the top was the moon and the bottom was us." Her feet don't move and don't listen. I don't blame them. Her toes might be under Sheetrock or a steel girder. There's only enough room in here for us. Everything presses down from above, or up from below. I keep talking and my voice fills our precious space. "Wait, it can't be the moon our building was built to. Maybe another planet with revolutions and rotations and orbital paths in sync with ours so the giant building doesn't get twisted and torn apart. Or maybe that's what happened, it did get twisted apart and that's why we're here." I stop talking because like the giant building, my words fall apart and trap me.

She flexes her calf muscle. Is she shaking me away? I move my hand off her leg and I immediately regret it. I feel nothing now. Maybe her movement was just a muscle spasm. I could ask her, but that would be an awkward question depending on her answer.

She says, "There are gods moving above us. I can hear them."

I listen and I don't hear any gods. It horrifies me that I can't hear them. Makes me think I am terribly broken. There's only the sound of my breathing, and it's so loud and close, like I'm inside my own lungs.

She says, "They're the old gods, and they've been forgotten. They've returned, but they're suffering. And despite everything, they'll be forgotten again."

Maybe I'm not supposed to hear the old gods. Or maybe I do hear them and I've always heard them and their sound is nothingness, and that means we're forgotten too.

I put my hand back on her ankle. Her skin is cool now. Maybe it's my fault. My chest expands and gets tight, lungs too greedy. My head and back press against the weight around me. I'm taking up too much space. I let air and words out into the crowded void, trying to make myself small again. I say, "Did the old gods make the building? Did they tear it down? Did they do this to us? Are they angry? Why are they always so angry?"

She says, "I have a story. It's only one sentence long. There's a small child wandering a city and can't find her mother. That's it. It's sentimental and melodramatic but that doesn't mean it doesn't happen every day."

She is starting to break under the stress of our conditions. I admire that she has lasted this long, but we can't stay in this no-room-womb-tomb forever. I should keep her talking so she doesn't lose consciousness. I say, "Who are you? I'm sorry I don't remember."

She whispers. I don't hear every word so I have to fill in the gaps. "Dad died when I was four years old. He was short, bent, had those glasses that darkened automatically, and he loved flannel. At least, that's what he looked like in pictures. We had pictures all over the house, but not pictures of him, actually. My only real memory of Dad is him picking up dog shit in the backyard. It's what he did every weekend. We lived on a hill and the yard had a noticeable slant, so he stood lopsided to keep from falling. He used a gardener's trowel as a scoop and made the deposits into a plastic grocery bag. He let me hold the bag. His joke was that he was transporting, not cleaning, as he dumped the poop out in the woods across the street, same spot every time. It was the only time he spent out in the yard with me, cleaning our dog's shit. I don't remember our dog's name. My father and the dog are just like the old gods."

The old gods again. They make me nervous. Everything seems closer and tighter after she speaks. My eyes strain against their lids and pray for light. They want to jump out and roll away. I say, "What about the old gods?"

She says, "I still hear them. They have their own language."

I wait for another story that doesn't come. Her head is next to my feet but so far away. Her ankle feels different but that's not enough to go on. Finally, I say, "Maybe I should go find the old gods and tell them you're here, since you seem to know them. Maybe I'll apologize for not hearing them."

My elbows are pinned against my chest and I can't extend my arms. I do what I can to feel around me and around her legs. I find some space behind her left hip. I shift my weight and focus on my limited movement. Minutes and hours pass. My body turns slowly, like the hands of a clock. If the old gods are watching, even they won't be able to see the movement. Maybe that's blasphemous. I'll worry about it later. In order to turn my shoulders I have to push my chest into her legs and hips. I apologize but she doesn't say anything. I make sure I don't hit her head with my feet. I pull myself over her legs, scraping my back against the rubble above me, pressing harder against her, and I'm trying the best I can to make myself flat. It's hard to breathe, and small white stars spot the blackness. I climb over her and reach into a tunnel where I'll have to crawl like a worm or a snake, but I have arms and I wish I could leave them behind with her. I can't turn around so I roll her back with my feet into the spot I occupied. Maybe it'll be more comfortable and after I'm through she can follow. I say, "Don't worry, I'll find your Dad," but then I remember that she told me he died. What a horrible thing for me to say.

In the tunnel opening I find a flat, square object. It's the size of my hand. The outer perimeter is metal with raised bumps that I try to read with my fingers, but they can't read. It's not their fault. I never trained them to do so. The center of the square is smooth and cool. Glass, I think. I know what it is. It's a picture frame. Hers or mine. I don't know. I slide it into my back pocket and I shimmy, still blind always blind, into the tunnel. Everything gets tighter.

My arms are pinned to my side. My untrained hands under my pelvis. My legs and feet do the all the work. Those silly hands and useless digits fret and worry. The tunnel thins. I push with my feet and roll my stomach muscles.

The tunnel thins more. My shoulders are stuck. I can't move. Should I wait for her? She could push me through. Do I yell? Would the old gods help me then? But I'm afraid. If I yell I might start an avalanche and close the tunnel. I'm afraid they won't help me. My heart pumps and swells. There isn't any room in here for it. The white stars return. Everything is tight and hard in my chest. I feel a breeze on my face. There must be more open space ahead. One more push.

My feet are loud behind me. They're frantic rescue workers. I hope they don't panic. I need them to get through this. My shoulders ache and throb. Under the pressure. Leg muscles on fire. But I squeeze. Through. And into a chamber big enough to crawl in.

I feel around looking for openings, looking for up. I still can't see. I'll use sinus pressure and spit to determine up and down. My legs shake and I need to rest. I take out the picture frame. My hands dance all over it. Maybe it's a picture of her father in the yard. He's wearing the flannel even in summer. I remember how determined he was to keep the yard clean. He didn't care if the grass grew or if my dog dug holes, he just wanted all the shit gone.

I need to keep moving. I pocket the picture frame and listen again for the old gods. I still don't hear them. There's a wider path in the rubble, it expands and it goes up and I follow it. Dad had all kinds of picture frames that held black-and-white photos of obscure relatives or relatives who became obscure on the windowsills and hutches and almost anything with a flat, stable surface. He told me all their stories once, and I tried to listen and remember, but they're gone. After Dad died, Mom didn't take down or hide any of the pictures. She took to adding to the collection with random black-and-white photos she'd find at yard sales and antique shops. She filled the walls with them. Every couple of months, she moved and switched all the pictures around too, so we didn't know who our obscure relatives were and who were strangers. Nothing was labeled. Everyone had similar moustaches or wore the same hats and jackets and dresses and everyone was forgotten even though they were all still there. I can't help but think, hidden in the stash of pictures, were the old gods, and they've always been watching me.

The path in the rubble continues to expand. My crawl has become a walking crouch. There are hard lefts and rights, and I can't go too fast as I almost fall into a deep drop. Maybe it's the drop I shouldn't be concerned about. What if I should be going down instead of up? The piled rubble implies a bottom. There's no guarantee there's a top. What if she did hear the old gods but her sense of direction was all messed up? What if they're below us? Maybe that's fine too.

I continue to climb and I try to concentrate. Thinking of the picture frame helps. In our house there was a picture of a young man in an army uniform standing by himself on a beach, shirtsleeves rolled over his biceps. Probably circa-WWII, but we didn't know for sure. He had an odd smirk and, like the Mona Lisa's, it always followed me. I also thought his face looked painted on, and at the same time not all there, like it would float away if you stopped looking, so I stared at it, a lot. If I had to guess, I'd say that's the picture in my back pocket.

My crouch isn't necessary anymore, and now I'm standing and level and the darkness isn't so dark. There are outlines and shapes, and weak light. My feet shuffle on a thin carpet. I avoid the teeth of a ruined escalator. I'm dizzy and my mouth tastes like tinfoil. There's a distant rumble and the bones of everything rattle and shake loose dust. She was right. The old gods are here. I imagine they are beautiful and horrible, and immense, and alien because they are all eyes or mouths or arms and they move the planets and stars around. I take the picture frame out of my pocket and clutch it to my chest. It's a shield. It's a teddy bear. I found it between floors. There's a jagged opening in the ruined building around me and I walk through it.

I emerge into an alien world. I'm not where I used to be. This is the top of the ruined building, or its other bottom. The air here is thick and not well. Behind me there is a section of the building's second or other foundation that is still intact. My eyes sting and my vision is blurry, but the sky is red and there are mountains of glass and mountains of brick and mountains of metal and I stand in the valley. Nothing grows here. There are eternal fires burning without smoke. Everything is so large and I am so small. There are pools of fire and a layer of gray ash on the ground and mountains. I'm alone and there's just so much space and it's beautiful, but horrible too because I can't make any sense of it and there's too much space, too much room for possibility, anything can happen here. I shouldn't be here. She was right not to follow me because I climbed through the rubble in the wrong direction and I think about going back, but then I see the old gods.

I don't know how she heard them. They're as alien or other as I imagined but not grand or powerful. They're small and fragile, like me. There is one old god between the mountains and it walks slowly toward me. The old god is naked and sloughs its dead skin, strips hanging off its fingers and elbows. Its head is all red holes and scaly, patchy skin. The old god must be at the end, or maybe the beginning, of a metamorphosis. There is another kneeling at the base of the mountain of glass. The old god's back is all oozing boils and blisters. Its hands leave skin and bloody prints on the mountain. It speaks in a language of gurgles and hard consonants that I do not understand. The old god is blessing or damning everything it touches. I don't know if there is a difference. I find more old gods lying about, some are covered in ash, and they look like the others but they are asleep and dreaming their terrible dreams. And she was right again; they are all suffering. I didn't think they were supposed to suffer like this.

I walk and it's so hard to breathe, but I shouldn't be surprised given where I am. There's too much space, everything is stretched out, and I'm afraid of the red sky. Then I hear her voice. Her falling dust in my ears. She's behind me somewhere, maybe standing at the edge of our felled building and this other world. She asks me to tell the old gods that I'm sorry I forgot them. My voice isn't very loud and my throat hurts, but I tell them I am sorry. I ask her if I'm the small child in the city looking for my mother in her one-line story. She tells me the old gods have names: Dresden and Hiroshima and Nagasaki. She knows the language of the old gods and I know the words mean something but it's beyond my grasp, like the seconds previously passed, and they all will be forgotten like those pictures, and their stories, in my mother's house.

I'm still clutching the found picture frame to my chest. There's a ringing in my ears and my stomach burns. The old god walking toward me spews a gout of blood, then tremors wrack its body. Flaps of skin peel off and fall like autumn leaves. Change is always painful. I take the frame off my chest and look at it. Focusing is difficult. There's no picture. It's empty. There's only a white sticker on the glass that reads: $9.99. I feel dizzy and I can't stay out here much longer. It's too much and minutes and hours pass with me staring at the empty picture frame, and how wrong I was, how wrong I am.

There's a great, all-encompassing, white light that momentarily bleaches the red sky and I shield my eyes with the empty frame. Then there's a rumble that shakes the planet, and well beyond the mountains that surround me a great grey building reaches into the red sky. They're building it so fast, too fast, and that's why it'll eventually fall down because they aren't taking their time, they're not showing care. It's still an awesome sight despite what I know will happen to it. The top of the building billows out, like the cap of a mushroom, and I try to yell, "Stop!" because they are constructing the building's second foundation in the sky. The building won't be anchored to anything; the sky certainly won't hold it. It'll fall. I don't want to watch it fall. I can't. So I turn away.

She speaks to me again. She tells me to leave this place and come back. I do and I walk, trying to avoid the gaze of the old gods. They make me feel guilty. But they aren't looking at me. They cover their faces. They're afraid of the great light. Or maybe they're just tired because they've seen it all before. I walk back to our ruined building, but she's not at the opening. She's already climbing back down. I'll follow. I'll climb back down to our space between floors and bring her the picture frame. I'll tell her it's a picture of my Dad in the yard with flannel and his poop-scoop.

I ease back into the rubble, dowsing paths and gaps, climbing down, knowing eventually down will become up again. Or maybe I'll tell her it's a picture of that army guy I didn't know, him and his inscrutable Mona Lisa smirk. Did he have the confidence and bravado of immortality or was he afraid of everything? She won't be able to see the picture so I won't really be lying to her. The picture will be whatever I tell her it'll be. I won't tell her about the new giant building, the one that was grey and has a foundation in the sky.

The gaps in the rubble narrow quickly and everything is dark again. I once asked Mom why we kept all those old, black-and-white pictures and why she still bought more, and why all the walls and shelves of our house were covered with old photos and old faces, everyone anonymous, everyone dead, and she told me that they were keepsakes, little bits of history, she liked having history around, then she changed her mind and said, no, they were simply reminders. And I asked reminders of what? And she didn't say anything but gave me that same Mona Lisa smile from the photograph, but I know hers was afraid of everything.

The picture is in my back pocket again. I am going to tell her that everyone who was ever forgotten is in the picture. We'll be in the picture too, so we won't forget again.

I'm crawling and the tunnel ahead will narrow. I can feel the difference in the air. There is another rumble above me and the bones of everything shake again, but I won't see that horrible light down here. I'll be safe. I wonder if I should've tried to help them. But what could I have done? I suppose, at the very least, I could've told the old gods that there is no light between floors.

ABOUT PAUL TREMBLAY

PAUL TREMBLAY is the author of the novels *Disappearance at Devil's Rock* and *A Head Full of Ghosts*. His other novels include *The Little Sleep*, *No Sleep till Wonderland*, *Swallowing a Donkey's Eye*, and *Floating Boy and the Girl Who Couldn't Fly* (co-written with Stephen Graham Jones).

His fiction and essays have appeared in *The Los Angeles Times*, *Supernatural Noir*, and numerous Year's Best anthologies. He is the author of the short speculative fiction collections *In the Mean Time* and *Compositions for the Young and Old* and the hard-boiled/dark fantasy novella *City Pier: Above and Below*. He served as fiction editor of ChiZine Magazine and as co-editor of *Fantasy Magazine*, and was also the co-editor of the *Creatures* anthology (with John Langan). Paul is currently on the board of directors for the Shirley Jackson Awards as well.

Paul is very truthful and declarative in his bios. He once gained three inches of height in a single twelve-hour period, and he does not have a uvula. His second toe is longer than his big toe, and yes, on both feet. He has a master's degree in mathematics, teaches AP Calculus, and once made twenty-seven three-pointers in a row. He enjoys reading *The Tale of Mr. Jeremy Fisher* aloud in a faux-British accent to children. He is also reading this bio aloud, now, with the same accent. He lives outside of Boston, Massachusetts and he is represented by Stephen Barbara, Inkwell Management.

THAT DAMNED CAT

NERINE DORMAN

H INDSIGHT OFFERED PERFECT CLARITY. I should have said something to my brethren when I noticed the two burly chaps standing outside Aunt Fustia's teashop, but we were in such a hurry to go down to the basement, that the significance of my observation was lost in the excitement of the moment. After all, it's not every day that a coven attempts to bring through a Duke of the Ninth Infernal Circle—especially not in a city where consorting with demons was an offence punishable by death. The Order of the White Rose was nothing if not dedicated in its defence of the Faith.

The ritual went so well at first. One of our esteemed brothers intoned the Nine Great Maledictions in his chthonic tones. The incense blend of blue rahash and porsephine musk enhanced the overall doom-enshrouded mood, and I could already detect faint disturbances at the edges of my vision. Perfection.

Things were going according to plan.

The vessel—a young woman procured from the Rash—lay bound and ready to accept the Duke. All we needed to do was complete the ritual.

Ours wasn't the first coven to attempt a summoning, but we were the first in more than a decade to endure the depredations of the knights long enough to make the attempt. The stars had aligned, both moons were gibbous. There was no better time than the present, though the Order's irrational fear of Infernal Entities meant we had to go to great lengths to maintain secrecy—hence the conversion of my aged aunt's basement into a makeshift temple.

The payoff would be worth it, or so the ancient texts assured us. Certainly worth the risk to become lords in this world rather than slaves in whichever afterlife those of the Faith proclaimed.

With a crack like glass breaking, the air in the basement was torn asunder, and a scintillating oval of light appeared above the vessel. Oh, how the girl struggled against her bonds, and her eyes rolled back in what must have been great terror. Thank goodness we'd gagged her, otherwise her shrieks would've burst our eardrums. She'd be of a different mind once the Duke was settled, however, so I shoved away my lingering doubts. We were about to bestow a great honour upon her. She'd thank us later.

The door splintered with a crash and a dozen black-clad figures shoved in yelling, "Halt! In the name of the White Rose! Hold your hands where we can see them!"

Before I could comply, I was shoved to the ground and all the breath left my lungs in a painful whoosh.

Worse was to come. The wondrous light of our portal flared once with a roar of compressed power then crumped into nothingness, along with our darkest dreams and aspirations.

Someone thought to flick on the switch, which flooded our makeshift chamber with the brilliance of a thousand daggers thrust into the back of my head—the downside of harsh lighting combined with the special blend of incense.

A frightful yowl pierced through the general hubbub of voices, thuds of fists on flesh and overturning furniture. Had something sneaked through the portal after all? I tried to look up, but someone kicked me in the ribs.

"Goddamn it! It scratched me!" a man shouted. "Careful! It might have rabies."

Another man stumbled and knocked over the altar, bringing with it the frightful crash of breaking glass and fallen idols.

I sighed deeply into the dusty stone floor. All ruined. Years of careful planning undone by the white-light, crystal-waving Knights of the Order of the White Rose.

***

The magistrate leaned into his palm, his wig askew. The way he was doodling with his pen did not bode well for me, while my attorney—some bloke called Edred Possenthirt—blathered on about obscure bylaws pertaining to religious freedom.

Aunt Fustia's loud sobs echoed in the courtroom, but I refused to turn around to offer her my trademarked death stare, because I risked the stern disapproval of hundreds of self-righteous glares. Trust my aunt to make a scene in public. If she carried on like that, the knights would have *her* bundled off, and a fine thing the tabloids would make of it.

PROMINENT FORTUNE TELLER CONNECTED TO UNDERGROUND CULT
TEA AND DEMONS IN THE GARDEN DISTRICT
CULTISTS LINKED TO KIDNAPPING, ATTEMPTED POSSESSION

The journalists had this way of twisting words to make our actions seem trite and somehow dirty. I cringed thinking of the unflattering black-and-white images that had been spread all over the front pages of the broadsheets.

Then again, I didn't expect to worry too much about the tabloids. Not where I was going: a short walk off the gallows at the wrong end of a noose, like my brethren who'd already been sentenced. So much for our religious freedom when adherents of obscure cults such as ours were viewed no better than insurgents and serial killers, of which this city had its surfeit. Oddly, I had passed beyond anxiety to dull resignation. This was it. The end. Each breath was measured in days—hours even—until the judge passed his sentence. So much I'd never gotten around to doing, like going back to varsity or moving out of Aunt Fustia's apartment building. Finding a nice girl. Marrying. Not having to pay for sex would be nice.

A murmur had me cast a glance to my left, to view a disturbance that turned out to be no more than a dark brown tortoiseshell with a kink in her tail. The feline sauntered down the aisle as if she had every right to be in the courtroom. She paused when she was adjacent to where I stood in the dock, and regarded me with her large, gooseberry green eyes. For a second they caught the light in that peculiar lambent way cats' eyes sometimes did, and gleamed red. Then she continued towards the judge without so much as a by your leave.

From the look of things, the cat's appearance had caught everyone by surprise; I mean, really, how in all the Unholy Hells had she managed to gain ingress in the first place? The courthouse was a bleeding fortress. Yet there she was, sashaying as only a cat could, until she reached the judge.

"Meowrp," said the cat.

This galvanised the man, because he looked up to one of the knights on duty. "How did this frigging cat get in here?"

The man shrugged, swallowed hard. I didn't envy him being the focus of the judge's ire.

"Well?"

"I'll remove it, yer honour."

Yet even as he strode forward, his plate armour clanking, the cat bunched and sprang, straight onto the judge's podium. For a moment the man's expression turned to horror—that a dumb creature would defile his most exalted position!—then he graced us with a beatific smile completely out of place on his saggy jowls.

The cat pirouetted on the judge's papers, tail in the air, arse end directed at his face, and the man reached out. The cat's purring was so loud and insistent, I was certain even the people at the back of the courtroom could hear it.

The knight stood, awkward, gauntleted hands flexing while he waited for the judge to finish petting the moggy. Even the prosecutor wore a faintly bemused smile, which only served to make his skinny features appear ghoulish.

"Your honour?" Possenthirt hopped from foot to foot like a constipated crow, clutching a ream of papers covered in his indecipherable scrawl.

The judge straightened with a small gasp and banged on the gavel. "Not guilty!"

"But what about the sentencing?" the prosecutor said. "This is highly irreg—"

Faint colour crept up the judge's neck. He made a show of glancing at his pocket watch. "It's tea time. I find the defendant not guilty. We'll adjourn for tea. That is all." He got up with a faint huff, and trundled out of the courtroom. A woman's shriek—it could only belong to Aunt Fustia—was the signal for everyone else to begin clamouring about this sudden turn of events.

I blinked, confused by this unexpected outcome.

Of the cat, there was no sign, but my nose prickled with the telltale tingles that presaged a sneezing fit.

***

A pressure on my chest and a burning in my sinuses nudged me from my slumbers, but it was when a cold, wet *something* was pressed to my nose that I jerked fully awake. A terrible sneeze exploded from me and propelled the small, dark brown tortoiseshell cat halfway across the room. Before I had a chance to yell, another sneeze racked me and a muscle in my back spasmed so hard I feared I'd slipped a disk.

Five eye-watering, nose-bleeding sneezes and two wet farts later, I was up. My eyes streamed and my nose was so thoroughly blocked I had to breathe through my mouth.

"Ged oud!" I ordered.

The moggy sat there on the centre of my threadbare Morcastian rug, and said, "Meowrp." She blinked, and those gooseberry green eyes flashed rubies in the light from my lamp.

"'Ow de 'ell?"

The courthouse was on the other end of the city. How the cat had found her way to my aunt's home in less than two days, I had no idea. Yet here she was.

And, no matter what I said to my aunt about my allergies, about the fact that cats had fleas and sucked the souls out of small children, it would appear that the damned cat was here to stay.

***

The knights were absolutely useless going undercover. It wasn't just the godawful haircut—straight back and sides—or the fact they sat on chairs as if they had a ruler shoved up their arses. The bastards never smiled, never showed even the barest twitch of emotion. The Order of the White Rose always ensured we had at least one supposed undercover operative at the teahouse, and we eventually grew accustomed to Sir Elric's hulking presence.

Aunt Fustia, being the kind of lady she was, eventually sent packets of shortbread and aniseed biscuits home with Sir Elric for his mum. Of course she had no biscuits for me. I was still in disgrace for bringing shame to the Wriggins family name through my nefarious dealings with a subversive cult. When I pointed out that my fifteen minutes of notoriety had brought more people over the threshold of her teahouse than the time when she'd read the First Princess's tea leaves back in '78, I received a glare worthy of a basilisk and wisely elected to keep my mouth shut in future.

The surviving members of the Brethren of the Onyx Circle had gone to ground now that its ringleaders were all dead, incarcerated or, as in my case, under effective house arrest due to round-the-clock surveillance. One of my first tasks was to clean out the basement—an activity that filled me with dread, for the basement was dank and gloomy, and the special blend still lingered to remind me of our failure.

All fragments of our idols that the knights hadn't confiscated were gathered and dumped into a bin—I kept the head off Purzzizi the Effulgent. It took me a day to scrape all the wax from the floor. Each sweep of the broom seemed to fluff more incense ash into the air than it did into the dustpan, which didn't help my allergies one bit. Aunt Fustia had me paint over all our lovely murals depicting the Nine Great Maledictions with a horrific shade of lime. (Her astrologer allegedly claimed the colour would help bring about beneficial vibrations from the planetary spheres. What utter hogwash.)

Yet it's when I began to sand the floor that I discovered the paw prints right where we'd had our altar, where the vessel had been offered. Three sets of paw prints had been singed into the wood, as if a small animal with scorching embers for feet had jumped down from…

Nervous, I glanced at the ceiling, but there was no portal, not even a ripple in the air. I shivered, then went about erasing this last trace of our attempt at summoning the Duke. The implications of my discovery laid a clammy fist over my heart, and for the first time since my arrest and subsequent trial, I tasted true fear.

Oh shit, didn't even begin to cover it.

***

Aunt Fustia called the moggy Tigrina and made her a special bed in the teashop, on an antique rocking chair that stood next to the grandfather clock. Tigrina could be found there most days curled so tightly into a round of fur that it was difficult to tell where the tip of her nose started and the tail ended. Other times she wove between the customers' chairs and legs or sought laps where she'd make bread and purr so loudly the rumble could be heard clear across the room.

What made it far, far worse was that her very presence seemed to attract all manner of clientele: people who never failed—in glowing terms—to tell my aunt, myself and anyone else who would listen, that seeing the damned cat somehow infused them with a greater sense of well-being and joy.

I'd thought nothing of this until the day I discovered the scorched paw prints.

What were the implications of a Duke taking up residence in feline form? And a female one at that? Esatiel of the Ninth Infernal Circle was known to appear as a brazen bull with three heads and a serpent as a tail. His eyes flashed scarlet and armies were said to wither before his smoky breath.

By contrast, Tigrina was no bigger than an ordinary housecat—perhaps a bit plumper, thanks to Aunt Fustia feeding her cream—and the worst she'd done since she'd come into our lives was to sharpen her claws on Aunt Fustia's favourite chaise longue and cause my sinuses to clog up.

The very same day I'd found the scorched paw prints, I approached the feline, my pulse hammering in my throat. The shop had hit the mid-morning lull, which meant Aunt Fustia was in the back sorting tea leaves, and I was supposed to be polishing tables.

Tigrina opened one gooseberry green eye as I neared her rocking chair, then uncurled herself sinuously and stretched in such a way that made me wish I could unkink my spine like that. Her mouth opened with a yawn that revealed ivory needles then she licked herself vigorously, as if my standing there were no more momentous than the ticking of the grandfather clock.

How did one approach a Duke of the Ninth Infernal Circle?

"Your infernal majesty…" I mumbled, conscious of my aunt's chatter in the kitchen. The last thing I needed was for her to catch me talking to the cat.

As if on cue, my nose started to itch.

Tigrina paused in her grooming to glare at me. Then she continued with her task, as if I were no more important than an empty bowl.

Was I mad to imagine that the Duke had somehow transferred himself to this small cat's body? How had a bloody cat found its way into the basement in the first place? All questions I wasn't sure I'd be able to answer, nor did finding the answers matter.

My nose felt as if it were turning inside out, and the first of many sneezes ricocheted off the ceiling and threatened to make my head explode. I should really stay away from that damned cat, demon or no demon.

***

Soror Althea was the first to come crawling out of the woodwork. Frumpy, frizz-haired and freckled, she was five years older than me, but the hideous olive green cardigan that swamped her slight frame made her appear as if she'd already slumped into middle age. She stood on the doorstep of the teahouse, suitcase by her feet, and peered myopically at me from behind thick glasses. "When I heard what happened, I went to go visit my niece in Partridge Point."

"Um… Ah…" I hated that I was reduced to monosyllables. Months had passed since the Unfortunate Incident, as I now called the catastrophe that had scattered the Onyx Circle. No one had contacted me during that time—to be honest, I couldn't blame them—and I'd resigned myself to a future where I obeyed my eccentric aunt's whims until she eventually kicked the teapot, leaving me sole heir to her not inconsiderable small fortune. (I mean, really, being a landlord at age fifty-two wouldn't be so bad—I only had another twenty years to wait, right?)

"But I've come back." She beamed. "We can start over! I have references too!"

"Um, I don't think—"

"The position is still open, right?" She fished in her handbag and produced a wrinkled scrap of newspaper.

I accepted the cutting from her, which smelled faintly of camphor and lavender.

ASSISTANT NEEDED:
MUST HAVE EXPERIENCE IN SERVICE INDUSTRY…

"I never placed an ad." I frowned at her.

"Look." She tapped at the bottom with a nail covered in chipped purple glitter varnish.

Our address was clearly printed at the bottom of the advertisement, along with Aunt Fustia's name.

"You didn't…" I mumbled and rushed back inside, abandoning Althea on the doorstep. If she took a hint, she'd clear off. I should be so lucky.

It was bad enough that the damned cat had upset the equilibrium of our existence. To have this ghost from my ill-starred past blow into our lives… Now *that* was a bridge too far, and I meant to have it out with my aunt. I would have none of this. We were doing just fine. Yes, a bit busy since my notoriety, but we didn't need *that* woman to come in here and upset things more than they already were.

Aunt Fustia pushed her horn-rimmed spectacles further up on her nose and studied the advertisement. "Mmm."

"Mmm, what, Auntie?" I clenched my fists at my sides and tried not to hop from one foot to the other like a possessed imp.

"I don't recall placing this advertisement."

Relief swept through me and I almost sagged against the kitchen table. "Then I can tell the woman to go, right?"

"There's a woman?"

I rolled my eyes. "Yes, Auntie. A woman saw this ad in the newspaper and she's responded."

"Mmm, '…must be single, of sober habits and available as live-in housekeeper'." Aunt Fustia said, tasting each syllable. Then she studied me over her horn-rimmed glasses. "Does she have references?"

I ground my teeth. "I don't…"

Aunt Fustia bustled past me in a swish of her pink floral print house dress. "Well, let's see this young lady. Now that I think about it, I could use…" Whatever else she said was lost in a mumble as she doddered off.

The hairs on my nape prickled, along with my sinuses, and I turned to my left to see Tigrina perched on the top shelf of the crockery unit. Something about the damned cat's demeanour seemed entirely too self-congratulatory, and I shuddered.

And I swore her eyes glinted red for a fraction of a second until she winked at me.

***

Despite my objections—which were plentiful and vociferous, have no doubt—Aunt Fustia employed Althea within the week. What made things worse was that the damned cat took an instant shine to the damnable woman. Tigrina would meow and butt her head against Althea's shins, and Aunt Fustia turned a blind eye when that damned woman fed the cat scraps of kipper off her plate at the breakfast table.

The only source of my relief was that Althea never once mentioned starting up the circle again; in fact, she was so busy composing menus and blending teas with Aunt Fustia, that most days mention of the word 'circle' barely featured in our conversations.

"We'll discuss this tomorrow," seemed to be the constant excuse.

I suppose it was a relief, in many ways. As much as I had once dreamt of raising armies of infernal minions to do our bidding—and a castle up in the Temple District would have been very nice, thank you very much—I had to admit that life under my aunt's thumb wasn't as chafing and as unpleasant as it had once been. Perhaps a week in the sub-levels of the city holding cells had done much to cause me to revise my opinion on the matter.

Despite a mere tremble of the cat's whiskers sending me into an epic fit of sneezing, I was—dare I say it?—content. Even our resident undercover knight thawed a bit to greet me on first-name basis, and I took Althea to the theatre. Her hands were very soft.

Which was possibly why I was less than thrilled when more stragglers from the circle pitched up on our doorstep one blustery autumn evening.

Feodor and Helna Burzumski had been satellite members. They lived in Thistledon, about four hours by bus outside the city—hence they'd only ever attended the main sabbaths and our AGMs. I had accepted they would assume that the circle had been disbanded, but evidently I was in error because now they stood on the doorstep of the teahouse, suitcases and all.

"Ezra! So good to see you!" Feodor greeted.

"We brought some preserves." Helna offered up a basket and a watery smile.

My veins iced over and I glanced back at Sir Elric, who hunched over a daily on the veranda, possibly still blissfully unaware of the small drama playing itself out right under his nose. This was exactly the sort of situation he was waiting to pounce on.

Then I turned back to the luckless pair. "You have *heard*, haven't you?" I pitched my voice low.

Feodor nodded then leaned closer, stroking his black beard. "We made a few discreet inquiries after the trial. But we assumed that you were being careful—hence the reason we didn't see a notice in the bulletin this quarter. It is the Red Sabbath tonight, we thought…"

Next to him, Helna shifted about, twitchy as a ferret. "We can rebuild and work to bring down the oppression of the church and their knights. We can bring back the glorious—"

The glare Feodor and I both levelled at the diminutive woman had her shut her mouth with an audible snap.

Dismay threatened to open a hole beneath my feet. "I should have written…I'm sorry. But I've been…" *Busy playing manager to a teahouse that I've been more concerned with muffins and jam than world domination?* I gestured vaguely around me, "…lying low."

An unearthly howl rent the air, and I gave a small yelp as the tortoise-shell hellbeast rocketed outside. Tigrina skidded to a halt and arched her back, and the low, ominous growling that emanated from her was at odds with her size. Her fur was puffed up in a way I'd never seen before and she turned sideways towards the Burzumskis, all the while making gargling and spitting noises that curdled my blood.

Naturally, I found this behaviour quite alarming, but because my sinuses immediately clogged up and my eyes started watering, I was more concerned with my impending sneezing fit than I was of the unexpected guests potentially suffering grievous bodily harm at the tender mercies of one small, apparently domesticated feline.

I was woefully unprepared for Althea's response, however. She bolted, shrieking out the front door, brandishing a rolling pin as though she were about to embark upon open warfare at a church bazaar. Her frizzy orange hair had come loose from its pigtails and fluffed around her face, giving her the appearance of an overexcited midwife.

"Get thee gone!"

I sneezed and locked gazes with the grim-faced knight as he glanced up from his paper, a frown creasing his forehead. I waved at him, as if to suggest that *no, everything's fine*, but then another vicious sneeze all but lifted me from my feet.

When I opened my eyes again, Althea was chasing the Burzumskis down the road, shrilling after them as she laid about her with her rolling pin. I would have laughed if it weren't for the fact that the knight had risen from his seat.

"Oh shit," I muttered.

At my feet, the damned cat stood poised, her spine less arched but her ears still plastered against her skull. The gargling had abated to a muttering.

Another sneeze, and I was certain I'd ruptured an eardrum.

"All right?" the knight asked. He had his notebook out and pencil ready.

Oh bother. He was going to log this as a suspicious incident. I looked up at him, smiled faintly, and gestured vaguely down the road. "Family. Dispute."

The man's frown reminded me awfully of that dank, vermin-riddled cell. I was in no mood to relive that experience.

"Meowrp," said Tigrina.

The knight's frown melted and he knelt with an audible click of his knees so that he could pet the now-calm feline. The little minx's purr rose above the rumble of a nearby tram as she wove between his steel-capped boots. The cat butted heads with Sir Elric and left fur all over the grey felt of his coat.

When the man rose, he offered me a beatific smile as he tucked the notebook back in his pocket. "You know, the tea here isn't half bad. I think I'll have another cup of redleaf."

I nearly sagged in relief. "I'll organise it right away, sir."

Somewhere, dimly in my past, an older version of me wailed and gnashed its teeth. I had just called a Knight of the Order of the White Rose 'sir'. Aunt Fustia looked askance of my smirk when I placed the man's order. Oh, how things had changed. Could I truly argue that life was so terrible? Sure, I was still under surveillance, but since that abortive summoning, I'd never lacked for money, I was the lord of my domain—albeit a teahouse under the nominal supervision of my aged aunt who read fortunes in tealeaves—and I no longer had to pay for the sweet comfort of a woman's affections.

I couldn't truly complain, could I?

My nose began to prickle as I returned to my office, and I paused on the threshold. There, crouched on my chair, was Tigrina, with embers lodged in the depths of her gooseberry green eyes.

***

The kittens came on the night before the Black Sabbath, when the branches of the poplars scratched at the windowpanes and snatched at the moons. Aunt Fustia and Althea sat up with Tigrina for hours while she circled in her nest—what used to be one of my underwear drawers. I withdrew to my office and made myself comfortable on one of the armchairs while the apartment building creaked and groaned in sympathy to that damned cat's labour.

At around about midnight, the storm struck with such ferocity that I cowered into my dressing gown and, by mistake on purpose, pulled the antimacassar over my head. The lightning bleached through the curtains and the thunder shook the apartment building to its very foundations. Never, in all thirty-two years that I'd lived here with my aunt, had I ever experienced such a tempest. It was apt, I supposed, considering the circumstances—that Tigrina, formerly Esatiel of the Ninth Infernal Circle, was being delivered of a litter of kittens on a bed of socks and undergarments.

Six they were in total, patchwork horrors just like their mother, and when I made a show of oohing and aahing over them at Althea's urging—standing at a respectful distance with a handkerchief over my nose and mouth—I couldn't help but notice that their eyes were already open. The smallest one, who, despite my misgivings, I had to admit was almost cute because of its little white paws, opened a tiny pink mouth and let out a teeny yowl. Then, like its littermates, it fixed its preternaturally aware gaze on me and I swore those eyes gleamed crimson for a fraction of a second.

"Sir Elric said he'd take two as mousers for the chapter house," Althea said, beaming.

Tigrina, reclining gracefully on her side to encompass her brood, seemed entirely too smug. Her rumbling purr was rapturous.

ABOUT NERINE DORMAN

NERINE DORMAN is a South African author and editor of SFF currently residing in Cape Town. Her short fiction has been published in an assortment of anthologies, including *Midian Unmade: Tales of Clive Barker's Nightbreed*; *The Endless Ages Anthology for Vampire: The Masquerade*; the Wraeththu mythos; and *War Stories: New Military Science Fiction*, among others. Her YA fantasy novel *Dragon Forged* was a finalist in the 2017 Sanlam Youth Literature Prize, and she is the curator of the South African Horrorfest Bloody Parchment event and short story competition. In addition, she is a founding member of the SFF authors' co-operative Skolion.

RIPTIDE

DAN RABARTS

1 – Winter

THE TIDE IS RUNNING OUT.

You can tell from the way the waters at the headland surge and chase each other. The current carves a line of froth between the reef and the ocean, before running away like a frightened child. In its wake are exposed the earth's wet bones, its soft flesh of sand and hair of seaweed, revealed by the moon's gentle yet irresistible tug.

I push the dinghy into the swell, sliding over the pontoon and dropping the outboard, comforted by its sputter and thrum as I open the throttle. Shortly the dinghy is nosing up on the swell, leaving the pale shore behind. Day by day I move from one spot to the next, marking out the grid, trading light and air for what lurks beneath. I must keep looking. Beyond the fish and eddies and crushing depths, there's a deeper place. Call it what you will, underworld maybe, but that's not right either. I need to believe the tide will turn and, when it does, it'll bring back what was taken from me.

The GPS blips. I wind back the throttle and drop the anchor over the blinking marker on the screen. The anchor warp runs out, sinking down and down, before hitting the bottom and going slack. Like I have every day for a week, I don flippers, mask, and snorkel, take a breath, and slide into the sea. She welcomes me back with a cold whisper.

***

2 – *Last Summer*

The tide was running out.

I yelled at the kids to come up to the campsite. Their shouts and squeals echoed beyond the flax, muffled by the staccato of cicadas in the *pohūtakawa* trees along the shoreline and the rumble of waves: the sounds of summertime at the beach. I swigged beer and turned the sausages, fat sizzling in the flame.

"*Kai* time," I said to Stephanie. "Go get the kids, will you?"

She was intent on some pristine moment frozen on the pages of her bargain-bin romance, though I could've sworn she hadn't turned the page in twenty minutes. She often lost herself in those pages, amongst those picture-perfect characters and their picture-postcard lives. "You go get them." She looked up, past me, past the flax and across the waves. Not looking for the kids. Just...looking. Like she'd heard some distant sound, beneath the crash of the waves. Then her face dropped again, curtains of blonde falling back into place as she sank into her book. "It's my holiday too, remember?"

I turned down the gas, breathing deep as heat rose in my cheeks. "Fine," I said, swallowing words I knew would only lead to an argument I couldn't be bothered with. We were on holiday; here to relax. Yes, there were things we couldn't just leave behind, but it was nice to imagine that out here among the cicadas and the sand and the sentinel *pohūtakawa* it could be different. Easier.

But some monsters never sleep.

I scuffed through the flax. "*E, tamariki!*" I called out, seeing they weren't under the trees where I'd told them to stay. I gritted my teeth and hurried over the sandbank. They were laughing and shouting near the water's edge, waves leaping around their feet. They shared my dark hair and wide brown eyes, and names from my people's tongue: Mārama and Rā, the moon and sun in my sky. But they wore their mother's skin, spoke her language. Whether they would grow up with her monsters or mine remained to be seen.

"I told you two not to go near the water," I growled. "The *taniwha'll* snatch you up and take you out to sea."

They stopped, eyes wide, their laughter stilled. Rā took a half-step in front of his little sister, looking up at me, quivering between fear and defiance. Brave Rā, standing up for his *taina*. I hoped it was something he'd learned from me, to be courageous and protective, because the alternative was troubling: that the look on Daddy's face might summon fear, require that a boy become a warrior. I'd never raised more than my voice to my kids. I wondered what he might see behind my eyes. *He's scared of getting in trouble for breaking the rules*, I reminded myself. Just because I saw monsters in every shadow didn't mean they were really there. Anyway, I'd only taught them about the *taniwha* in the world around them, not about the ones that lived inside people. Not about how much harder those ones were to hide from.

How much harder they were to fight.

Either way, I couldn't stay grumpy with my *tamariki*. It wouldn't be the first time silly kids had gone playing in the *taniwha's* garden. But I, of all people, had no excuse for forgetting what might happen if they did. Mock fierceness dissolving into a reassuring grin, I bounded across the sand and scooped up one child under each arm, spun in a circle and spilled them onto the beach in a giggling bundle of limbs. Then they were on me, in the blitz of arms and legs fondly known as 'Taking Daddy Down.'

I let this go on for a minute before carrying them up to the campsite, quelling their protests with promises of fizzy drink and chippies, because it was a summer holiday after all.

"Daddy?" Rā asked me over a mouthful of sausage and bread, his lips sticky with sauce. "Is there really a *taniwha*?"

I ignored Stephanie's withering glance. "'Course there is, son. Every place has its *taniwha*. Some we can see, some we can't. Some live under the ground, and some swim in the sea, and in the spaces in between. They come in all shapes and sizes, and they're really good at hiding, so they can pop out and gobble you up when you least expect it."

"Do they really eat people?" Mārama asked, frowning in worried concentration. That was her mother in her, I thought. Less wonder, more worry. Although much as I didn't like to show it, I worried a lot, too.

"Not all of them," I said. "Some watch over us, keep us safe. But then there are other ones, the *hungry* ones…" I grinned, stuffing my mouth with sausage and bread and chewing noisily. "They'll chew you up in one bite. Mmmm! I love eating people! Nom nom!"

More giggles from the kids, more furious silence from Stephanie as she pushed a blonde lock behind her ear. I washed down the carnage with more beer and laughed, long and hard, with my kids. My sun and moon.

"You're filling their heads with nonsense."

Behind her book, Stephanie's face glowed orange in the ember of her cigarette, her first for the day. I never saw a smoke in her hand until the kids were asleep. There were things they didn't need to see, she'd say.

"It's not nonsense," I said, rummaging in the chilly-bin for another beer. I'd have to bring another case down from the car, and the carpark was a wee hike away. "There *are taniwha*, and they *will* eat our kids, if we aren't watching." Maybe if I'd told her about Tamati then, and she'd believed me, it might've been different. Probably should've told her years ago. But my monsters weren't hers. Mine were older, though no less deadly.

"I knew where they were the whole time." Her voice harboured a dangerous undercurrent while she treated me to that cold, careful smile which told me it wasn't worth making an issue of. "Mother's instincts." She dragged on her smoke, the hot ember making her eyes shine.

"Bullshit. You had your nose buried in your book all day."

"I could *hear* them, then."

"There's a hell of a rip out there, and if it catches one of our kids that'll be that, end of story. *That's* the taniwha. It swallows people whole." There was more I should've said, but every time I came close to stirring those currents, my throat closed over, like water rushing into my lungs. I cracked open the last beer—cold, wet, fresh as the ocean.

"I didn't see *you* down there with them," she said, flicking on her reading light and opening her book. Smoke swirled around her, rising ghost-like into the night. "Tomorrow you can tell them they can't go to the beach without one of us there. Easy fixed."

"I'll take them," I grumbled. "Spend the whole day down there if that's what they want to do."

"But darling, I'll miss you." Then she sank back into her reading, that tiny smile on her lips. I wish I'd seen it then, the way her monster had changed, how it had crept from its cave and taken on a new form. But I didn't. Or maybe I just couldn't bring myself to believe it, because after so long living with the monster, you no longer see its face, you only see what you want to see: the perfect smile you fell in love with, and not the carmine cigarette glow in the back of the eyes.

Besides, I had my own *taniwha* to worry about.

Instead, I listened to the beating waves and drank my last beer and thought how *nice* it was that we could get away to relax and have a break from it all, our shared monsters so far, yet so very near.

***

3 – Winter

The tide is turning.

It's the slack, when you can hang in the water, barely moving. When the kelp and Neptune's Necklace still their swaying, waiting for the world to turn. It is to the magic of the sea what midnight is to witchcraft; that time when the fabric separating our world from the one beyond is at its thinnest.

I spin slowly, searching, my torch flickering as it does every time I pass through this mystic eye. My lungs burn. Years ago, I dived everywhere I could. It was all I worked for, to save enough to dive another coast, another atoll, another reef. I remember floating in the sea in Fiji, off the Yasawas, watching the manta rays hanging in the current like razor-winged aliens. They were hardly swimming, just holding their position in the tide, which carried plankton straight into their open mouths. It was mesmerising, and magical. This is how the *taniwha* has escaped discovery for so long. It lurks in the shifting tides where the worlds of us and other scrape together like rocks in the surf: grinding, hungry, patient. It knows that in time someone will grow careless, or reckless, or murderous. In time, it will have its fill.

Not of my blood, taniwha. *Not again.*

Something moves in the corner of my eye and I turn, stale air screaming to escape my chest. I swing the torch, but whatever it was is gone, and I must breathe. I burst to the surface, sucking in life. I'm getting closer, I know it. I dive again.

This time, there's nothing to see.

***

4 – Last Summer

The tide was turning.

Early morning, high water, the surf rattled along the rocks and drift-wood at the tideline.

I threw the ball overarm and grinned as Rā sprinted after it, kicking up sand devils in his wake. He was an early riser, like me. It was good to get out of the tent and have a walk with my boy in the quiet hour before the girls roused themselves. I took the time to sneak a secret cigarette, the one that even Stephanie didn't know about or, if she did, she didn't mention. Why did I still need one every day, cupped inside my fingers like a guilty pleasure so Rā wouldn't notice? I didn't know, except that none of us were perfect. We're all just collections of imperfections that we make the most of, day to day, like the tide creeping in overnight and stripping away the footprints that mar the beach. But after every tide, the footprints return.

"*E tama*," I called, crushing the butt into the sand with my heel. "Don't go too far." I paused, letting my lungs clear, the *pohūtakawa* casting its tall, gnarled shadow across my shoulders. Standing right here I could see the calm patch between the rollers, the waters deceptively still, as if something drifted just beneath the surface, waiting. That dark lurking spot, like Stephanie, the unruffled surface hiding the violent rip current below.

"Rā!" I called. It was time he saw something that maybe I should've shown Stephanie long before now. Something that, if she'd seen, might've helped her understand me a little better. But I'd kept it from her for too long, and every year it got harder to find a way to talk about it. "*Haere mai!*"

With my boy at my side, I pushed aside the undergrowth around the *pohūtakawa's* trunk, revealing the small wooden carving, now dark with salt and age, but no less meaningful for it. Koro Tipene, my grandad, had made it, using the old tools and the older ways, the ancient *karakia*, then he'd shown it to me when he thought I was ready.

"What's that, Daddy?" Rā asked, reaching out and running his fingers over the whorled patterns resembling wave and wind, and the fluted shadows beneath that might have been fins, or claws. Or teeth. A small yet unafraid figure in the traditional Maori style faced the carved ocean, tongue thrust out proud and sharp, fingers splayed in the ancient *wero* of challenge, a stance with its origins in the martial traditions of a warrior culture, yet which most people would associate with the All Blacks doing a haka on a rugby field.

"*Whakairo*. A special carving, made by my *koro*, so your Uncle Tamati can find his way home."

"Is that Uncle Tamati in the carving?" he asked, pointing at the leering figure. "Or is it Koro Tipene?"

"No, son," I said, and then I told him about my brother, the uncle he'd never known. I didn't answer his question, because I didn't want to tell him who I thought that figure was, standing on this beach under a wind-torn sky, throwing challenges at the *taniwha*.

I told Rā how I'd come down here one day with my *koro*, and how we'd nailed the *whakairo* to this *pohūtakawa* tree. Koro had sung a *karakia* in his gravelly old voice, making the ancient prayer sound like rocks grinding in the tide, while I cried. I'd done all my crying a long time ago now. Take a tear, drop it in an ocean, and see if it makes any difference. There was no point crying, not for those the *taniwha* took. But the *taniwha* heard that *karakia*, I'm sure, and in the dark and the whisper of waves I reckon it came up this beach and tasted a grieving boy's tears. I reckon it saw that *whakairo*, saw its own face carved there, together with the warrior's *wero* and the whorls that turn upon themselves and bring everything full circle: time, sun, moon and tide. A prediction of sorts, or perhaps a prophecy. That what was begun would also have its end.

And *taniwha* have long memories, endless like the ocean.

***

5 – Autumn

That summer holiday seemed like a long time behind us the day I felt the monster's breath on my neck. It was a rainy Friday afternoon when I came home to an empty house. No Mārama, no Rā, no Stephanie. She didn't answer her phone. I tried the obvious places first—her office, the hospital—before I started calling her family and friends.

Sometimes, in the early days, when she got tired of how the meds sapped all the colour from her world, she'd take the car and drive and I wouldn't hear from her for days. But she hadn't done anything like that since the kids had come along. Although a coldness gnawed at me, I couldn't believe she would harm them. Whatever else, she was their mother.

I got no clues by checking the bank account and the credit cards, except that she'd probably filled the car with gas before leaving town. The cops told me to call back after she'd been missing for twenty-four hours. *The children were with their mother, weren't they? So they would be fine. Did she have any history of violence? No? What about mental illness? Was she taking her medication?*

An agonising week later they called about the car.

I sped up the coast, stomach churning and heart thundering. Her silver wagon sat alone on the gravel, grey under a slate-dark sky. The carpark wasn't visible from the road, and since it wasn't exactly boogie-board season, the police were deliberating over whether it had been there one day or many.

They hadn't found any bodies, they said.

Those words had crashed over me, driven the air from my chest the way a breaker can slam you down and leave you with that deep, hammering deafness. There was nothing to suggest they'd gone into the sea, they said, but a boat was running a coastal search just in case. More likely someone had met them here and they'd left in another vehicle. *Is there any chance your wife might've met someone here, sir? A sister? A friend? Is it possible she was having an affair, sir?*

I walked down the path to the beach, to the stubby flax and the looming *pōhutakawa*, to the sandbank overlooking the rasping waves. Fumbling, I lit a cigarette. My hands were numb as I gazed at the deceptively calm patch between the waves where I'd watched my brother go down, slipping through the water into the deep places between.

I tried to convince myself I was wrong. That the *taniwha* had not sung its haunting song—my monster calling out to hers across the thin places where the worlds scraped together like rocks in the tide—and drawn her to it with promises; promises of peace and of freedom from life's imperfections. That it hadn't lured her down with lies about its world being an escape from the washed-out vistas of former passion and pain; a landscape now reduced to little more than bland monotony. Unlike my monster, hers had not taught her to love without restraint. All hers had taught her was that tomorrow would be as harrowing as the day before, her yester-days as hollow as the promise of days to come.

Even with her history, I doubted the cops would've believed me if I'd told them that she might've walked into the waves, holding one of our children's hands in each of hers, and just kept going. I could almost see her, taking those inexorable steps down, Rā and Mārama tugging at her grip like iron, like ice.

All I wanted to know was why, and all I wanted was them back.

***

6 – Winter

The tide is coming in.

This is my seventh day, the thirteenth slack tide I've been on the waves. It should be symbolic, like some sort of talismanic charm, except that *taniwha* don't care much for numbers.

I haul myself back into the dinghy and strip off my mask and flippers. Taking a moment to breathe, I scan the horizon, the rocky shoreline, the foaming white backs of the breakers as they thunder home. There stand the *pohūtakawa*, tall and bent and dark, brilliant red flowers long since gale-shredded, scarlet gone to rot upon the sand. How long have those trees stood their lonely vigil over this stretch of beach, and what have they seen?

I check another square off my grid before cranking the motor. Every inch of the bay has now been marked, except for that long, dark stretch where the rip current sucks back through the sandy trench: the killing zone. I haven't looked there yet because the rip spits out everything it takes into more settled waters, to be collected by other tides and carried where the sea wills. I've snorkelled all the way along these rocky headlands and every place in between, except for the rip. I can't put it off any longer.

I'm not afraid. I've been diving a long time, and even though family life and the day-job have added a few extra kilos in places and maybe my lungs aren't what they used to be, I once dived Thailand, the Great Barrier, and Mozambique. I know how to swim a rip current; I know not to fight it. There's more power in a riptide than even the strongest swimmer can overcome. The trick is to ride that power, letting it carry you until it exhausts itself.

I haul in the anchor and head back to shore. High tide is only a few hours away, and I want to be ready.

***

7 – Summer, Twenty Years Ago

The tide was high.

I surfaced and shook water from my eyes, realised I couldn't touch the bottom. I hollered in excitement, not afraid; not yet. It was too soon for fear. I kicked around until I could see the beach, there between the backs of two rollers raging away from me in the moonlight, giving the impression the beach was receding. The waves sounded louder in the dark than during the day: Deeper, somehow. More menacing. I should've been frightened, but I was with Tamati. Whatever my big brother did, I did. We had fun together, we got into shit together. That's how it was. He wouldn't let anything bad happen.

Then the waves broke, and the shore kept retreating. I found the breath to yell.

Figures were running along the beach, Dad and Uncle Hohepa come to give us a hiding for going in the water after dark, and there was Tamati, powering through the waves towards me. He was big, so much stronger than me, him with his rugby-scrum shoulders. I heard Dad shouting, just before I went under again, inhaling seawater.

The world roared in my ears as the sea pulled at me. I fought it, arms and legs and lungs burning with the effort. I tumbled over and saw Tamati getting closer, closer, arms outstretched. I'll always remember how he looked that night, cutting through the waves like a fish, like he was born to the water. I remember thinking that it was going to be okay, because my big brother wouldn't let anything happen to me.

I saw it out of the corner of my eye just before his hands could grasp mine. It was no beast, no tentacled or serpentine horror. All I saw was the flash of white, curves and barbs twisting up from the depths as if carried against the current by an even more powerful force; *hei matau*, a bone fishhook, cut from something sharp and ancient. It snapped around Tamati, passed through him, *into* him, and then whatever invisible line it was that held that jagged barb pulled taut. Tamati jerked, and was gone. Not dragged down, or away; just gone. Slipping into the dark spaces between the waves.

I screamed, and the air burst from my lungs, and the sea rushed into its place.

I'm not sure why I never told Stephanie about Tamati, apart from how he died when I was a boy, but not where, or how. I guess I wanted her to believe that I really was the man I pretended to be; that I didn't carry the fears and weaknesses which crippled other men, preventing them from being good fathers, good husbands. If she knew about Tamati, would she think my passion for diving something more; an obsession, maybe? An impossible hunt, dangerous and disturbed?

So instead it became an anchor buried somewhere deep to hold me against the current. Stephanie had enough demons of her own—demons which I had been forced to face—without also worrying about mine. I'd thought that our two beautiful children, who bridged the divide between our worlds, would have been enough to drive those demons back into the dark where they belonged.

But maybe the dark was where those demons had always wanted to be, like my *taniwha* who hides in the shadows between tides, between worlds.

***

8 – *Winter at the Edge of the World*

There is no tide.

Here above the rip the sea only flows one way: out, and down, and deep; forever. My anchor is buried high up the beach, a long silver strand binding my vessel to life and light and air. I have my tank this time, because I know the rip won't release me just because this frail mortal needs to breathe.

There's no need for the motor; the current pulls me out as I ease the warp, the troubled waters darkening beneath me. I cinch the nylon cord and feel the drag under the hull, like a river. I raise a blue-and-white diver's flag and knot on a marker buoy, which draws away until the rope pulls taut. If I don't come back, at least they'll know where to start looking. Not that they'll ever find me, like they never found Tamati, or Stephanie, or Mārama, or Rā; like they've never found so many who go into the sea and don't return. Because it shouldn't have been Tamati that night, like it should never have been Stephanie, or our children. It should always have been me. I should've faced my monsters sooner, instead of hiding from them. In that way, I've always been a boy, flailing in the current, panicking as the riptide dragged me under. I sit on the pontoon, fit my breathing mask, nod to the sentinel *pohūtakawa*, and tip backwards.

The sea grasps at my limbs, trying at once to crush me and pull me apart. I get my bearings, fight the clutching fear. The rip propels me along and I sweep my torch every way, hoping to see something, *anything* to prove this isn't a fool's venture, just my own quiet madness; a sad and desperate insanity serving only to drown my grief, a means to bury my guilt—inter it somewhere deep, dark and impossible to find.

The current ejects me into the head of the rip, leaving me to drift. I look up through the distorted watery lens as the swell builds above me, an inversion of sea and sky, and I wonder if this is how she sees the world. Is this what she went searching for—an *otherworld* of perfect stillness where she could silence the *taniwha* in her mind? A place to escape the darkness into which even our sun and moon hadn't been able to cast their light when they graced our lives? Maybe she saw a path to perfection, a rebirth in the turning tide.

I check my watch, its hands glowing ethereal in the murk. Mystical, magical slack tide is almost upon me. I kick towards shore, tracing the edge of the rip, identifying from the drift of sand and weed where the waves turn deadly.

I slide into the rip. Even as the rest of the bay slumps into the languor of the slack it continues, relentless. The current twists me, rolls me over. For a moment, I'm not sure which way is up, and panic swells in my chest. I kick out, turning, but everything is black. Through the vortex I glimpse shifting sand below, then it's falling away, as if the ocean floor is opening up—a crevasse, the sea falling into it—and I'm rushing down into something beautiful, transcendental, horrific. It's the monster I've come here to face. Maybe it's Stephanie's, maybe it's mine. Maybe it's something more ancient and perfect than we can ever be, lurking beneath the drowning horizon.

As the light flees, I see the bone-white flicker of barbs as something snaps past me, through me, *into* me. The crevasse—the *mouth*—opens wider. I can't scream, although I should. It's not the underworld down there, I repeat to myself. It's a place to be reborn. A place for lost brothers, children, lovers to be found, their broken pieces fitted back together, made anew. Made into something perfect, like the turning of the tide.

Is this what you were looking for, Stephanie, when you led our kids into the deep? I could've told you there's no perfection in death, that all it leaves in its wake is broken lives. I could've told you that nothing was perfect and never would be, no matter how hard you tried. I could've held you as you fell apart, then picked up your pieces and put you back together, and still I would've loved you, all your scars and imperfections. Because nothing can be perfect forever; not the beach or the reefs I used to dive. Not the dreams we cling to as the years wear us down. Not even the love that seemed so flawless when it bloomed. Like the *pohūtakawa* that grow ever more bent and twisted, their brief summer beauty stripped away by autumn winds.

I let the torch float free on its lanyard and draw my eight-inch dive knife from its quick-release sheath. Through my left-hand glove I grip the hard edges of the *whakairo*, plucked from the *pohūtakawa* before I made this final plunge. The *taniwha*'s carven face presses into my palm, cut there with the old tools, the older ways; ways ancient as the *taniwha*, from a time before time when men fought monsters and won. I feel those whorls carved by my *koro*, symbols of the cycles. They represent the changing of the seasons; the power of life over death, the turning tide, and of eternity. Symbols carved as much for me as for my lost brother, to lead us both home. I do not go unarmed into this battle, but clutching cold steel and a talisman of ancestral magic engraved with the *rotu*, the ancient words that were once used to drive the *taniwha* back into the darkness.

Rotua! Rotua!

Tū te ihi, tū te wehi, tū te wana, e taniwha, e; mate atu koe ki te rau o te patu

(Feel my magic, taniwha, *and the blade of my weapon)*

I'm not coming back until I've torn this monster from the sea, and from the dark places behind my eyes.

Hūhutia mai koe i te moana...

(You are cast from the sea...)

Better to be left with a hollow place where memories used to be, than the aching pit that fills me now. Rather that, than to come back to this empty world. No Rā, my sun. No Mārama, my moon. No Stephanie, my beautiful monster.

...kia tīraha tūpāpāku koe ki te ākau...

(...your corpse laid out on the shore...)

There's a roaring in my ears, a boiling in my blood, and I can hear the *karakia*, the *rotu*, calling out my name.

Not my blood, taniwha. *This time, it will be yours.*

The tide is turning.

ABOUT DAN RABARTS

DAN RABARTS' science fiction, dark fantasy and horror short stories have been published in numerous venues around the world, including *Beneath Ceaseless Skies, StarShipSofa* and *The Mammoth Book of Diesel-punk.* His writing and editing work have earned him both New Zealand's Sir Julius Vogel Award and the Australian Shadows Award multiple times. Together with Lee Murray, he co-edited the anthologies *Baby Teeth - Bite-sized Tales of Terror* (Paper Road Press, 2013), and *At The Edge* (Paper Road Press, 2016). *Hounds of the Underworld,* Book 1 of the crime/horror series *The Path of Ra*, co-written with Lee Murray, is available from Raw Dog Screaming Press. Find out more at dan.rabarts.com.

THE IMMORTAL DEAD

J.C. MICHAEL

"A GHOST WALK? SERIOUSLY?"

A pout, a narrowing of the eyes, and then a smile "And why not? This city is famous for the ghosts, and I find the paranormal very interesting. Besides, it will be fun. We need some after today. And tomorrow will be no better I am sure."

Tasha couldn't help but grin. Her friend's enthusiasm was, as always, infectious, and the day had been undeniably dull. A whole eight hours training in customer service from the most boring man on Earth, who no one in their right mind would employ as the public face of anything, had been draining for both of them. To make matters worse, there was a second day of it to come.

"Come along, how can we not enjoy Harlan Marshall's Ghostly Gallivant? A tour of Spooks and Spirits." Tasha's friend, Esme, held out a flyer as she spoke. It was cheaply produced and advertised what looked like a hybrid ghost-walk-cum-pub-crawl.

"You're sure you want to do this?"

"Quite sure. I have been on similar tours back home and they have been excellent. Look, he has even won awards."

"Hmmm, from the local tourist board eight years ago. And even then it was only a bronze."

"And he is still in business, so by now he must have improved to gold standard!" Esme proclaimed as she first tried to put the flyer into the pocket of her skintight jeans and then, giving up on that thankless task, stuffed it into the pocket of her leather jacket.

Esme was a long way from her home in Poland, and even though she'd been in the country a good six months she still acted as though she was on an extended vacation. When she was at work she was the best member of staff on Tasha's team, and outside of work she had soon become her best friend.

Tasha finished her drink. "I don't know Esme, I'm tempted to have one more and call it a night. We're supposed to be here for the course, not a fun-filled city break for two."

"Natasha Wood, I am so disappointed in you. All you've done for weeks is complain about never getting the chance to let your hair down, and now we have a golden opportunity to do something different." The flyer was back in her hand and she waved it under Tasha's nose. "Look, that's him over there. He looks just like his picture on the leaflet."

***

A couple walked past where he sat, glancing at the empty chairs. His presence clearly put them off taking a seat. He didn't care. He wasn't in the mood for company, though soon he'd have no choice. He stared at the film of whisky covering the side of the tumbler and swirled the remainder of his drink around the bottom of the glass. It was always the same. A slowly sipped shot before the tour began. A drink that seemed to take an eternity to finish. A ritual that seemed to take longer each time he took his seat in the corner and started to drink. He looked up and spotted the two girls at the bar, one staring at him, the other waving. He tipped his glass toward them and smiled. They would be ideal.

Outside the crowd was gathering, the ten of them waiting for him like they always did. The theatrics of the evening had worn thin. The nightly repetition of the same tour, the same words, the same actions, all wearied him, yet he had no option but to continue. It was what he did, what he had chosen to do. But tonight would be different. He had plans. Plans that hinged on the eleven becoming thirteen.

Harlan stood, shrugged his shoulders within his heavy overcoat and headed towards the front door. His route took him past a drunk punching the side of a fruit machine who turned to look at him as he walked by, and then he was at the bar with the two women. He smiled at them. They were perfect. The one who had waved at him waved again, his flyer held in her hand. His smile broadened as he headed outside.

***

"Bloody hell, Esme. He thought you were waving at him."

As Harlan passed, a second man followed a few feet behind. His gait was unsteady, but his eyes were locked on the two girls. He was spilling his pint as he approached.

"All right ladies." He rested his tattooed hand on the bar between them, his leer moving from one to the other with no attempt to conceal the fact he was more interested in what was below their necks than above.

Esme looked at Tasha and smirked. "Shall I go on the walk on my own and leave you with your new friend?"

A puzzled look crossed the drunk's face as he attempted to process what Esme had said. "Yeah, that's right, your new friend. How 'bout I buy you girls a drink?"

Tasha was already off her bar stool. "No thanks. We were just about to catch the ghost walk."

"Come on, my treat," he drawled. "There's no walk tonight." But the girls, now arm in arm, were already halfway to the door. "Fucking lesbians."

"You soon changed your mind," Esme said with a giggle as they made their way outside.

***

"Just in time, ladies, just in time."

Harlan stood, slightly elevated, on the step of the shop opposite the pub. "You bring our number to an unlucky thirteen, the perfect number for tonight's stroll." He gestured the group to come closer. "So, welcome ladies, gentlemen, and those who be neither, to my ghostly gallivant through the streets and snickleways of this fine and ancient city." He flourished a bow. "I am Harlan Marshall. Your guide and protector for the evening.

"As you can see, the sun is bidding us farewell and the night is all but upon us. We are between times, at the point betwixt night and day. And tonight I shall tell you the tales of those who inhabit the between—those between life, and death. Those who have not crossed over, but remain on this earthly plane as the immortal dead. Yet do not fear, for once the stories are told and the cold shivers have run down your spine to chill you to your very core I shall allow you respite in some of the finest hostelries in the whole of England. For this is a night of both spooks and spirits, and I am a fan of them both." He winked and took a small black hip flask from his pocket. "Let us steel our hearts for the expedition we are about to undertake, for I fear I cannot guarantee your safety this evening. Sometimes the dead themselves like to make an appearance to listen to their tales as they are told, and though most are benign, and some may be playful, some, I cannot deny, are simply evil."

The flask was passed around the group, and all took a sip of the warm liquid.

"What the hell's that?" shouted a man to the rear of the group.

Harlan smiled. "That, sir, was the finest Absinthe. And not your Tesco imitation, no. That was the genuine article. Imbibe too much and the green fairy shall drive you insane, but drink the right amount, just a sip on a cold damp evening, and it can help you see what lies between worlds." His words had addressed the man who had shouted out but his eyes were fixed firmly on the girls.

Tasha pulled Esme close. The roguish charm of their guide appealed to them both, and liquor-fuelled smiles played across their lips. Esme felt Tasha give a slight shiver and squeezed her arm in return.

"Now enough of this, for night is falling, and it is time we were off."

***

Harlan was no novice and held the group captivated as they swept through the night.

"There's no time to lose," he said as he strode down a cobbled street. "There are enough pubs within the city to allow you to drink in a different one each evening for a year, and enough ghosts for you to see a different one each night for half as long again!"

"A year's a little longer than we were expecting for a fiver," said one of the group, a comment which earned him a nudge in the ribs from the woman beside him.

"Never fear, we shall be done by twelve," said Harlan as he came to a stop. "That will give me plenty of time to cover the bloody history of this city and its tales. Some of which you may find gruesome and grotesque, others tragic, humorous, or plain bizarre.

"A lord of the realm once watched an apparition of a sheet of paper blowing in the wind. The sheet turned into a monkey and then a bear, before disappearing in front of his very eyes as he stood on the steps of the city's Crown Court. Personally, I think he was probably drunk."

"Sounds more like he was trippin' to me," said a young man of about twenty.

"Perhaps," Harlan said, "but we want no tripping tonight, so watch your step on the cobbles. Now come along." He was off again, moving faster than before, the group scurrying along behind him.

"It's like following Willy Wonka through the Chocolate Factory," Tasha said.

Esme's brow furrowed a little, "Or the Pied Piper. And we are the rats."

"You know a pair of elderly ladies once claimed to have witnessed a battle between a Roman legion and a barbarian horde on this very spot," Harlan said, coming to a stop outside a tea shop. "If you listen carefully, you too may hear the sounds of battle carried faintly on the air."

"Do you hear it?" Esme asked, her head cocked to a side. "The yelling and clashing of metal? I believe I can."

"Yes," Tasha said. "So can I. I can ask him to lend you the iPod he's playing it on if you like."

It wasn't long before the Romans featured again as the group passed a house where a workman in the cellar claimed to have seen a spectral cohort silently marching by, the soldiers visible only from the knees up as they headed north. At a later stage of the work, an old Roman road had been discovered beneath the cellar floor, at just the right depth to put the more recent floor level to be at knee height.

The tour was part history lesson, and Harlan either knew his facts, or was so confident reeling them off that any inaccuracies were swept away by the narrative. He told how the Romans had left their fortress and the grand buildings had fallen into ruin under the rule of the Anglo-Saxons, and then the Vikings, who "categorically did not wear horned helmets, whatever Hollywood may have you believe."

It seemed, however, that the medieval period was the most fertile for ghost creation. There were stories of ghostly monks and headless lords, of queens and paupers, soldiers and sinners. There were those who had murdered and those who had been murdered. The victims of accidents and those whose lives ended at their own hands.

As the group stood and looked at the sole remaining tower of the Norman castle, the chanting of the Jews who had barricaded themselves within its walls to escape a baying mob drifted through the night.

"That is not coming from him," Esme said.

"He must have a speaker hidden somewhere nearby. He'll have friends going around ahead and behind us," Tasha said. Her words conveyed certainty, but her tone did not, and the chanting ceased at the exact moment Harlan mentioned they had committed mass suicide before the mob broke down the castle gate.

"It is claimed that the earth of the castle mound remains stained red with their blood to this very day," Harlan said.

***

"Come on Harlan, join us for one," Tasha said as they stood outside the Golden Fleece—a pub with a five-hundred-year history and fifteen ghosts including a Canadian airman who fell to his death from an upstairs window; a young boy trampled to death by a horse; and One-Eyed Jack, a pistol-wielding Redcoat.

"I don't think so, not when I'm working."

She brushed her long blonde hair behind one ear and gave him a flirtatious smile, "You've skipped the last three, surely one won't hurt? And you can't expect me to stay standing out here chatting to you, it's freezing."

"Maybe later, but right now I need a smoke. You're right though, it's bloody cold." He took off his long black overcoat and passed it to her. "Take this, I've enough to remember without adding in The Tale of the Frozen Maiden."

"I can't."

"Yes, you can."

"Okay, but you'll have a drink with me before the night's through or you're not getting this back," she said, putting on the heavy coat. "That's better, I can stand it out here a while longer now."

"Well, if you insist on keeping me company, who am I to disagree?"

They smiled at each other before the silence became awkward and Tasha asked the question that she'd been wondering for a while now. "So Harlan, do you believe in ghosts or are you simply a storyteller? I'll give you that the effects had us unsettled for a while, but come on, are you an out-and-out showman or a true believer?"

Harlan dropped his cigarette on the floor and ground it out with his boot in a way that hinted at annoyance, even if his continued smile said otherwise. "Effects? All that you see and hear is genuine I assure you. And of course I believe. It's a fascinating topic, how people may die yet live on. Not just as stories, but as a real presence. Don't you see how it is a kind of immortality?"

There was an intensity in the answer that made Tasha uneasy. "What? Doing the same thing over and over? Haunting somewhere? Doesn't sound like living forever to me."

Harlan stepped toward her, resting his hands on her shoulders. "Not all ghosts are like that, as the stories I recount clearly demonstrate. I'll grant you that some, indeed many, are mere images burnt into the fabric of a place through the traumatic nature of their deaths. These images are then played on the film of the past that exists on the fringe of what the living can comprehend. But others are more than simple re-played scenes from the past. These others are special, they can interact with and influence the world of the living. Those are the ones who left their bodies behind but have become more, become immortal."

"I see."

His hands pressed down, his fingers clamping ever so slightly. "Why are people so quick to condemn those who believe? To poke fun? Many people have encountered spirits throughout history, but the modern world ridicules those of us that see them now." He moved closer. "Yet thousands more believe in a God that has never been seen, and that is simply accepted as faith."

"That's an interesting view," she said, stepping back.

"It is. But it doesn't make for fun small talk does it?" He grinned. "Now get in there and get a drink down you to warm you up."

Tasha relaxed. For a moment, there had been an almost tangible darkness about him, but it had evaporated. It was the theme of the night, that was it. She'd gone and spooked herself and felt silly for it. "You're the boss," she said as she pushed open the door and walked inside, almost bumping into Esme.

"Careful! I was on my way to bring these out as you seemed too busy to join me," Esme said, raising the glass she held in each hand before sitting down at a table just through the door. "You know, I swear I saw a man in an old-fashioned red military uniform walk past the cellar door while I was at the bar."

Tasha giggled. "It'll be another of Harlan's mates he's roped in to creep us out. You'll be jumping at shadows before the nights out Esme-Rose."

"You are the one interested in the jumping," Esme said before catching the giggles herself.

***

The tour arrived outside the gothic cathedral that dominated the surrounding skyline. They could hear a dog barking. It sounded like it was coming from inside.

"That'll be Seamus," Harlan said. "Poor bugger's sealed up somewhere in those walls. The stonemasons did it to get at his owner, a mason from down south who they blamed for their tools going missing. He'll give over soon." Sure enough, the barking stopped, and Harlan was onto his next story about the soldier who had appeared at his sister's side as she prayed for his safe return from war. An apparition that coincided with his death thousands of miles from home.

It was typical of the tour, a bewildering array of historic sites and haunted hostelries with Harlan regaling them with a multitude of tales along the way. They visited the six-hundred-year-old Black Swan where a pair of disembodied legs were said to descend a flight of stairs and a bowler hat-wearing ghost was claimed to frequent the bar. There was The York Arms where a nun had been bricked up in a small room and left to starve in the dark as punishment for falling in love and forgoing her vow of celibacy, her sin betrayed by her subsequent pregnancy. And then there was The Punchbowl, a pub haunted by a woman who had died of a broken heart, a murdered prostitute and a landlord who died in a fire on the property but was still said to work the odd shift behind the bar. It was a lengthy list, and testament to Harlan's skill as a storyteller that he held the group's attention throughout.

As always Harlan refused to enter any of the pubs and bars on the route and, after asking him to join her at each, Tasha was close to giving up. She found him interesting and undoubtedly attractive, but, as she had stressed to Esme, she was neither besotted nor desperate.

"Do not feel bad," Esme said as they sat in the White Swan, watching the fireplace and keeping an eye out for the joyfully inebriated spirits alleged to meet there. "I am sure it cannot be you. He has barely paid me any attention at all," she said with a look of mock contempt. "It can mean just one thing. He likes the boys."

"Maybe," Tasha said, "but it's typical. I get nothing but unwanted attention from here, there, and everywhere back home. But when I try to chat someone up? I get nowhere." She took a drink.

"More fool him. Look, he is cute, and he is smart, but there are plenty of cute, smart men. And most of them do not smell of burning. I do not know how you can wear that coat of his. It reeks of smoke."

"It weighs a tonne too, but at least it's warmer than this thin cardigan."

"Well, we did not expect to be walking the streets did we?"

"No, we didn't. I wouldn't be wearing a skirt and heels if we had. You know, I think he'd like me better if I was dead," Tasha said, shuddering at her own statement. She looked at her wrist "What time is it? I think my watch's stopped."

"Half past ten."

"It must be later than that. We've been out for hours."

Esme checked her phone and then her watch for a second time. "No. Half past ten. Time for many more spooky stories. Come along. The group is gathering outside."

As they left the bar a glass smashed behind them. "That will be the poltergeist he told us about," Esme said. The way she said it gave Tasha pause for thought. Perhaps she had imagined it, but she was sure her friend's usually limitless good humour was beginning to fade.

***

As the night wore on, the sense of unease the girls felt increased. In Ye Olde Starre Inn they left their drinks virtually untouched, for the screams and wails they could hear coming from the basement, which had been used as a field hospital during the Civil War, were unbearable.

"How can people ignore that noise?" Esme asked once outside.

"They'll be in on it, and pissing themselves laughing at us now." But Tasha didn't sound convinced, and there were no such signs of such hilarity when she peered back in through the window. Just a normal pub full of normal people and a puzzled looking barman clearing away their unfinished drinks. A bout of sneezing caught Tasha before she could speak again.

"Cat allergy?" Harlan said, laughing, "There's two walled up in there between the door and the bar. Drives dogs mad. One even knocked itself out throwing itself against the wall."

The girls looked at him, Tasha alternately wiping her nose and rubbing beneath her eyes. Esme was shocked. "What is it around here with walling living things up in buildings?"

"It prevents the place burning down of course," Harlan said in an entirely matter-of-fact tone. "Now it is nearly twelve, and we only have a couple more stops to make. Follow me!"

With that, he set off at a jog and the tourists followed, all but Tasha and Esme. "Are you okay? I think we may have had enough, yes?"

They heard Harlan shouting in the distance. "This used to be called Mad Alice Lane. She was hung in 1825 for no crime other than her insanity."

"This whole tour is madness." Esme continued. "I am sorry even for the mention of it."

Tasha took her hand. "Mad or not, it's an experience. Come on, we may as well see it through."

***

They caught up with their fellow tourists outside a small stone house in the shadow of the great cathedral they had visited earlier. Harlan was smoking a cigarette. The rest of the group were eerily quiet.

"I'm glad you could join us, ladies, for this is the final tale of the evening before we return to where we started, and where I shall join you for one last drink. Here, in this very house, resides the spirit of a young girl who lived during a time of plague. A time when a great pestilence swept through Europe claiming the lives of tens of thousands. The plague doctors in their waxed robes and beaked masks could do nothing to stop it. The church, with young boys sleeping at the feet of its bishops—so as to catch the bad air, the miasma, before it reach their holy selves—could do nothing. Only nature itself could bring an end to the death, or an avoidance of it. And Mother Nature, she was kind to the girl as she never caught the disease. Her parents, on the other hand, were not so fortunate.

"They barricaded themselves in their home to avoid the infected. But doing so didn't save them. For they contracted the disease. And they died, thus leaving the girl trapped. Boarded up with their plague-ridden corpses. It's said that she looked out of a small window, the one right there." He pointed at the window as the minster clock began to chime twelve.

"It is said that her neighbours could see her." He raised his voice slightly to contend with the chimes. "But they feared she was infected too." His voice heightened further as he continued, the chimes themselves appearing to increase in volume as they rang out. "They did nothing, according to some. But others tell how they boarded up the door still further to keep her and the plague trapped within." He was now shouting. Goosebumps ran across Tasha and Esme's bodies. "The poor girl starved," he said as the eleventh chime rang out. "And she so needs our help!" The clock chimed *twelve* at an almost deafening volume, and Harlan's voice dropped to a whisper. "Even now."

All was quiet. Harlan was stood, rocking, his arm ramrod straight pointing at the window. The window from which a small girl's thin face peered. Tasha gasped and grabbed Esme as the face began to fade. Then vanish. The group broke into a round of applause.

"She looked so real," said Tasha as she half-heartedly clapped along while Harlan took an exaggerated bow, the twin of the one with which he had introduced himself.

"Yes. A clever trick I am sure," Esme said before adding, "I am glad we are done. This evening, it has not felt right for some time."

***

Five minutes later they were back in The Awkward Turtle, the bar where the tour had started. Their companions on the tour stood around Harlan in the far corner, congratulating him on his performance, but Tasha and Esme had said a polite goodbye and sat themselves at the bar. They sipped at their drinks quietly, and when Tasha moved to visit the loo her friend followed.

It was as they returned that the blast hit them. A wall of pressure, heat, and noise knocked them off their feet, slamming them against the toilet door that had closed behind them. They were deafened but to the ringing in their ears, and a concerned crowd gathered round and helped them to their feet. Hands guided them to a nearby table and sat them down. Tasha touched her scalp, there was blood on her fingertips. "What happened?" said her silent lips to Esme. Esme looked back at her, fear in her eyes.

"Step aside, give the lasses some air." It was the barman. A solid guy who made his door staff look in need of a steroid or two. "Are you girls all right?"

The crowd was moving away. The show was over.

"What happened?" Tasha asked.

"Buggered if I know," he said.

One of the door staff was at his shoulder. "Everything all right, boss?"

"Fine, John. Bring the first aid kit for the little cut on this lasses head. It won't kill her but we don't want her dripping on that white blouse, do we. And while you're at it, get the girls a Bacardi and Coke each. Double. They seem a bit shook up."

"There was an explosion." As soon as Esme said the words the colour drained from the barman's face. It left him as pale as the little plague girl that had closed the tour.

"I was being nice, ladies, but that isn't the kind of thing to joke about. I'll put it down to the pair of you collapsing and being all confused and that, but any more comments of that sort and you'll need to leave."

John was still at his boss's side. "You girls taken anything we should know about?"

"John, get the Elastoplast and the drinks yeah? I served the ladies not ten minutes ago and they were a bit tipsy but nothing more. Training course, isn't it? I remember the pair of you from earlier."

Tasha nodded. "But there—"

Esme was speaking at the same time. "Yes. That was us. And then we went on this."

The colour returned to the barman's face as he looked at the crumpled and burnt flyer. The printing blistered, the edges singed.

"Where'd you get that?" he asked, his voice shaky.

"The rack by the door. But it was not burnt when I picked it up." There was a tremor in her voice.

John was back with the drinks but the barman took one, downed it, and then polished off the second. "Bring three more."

***

"First things first. I'm Cliff," he said, offering his hand to Tasha and then Esme. "Do you know where you are?"

The girls nodded.

"Really? What's the name of this pub?"

"The Awkward Turtles," Esme said.

"Close enough. It's Turtle. One awkward turtle's quite sufficient, I'd say. Hasn't always been that though. Ever hear of The Turks Head?"

The girls looked at him blankly.

"You might not of done, Miss. Not from around here are you? But you have, you just don't know it." He gestured at Tasha as he spoke, and then took a long drink. Behind him the atmosphere in the pub had returned to normal, but there was no sign of Harlan and the rest of the ghost tour.

"I don't think so," Tasha said.

"No. I have not heard that name," said Esme.

"You have," he said, gesturing at Tasha again, "unless you were living in a cave or out the country eight years ago."

"No."

"Then you saw it on the news, must have done. You remember the bombing? Eight years ago?"

Recognition flashed across Tasha's face. "That was here?"

Cliff leant forward over the table, the flyer held in his hand. "Eight years ago, thirteen people set out from The Turks Head on Harlan Marshall's Ghostly Gallivant. It set off as usual, at dusk. I knocked off early that night around the same time and remember Harlan saying to me as I left 'Thirteen tonight, how's that for luck?' They would've come back at just after twelve. Always did after he told the plague-house story while the bells chime."

"He did that tonight," Tasha said.

Cliff raised an eyebrow and looked at each girl in turn. "No he didn't, love. The bastard's been dead since that night. He set the bomb off at about ten past twelve. All the papers said it was a terrorist attack at first. The pub's name didn't help as people guessed we'd been targeted because of it. I suppose it wasn't exactly inclusive, but hell, it'd been called that since afore such things mattered so much."

"Harlan was the bomber? And he was killed?" asked Tasha as Esme sat in silence.

"Aye. Him and seventeen others, including ten of those that had done the tour with him that night. The explosion was centred in his favourite corner over there. He always had a glass of whisky there afore setting off, and finished the night with another when he came back."

"He didn't drink the rest of the night did he?" Tasha's voice was little over a whisper as she spoke, but Cliff had learnt to lip read during his years working in noisy pubs and clubs.

"Oh he drank all right, from his flask, but he never went into the pubs. Wasn't allowed. He was barred from every pub in the city centre other than here, and that's only because the owner used to go to bingo with his mother."

"Why was he barred?"

"Oh, for getting drunk and pissing off the customers by saying he could see ghosts at every turn, shouting his mouth off about death and disasters. His tours were highly thought of, I'll give him that. But the rest of the time he was a grade-A wanker. Turned out he was heavily into all sorts of black magic and voodoo shit. Probably had a lot to do with why he did it but we'll never know for sure."

"He wanted to die in a way that would make him a ghost," Tasha said, the comment causing all eyes to turn to her. "He seemed so nice."

"Seemed's the operative word there, love. He had a way with the pretty girls when he was sober. There were a couple with him that night as it happens, the two that survived other than a few bumps and scrapes. They'd gone to the toilet you see, walked back just as the bomb went off."

At that Esme stood, her fists clenched at her sides and her face red with anger. "Do you think this to be funny? An amusement added to the tour to end the evening's entertainment at our expense? Let me tell you…" She paused. "If this is true. Then how can… Tasha, we should go. Now."

"Calm down lass, have your drink," Cliff said.

"Sit down Esme, my head still hurts," Tasha said.

"You don't understand." Esme was hysterical, tugging at the coat her friend was wearing. "Get outside, now. Get it off!"

Tasha understood. She was still wearing Harlan's coat. A dead man's coat. An unusually heavy coat…

***

Harlan Marshall stood outside what to him would always be The Turks Head. People had begun to forget his name, and he couldn't allow that. But they were reminded of him once more, to be sure. He had claimed two lives in atonement for those that had eluded his first attempt. He had proven his theory—a violent death of his own making whereupon he turned his back on the light when it had opened up for him. He had made a choice he regretted at times, yet revelled in at others. He took a drink from his flask. The alcohol burnt his throat, like the blast behind him a few moments ago had burnt his body just the same as the one eight years previously.

But this time there was no pain. He was already dead and could never die again.

He was immortal.

ABOUT J.C. MICHAEL

J.C. MICHAEL is a horror author from North Yorkshire, England. His writing credits include the novel *Discoredia* and the *Double Barrel Horror* shorts "Just One Pound" and "Meetings with the Devil." Since the publication of *Discoredia* he has appeared in a number of anthologies, including the Amazon bestselling *Suspended in Dusk: Volume One* that features his own take on the vampire genre in "Reasons to Kill."

DEALING IN SHADOWS

Annie Neugebauer

T HE SHADOWS BELOW SEEM TO HOLD THEIR BREATH at
my approach. I always seek them out, something to do with grief,
maybe. Does my sadness draw me to dark corners? I don't know
why exactly, but ever since I started noticing shadows, they seem more
and more alive to me, as if they're waiting just for me. Waiting for me to
walk by so they can let out their breaths.

"Where are you going now?" Charlene's voice whines in my ear like a
moped. I'd almost forgotten she's on the line.

I fidget with my necklace, wanting to finish the conversation so I can
go down into the metro without losing cell reception. "Home. I'm exhausted."

"Are they still overworking you? I thought you said you'd talk to them
about cutting back your hours."

"I was going to, but then two of the new nurses left. I can't just leave
them high and dry."

Charlene huffs. I picture her pressing the phone between her ear and
shoulder as she picks at her nails. "So you're not coming out with us?"

"No, I'm going home."

I brace for her rebuke, but she sighs and says, "That actually sounds
good. I kind of wish I was too."

"Then go," I say absently, eyeing a deep shadow at the bottom of the
stairs. It almost looks like something is moving in the pit of it. "You're not
obligated to go out with them."

"Yeah. But I hate my apartment. You're so lucky to have your own place, Eva. How many twenty-six-year-olds own a house in the city?"

My face flushes. "I think I hear my train. Gotta go." I hang up without waiting for a reply, but it's either that or explode at my best friend. I know she didn't mean anything by the comment. Her life still bustles with dates and drinks and one-liners, like it should. Like mine used to. I can't expect her to understand.

I tuck my phone back into my purse and descend into the griminess of the metro. I try to ignore the shadows as I pass.

You're so lucky, she said. Lucky to have my own place. In a way, on some level, she's right. But the problem with that statement is that to get so 'lucky,' my dad had to die last year. I can only afford my house due to the inheritance.

My train pulls up to the stop, and I slip through the doors. The metro is almost deserted, which isn't too unusual this time of night. The car I sit in is empty.

I lean my head back and close my eyes, trying to let go of all the worries I carry home from the hospital. Since I'm a physician's assistant in the hospital's psych ward, I deal with many disturbed and disturbing patients. There is one man in particular, Jerry, who came in today claiming he's forgotten just one person. How he knows he's forgotten the person, we still can't figure out.

I shake my head. No work outside of work. But without the distraction, I'm left with thoughts that circle like vultures. Charlene's comment bites at me. Am I lucky? Is a house, some furniture, and financial stability worth the death of my dad?

I squeeze my eyes tighter as the train rocks me from side to side, an oversized bassinet making its way through the dark tunnels. The mechanical sounds of the inner-workings of the engine are bleak and familiar. My chest stays tight.

It's not worth it, I vow. *I miss him so much. I'd give it all back just to see him one last time. Everything.*

A soft scuff draws my eyes open. I look down my nose at the deep shadow under the seat across from me, where the lights of the train can't penetrate. Detecting a small rectangle, I lean forward and pick it up.

It's a slip of black construction paper about the size of a large match box. I hold it up to the light and angle it to read the words scrawled in pencil: SHADOW PEOPLE. That's all it says.

I slide back into my seat, shutting my eyes again. There's the faint smell of smoke in the air, tickling my nose. "Shadow people," I whisper.

"Oh, dear," comes a warbling voice from my right. My eyes fly open. A lady hunched with age is looking at me in sympathy. "Who have you lost?"

Can she read minds? is my first, irrational thought. And of course, the thought of her knowing what I'm thinking sends my mind tripping through all of the things I wouldn't want anyone to know. They play in my head like a flip-book: watching porn, lying to my mom about having plans for Thanksgiving, stealing soda from the broken vending machine at work, the last thing I said to my dad before he died.

"How do you know I've lost someone?" I respond, trying to shove the guilt out of my head. Where the hell did she come from? Hadn't the metro car been empty? Didn't I scan the seats before I sat down?

The tunnel just beyond the shelter of the train races by in a dark cement blur. The woman's eyes are a startling amber, as if somewhere down the line one of her ancestors was a wolf. But the look she gives me isn't predatory, it's appraising.

"It's in your eyes, dear. They bespeak your grief."

"My eyes were closed." My skin is detached from my muscles, trying to crawl up my body to hide under my scalp. I wrap my arms around my stomach, hunching in on myself, trying to hold it down.

She laughs the sultry chuckle of a much younger woman. "It's just an expression, dear."

I stare at her, wishing I were home. I consider snapping, '*Don't call me dear.*'

She continues, "So who was it, child? Someone close?"

"My father." I'm surprised by the words. Why am I humoring her?

She nods as if she's known this all along. "And did he die unexpectedly?"

I squeeze my lips together, tucking the black slip of paper into my pocket. She gets no more from me. The train is coming to a whooshing halt. I'm still two stops from home, but I say, "I'm sorry. This is my stop." I stand and edge toward the sliding doors. *Open, open,* I urge them.

"Well there's no reason to lie, child. I can call you *that*, can't I, dear?"

I can't keep the surprise off my face. My mouth gapes just as the automated doors fly open. A strange sense of dread creeps through me like the first stirrings of a storm. I step out onto the platform, her stranger's laughter slipping through behind me.

Just as the doors whistle closed, she winks, the quick glint of a wolf through trees. I stare at the well-lit interior of the car as the train pulls away. I cannot spot the small hunched figure of the woman.

***

It's not until the next day at work that I realize how she must have known I'd lost a loved one: around my neck is a tiny silver vial that contains a sprinkling of my father's ashes. Engraved in the metal is the phrase ALWAYS REMEMBER. She must've been familiar with cremation jewelry. Maybe she even works in a funeral home.

Now I'm in one of the examining rooms with Jerry. He's old and sad and all worked up. I fiddle with my necklace as we cover the same ground for the tenth time.

"I forgot all about her," he says, looking at me with a face that would have terrified me as a child. "It's very important that I remember her."

I stifle a sigh, trying to be respectful. It's obvious to me that Jerry is suffering not from a neurological disorder but from simple age-induced dementia. I'll have to go back into his chart and find out who admitted him later. Whoever it was deserves a good talking to.

"Sir," I say in my best calming tone, "How do you know you forgot someone if you can't remember her?"

"Well I remember everything else," he begs. "And Eva, look." My eyebrows hitch at his use of my name; I'm impressed that he's remembered it. He slides off the examining table and I grab his elbow to steady him. Next to his, my arm looks strong and unblemished. In his black socks and hospital robe, he pads to the chair that holds his pile of clothes. He moves slowly, but with great stubbornness.

He rummages through his khaki trousers, fishing through the pockets until he pulls out his wallet. His trembling fingers reach into one leather recess, and he hands me a small sepia-toned photo of a lovely young woman.

"Who's this?" I ask him.

"I don't know," he says, tears filling his wrinkly-hooded eyes. "I remember everything but her. I remember everything but her!"

***

I decide to walk home from work. I tell myself it's because I'd like the fresh air, but the truth is the metro makes me nervous after last night. But now, as I move briskly down the sidewalk, my low ponytail creating a warm damp spot on the back of my neck, I wish I'd just sucked it up and taken the train. The city is not a friendly place after dark.

The streets are desolate tonight. I clutch my necklace and keep my head down, passing one dark alley after another. There's the faint scent of smoke in the breeze, and it reminds me of the rail car. I slow my pace and look nervously to the next dark opening between buildings.

From deep in the shadows, comes the soft sound of paper scuffing on concrete. My steps come to a stop a few yards away. For some reason that I can't understand, I find myself whisper-calling, "Shadow people?"

Nothing.

Then a small figure steps onto the sidewalk from the alleyway. It's a little boy of about eight, thin and pale. His rich amber eyes are cupped by dark circles.

I feel foolish for my pounding heart, but worried about the child. What is he doing in an alley so late? He doesn't look homeless. He appears to be alone. I don't move forward.

Staring straight at me from a couple of yards away, he says, "You spoke of us."

"Who?" I get the impression it's not a child I'm speaking to.

"You know who," he chastises. "This is the second time you've summoned us."

There's a lump in my throat the size of a golf ball. It's the eyes I can't look away from, piercing and startling like the gaze of a wolf. "The metro? The old lady?"

He nods. "Speak of us and we appear."

"I didn't mean to," I say lamely. The words just sort of slipped out on their own.

"Sometimes," he says softly, "thoughts can be wished so intently that they gain the power of words."

I swallow in a painful gulp. The shadows around the buildings lengthen, stretching for my ankles. I fight the urge to run. "What do you want?"

"To help. We can give you what you desire."

"How do you know what I desire?"

He smiles an old, sad smile—as if I'm the child—nodding to my hand where it grasps the vial at my chest. "We want to make a trade."

"What kind of trade?"

He smiles. "Nothing more than what you claim you would be willing to sacrifice. We will allow you to see him, once, in return for everything he's given you. Nothing less, nothing more."

Dad? My lungs contract in a jerk. I place both hands out to the side to regain my balance. I look around once, quickly, but we're still alone. The child-who-is-not-a-child hasn't moved, hasn't even blinked. The very ache of my craving for this to happen is sign enough that it's wrong. Bad. Evil, even. Not to mention impossible. I don't know who or what this is, but I want no part in it.

"No," I say. If only my voice didn't waver as I said it. I clench my fists at my sides and repeat, "No. Please go way."

The boy nods once, then steps back into the darkness of the alley. His voice echoes from within. "If you change your mind, you need only to speak of us."

I dash past the passage. It's empty but for shadows so thick they seem alive.

When I get home, I turn on all the lights even though I can hear my father's voice echoing in the back of my memory: *You're wasting electricity. Turn off the light when you leave the room.* His absence is in every breath. I consider calling Charlene for company, but the fullness of her life makes me feel even emptier.

I try to keep busy; try desperately not to think of the shadow people. Try mournfully not to think of my dad. Try frantically not to think of their offer. I don't sleep for fear that my dreams will betray me.

***

The next day at work I'm so tired I feel my bones sleeping of their own accord, pulling my flesh around them like blankets. I tell myself I'm making too much of the encounters with the woman and the boy. I tell myself I'm just depressed and lonely and overworked. I even tell myself that none of it was real, but I don't quite believe it.

To pass the time, I check out old Jerry. All of the details he's given us, from last name to residence to date of birth, are accurate. He knows my name and his, the year, the president, what happened yesterday and on his fifteenth birthday. What he doesn't know is who the picture in his wallet is of.

And no, he says, it couldn't have come with the wallet. On the back is scrawled, LOVE ALWAYS. Everything else in the wallet is his.

I still suspect that this is a therapy issue rather than a neurological one, but Jerry intrigues me, so I ask him to stay another night or two and order an MRI.

***

I stay late. I tell myself that we're short on nurses and I have a lot to do. I'm getting pretty good at telling myself things without listening.

I'm in the break room, meandering through Jerry's file yet again. I examine his charts, searching for clues, but I keep going back to the photo of the woman he says he forgot. It's not the original picture; Jerry wouldn't let me keep that. In fact, he became almost frantic at the suggestion. "It's the only thing left," he cried. "I have to remember her!" I allowed Jerry to accompany me to the front desk so I could make a color copy of his photo.

So now, in the quiet dimness of the hospital at night, this strange, nameless woman whom I've never known and Jerry can't remember stares back at me from a rectangle of sepia surrounded by a large border of white. The depth and shadows in the background are crisp in contrast with the empty border. I scrawl pretty lines in it with my pen, absently drawing scrolls and loops as I study her.

"Who are you?" I murmur. Her eyes, which must have been some pale color in life, are amber in sepia, and I imagine the wolf-eyed woman on the metro. The little boy in the alley. Faintly, I smell smoke.

I stop the flow of ink, jogged out of my daze. Among my scribbles are cursive letters. "The shadow people," I read aloud, dropping my pen. "Did I write that?"

A sound in the room. My head jerks up to find a man standing in front of me. I gasp.

"Oh, my goodness you scared me." I try for friendly through my fluster. "I'm sorry, sir. You can't be in here."

The man raises an eyebrow at me. He is tall, handsome, young. Unwanted adrenaline seeps along my spine. Young means it's probably not a memory problem, which means it's probably a scary problem. Like schizophrenia. I'm supposed to be professional, but I hate dealing with the schitz patients.

I sit up straight, hoping it will jar him into motion. "Can I help you find your room? Are you a patient here?"

He shakes his head. My fingers find my necklace. God, I wish I weren't alone.

"A visitor?" But visiting hours are over.

"Why are you playing games? You know who I am." His voice is smooth and cultured, like an actor in a period piece.

The words SHADOW PEOPLE stare at me in my own handwriting. Why did I write it? I snap the file closed, stand, and toss it on the break room sofa. "I made a mistake," I say. "I didn't mean to speak it out loud."

His lips quirk just a bit. "You would not have been thinking of us to begin with if your yearning were not so great. The bereaved always notice shadows."

That comment takes away my indignity and frustration, and sorrow seeps into their place. It's true. In the end, this is not about my willpower not to speak of them; it is about how much I miss my dad. How much I wish I could make right what went wrong.

"I won't do it," I whisper.

He smiles now, really smiles. He's startlingly attractive, his eyes a familiar burning amber, his teeth in straight white rows. "Come now. Surely you are not so attached to what he's given you that you would choose your possessions over him, are you?" He spreads his palms face-up like a graceful maître d'.

"Where's the catch?" I fire back. "He gave me life, you know. Is that it? I get to see him but you take back my life? Everything I am, genetically and emotionally. All he's taught me too? I won't be fooled."

He laughs now, stepping forward. I stiffen. "Child," he says, and I wonder if he's older than he looks, "What do you think we are? Leprechauns? Genies? There is no trickery here. It is an agreement of simple terms. You get to see your father one last time, and only once—I do not promise you a lifetime with him alive again, mind you—and in return you give up all he's given you. Not your life, not your genetics, nothing so sneaky as that. Simply your physical possessions, your wealth and, of course, your memories."

"My memories? All of them?"

"No, of course not. Just the ones of him. He did give them to you, after all, and thus they are possessions."

He looks so calm and reasonable that I could punch him. Instead, I cross my arms over my stomach and say, "That's not fair. How can I trade one interaction for a lifetime of memories?"

He gives a Gaelic shrug. "It matters not to me. The choice is yours."

I think of the last thing I said to my father. My eyes water. The man examines his fingernails.

"How long do I have to decide?"

"Why, as long as you wish. But hear this. You have already contacted us three times. You may only contact us once more, so choose wisely."

He walks toward the storage closet: a liquid puddle of darkness at the corner of the room.

"But how do I reach you?" I call as he slips through the partially open door.

His body disappears in shadows. His laugh echoes from within. "How do you think?"

Of course, I check the closet later, once I build up the nerve. It's empty. There are no air vents, extra doors, or secret tunnels. Somehow, I knew there wouldn't be.

***

The first thing I do is take an MRI of my own brain. Even people who work in neurology go crazy. It's against the rules to use the equipment for personal reasons, of course, but I must know. The results come back normal.

It occurs to me that if I'm so delusional as to make up imaginary shadow people, I'm likely also delusional enough to see what I want to see in my brain structure, but if that's the case, I can't do anything about it without "turning myself in" and risking my job.

So I move on to the next consideration: if I am losing my grip on reality, does that change things?

The scariest thing about my schizophrenic patients is that the ones who experience hallucinations don't imagine they hear voices; they actually physically hear them. I've seen neuroimaging taken during such episodes. The patients don't use the creative part of their brain as it's happening. They use the auditory reception part. In other words, their brain is literally hearing voices. The fact that they're not from a real source doesn't make them not a real sound.

How can you know what's real in life if it's all real in the mind? And at that point, does the distinction even matter?

If I am going crazy, does that make this choice any less important? It's real to me. The shadow people are real; I saw them, spoke to them. Was made an offer by them.

And in spite of my training, my education, my reason, and my fear... I can't help but consider that offer.

***

I do what I always do when I have an important decision to make: I try to take the emotion out of it. The best way to do that is with a list.

On the back of the photocopied picture of Jerry's forgotten person, I write, REASONS NOT TO TRADE. Under it I make a list: can't trust shadow people, can't change what happened, just one conversation, won't know what to say, loss of money and possessions, no more memories of us, fear. To the right, I start a new column that says, REASONS TO TRADE. Beneath it: see Dad again.

The first column is longer, heavier, the clear winner. But the second calls to me like the lure of someone else's skin, like the knowledge that I could try on a robe of Other, be lost inside it, and only within that find my peace. If I am honest, I have already chosen.

I pretend to think about it for three more days.

***

Jerry's eyes are those of an unbroken horse saddled for the first time. He looks at things I can't see, mutters his loss, slabbers spit upon his lips. I try to calm him with the stroke of my hand on his withering arm. He does not see me.

I look around even though I know the room is empty but for us. "Jerry," I whisper. He moans and his nostrils flare. "Jerry, do you regret your deal? Do you regret making the trade?"

He looks at me. His hooded eyes, for one moment, hold clarity like I long to feel. "Oh, Eva. I cannot regret accepting the deal," he quavers. "It is not accepting the deal that I regret."

"What does that mean?" I ask him, but his eyes have returned to roaming the ceiling. If he were an animal, we would have him put down. Patients do not return from this level of senility.

"I miss remembering her," he cries. "I must remember her!"

"I'm sorry, Jerry."

I can't look at him any longer. I call a nurse and leave his room.

***

I decide to contact them in the brightest place I can think of: my kitchen. Four sets of fluorescent lights line the ceiling, and there are no dark corners. I turn on every fixture in the house. I lock the doors and windows, turn off my phone. When both stories of the house are filled with a strange, sacred hush and the indiscernible hum of light bulbs, I sit down at my breakfast table and cross my arms in front of me.

"Okay," I say hesitantly. This is weird. Shouldn't they have given me a magic token or something? I look around, but see no one. "I, um… I accept your deal. I'd like to see my dad again."

The hollows between my ears and jawbones thump with blood. Nothing happens. "Shadow people?"

It must be too bright for them. Feeling the pulse rise into my eardrums, I close my eyes and count to five.

When I open them, I expect to see a person with amber eyes sitting across from me at the table. I sniff the air for smoke, but there is nothing. What am I doing wrong?

A sound comes from upstairs. Something familiar: the scraping of a chair against the carpet.

The pulse racing in my inner ear stops. I taste metal on my tongue. Grasping the vial of my necklace in my left palm, I swallow the flavor of pennies and head toward the stairs.

***

The light at the top of the landing—that I *know* I left on—is out. My right hand is clammy on the banister. I crane my neck, but only thick shadows await me.

This is it. I agreed to a deal with the Devil. He's probably waiting at the top with a contract he wants me to sign in my own blood. Why am I going up there again?

I take each step slowly, matching both feet on the next surface before lifting my leg again. *Dad*, my heart whispers. *That's why. Because this is the only way to see him.*

This could be a trick. This could have all been a lure. But if all they want is me in a certain place, they could have come and snatched me at any time. They didn't have to promise me false, impossible things.

"Shadow people?" My voice is squeezed through a throat so tight it hurts. I'm almost to the top of the staircase. "I'm ready to accept your offer."

I whistle in one deep breath and take the final step onto the upstairs platform. "What do you want me to do now?" I ask them. All of the doors in the hallway are now closed.

A voice straight from my memories echoes down the passage. "Give me a hug."

I whirl. There, at the end of the hall, sitting in an antique armchair from his own house, lit under the soft yellow glow of his great-grand-mommy's lamp, smiling at me like he used to every day of the first eighteen years of my life, is my dad.

***

"Dad?" My limbs turn to clay. I stare at him, ready to be horrified. I prepare myself to see autopsy scars, but there are none. I look for signs of dirt and decay on his skin, but then I remember that he was cremated, that this isn't a resurrection. This isn't possible at all. Magic or hallucination, he looks real. A little thin, like before he died, but whole and solid.

All of this passes in the space between blinks. He stands, holds out his arms. I run to him. I fling myself into the hug, trusting that he's not a ghost and that I won't fly through him like a hologram. His arms wrap around me, strong and sinewy, as I tuck my face into his shoulder.

I know he's real because he smells just like he always did: like cedar, cigars, and deodorant. His hand smooths down my hair as I cry into his shirt. "Shhh, Eva. It's okay, sweet pea. It's okay."

I can't say anything. I have a million thoughts, but my throat is busy with great hiccupping sobs. Dad squeezes me tightly, rocks us both side to side as I fight to overcome my emotions. I don't know how much time we have.

As I pull out of the hug, his bristly cheek scratches against my temple. I take one giant sniff, swallow my next sob, and step back so I can look at him.

He has gray hair, the color of hay under moonlight. His skin is old and smooth, folding over in places like a cotton quilt. His dark eyes gleam with intelligence and life, and I'm grateful for that. Glad that he is as I've chosen to remember him and not as he was for the last years before he died.

"Oh, my God, Dad. I've missed you so much." The last word breaks over a hiccup, and we both chuckle in that nervous, overwrought way people have at important moments.

A few tears escape his eyes too, and he pulls me back into one more hug as he says, "I know, sweet pea. Me too. Me too."

I allow him to wrap his arms around me so I can just stand here, basking in his protection again, remembering how much I've missed by not having a father.

This is good enough. If all we have time for is one more hug, it's been worth it. A salve has been smoothed on my soul.

But Dad pulls away sooner than the first hug, patting me on my shoulder. He gestures to the chair on the other side of the lamp, and I pull it up so we sit facing each other.

He settles himself into the chair, crossing one ankle on top of his knee. He folds his rough hands gently across his lap—that strange combination of blue-collar worker and late-night scholar that he's always had—and pins me with his gaze. I sniff, then swallow.

"But you didn't bring me here just to tell me that you miss me, did you?"

"No. Well not only. I do miss you."

He nods calmly. "That goes without saying."

I nod too many times. I'm raw with the guilt of what I said the last time I saw him. It echoes in his sad, dark eyes.

"I'm sorry," I blurt. "I'm so sorry for what I said to you. I was angry at you for not pulling yourself out of the addiction, the depression, but it wasn't true that I might as well have not had a father those last years. I know that, now, actually not having you." The words are tumbling over each other like eager tadpoles, and I can't stop the tears from rushing back. "I guess I was trying to scare you sober, but it didn't work. It just pushed you further over the edge. I'm so sorry, Daddy. I didn't mean it."

He looks at me with a measure of wisdom that I've never noticed before. He clasps his hands more tightly around his knee and leans forward. "But you did mean it, Eva. And you had every right to mean it."

And the most horrible part is that he's right. I didn't mean to hurt him, but I was desperate for him to recover—and it did feel like I'd already lost him. In his addiction to pain killers and subsequently alcohol, I was forced to begin grieving my father years before he died.

So is this a waste? Have I given up everything he's given me for nothing?

"But that doesn't make you bad, sweet pea. Say you hadn't told me how you felt. What good would that have done? I'd dug myself too deep. I couldn't find a way out. There was no winning, no happy ending left for me. I would have done it either way."

And that's the answer I wanted to hear and was terrified to hear. It wasn't my fault. He would have killed himself either way. I'm not sure which is worse.

I feel like such a child asking what I'm about to ask, but it must be said. "But, Dad... Didn't you love us? How could you leave me when you knew how much I loved you? How much I would miss you?"

And now, finally, Dad breaks. He drops his face into his palms and weeps. I have never in my life seen him cry. It makes me scared, and I shift in my seat, wanting to reach out to him but suddenly too nervous.

Through his fingers he says, "Of course I do, Eva. That's why I did it. I couldn't keep holding you back from happiness when I knew it was too late for me. I was lucky that I had security and possessions to pass on to you, unlike some in my position. It was the only choice I had left. It was all I could do to spare you some small amount of pain."

I am left staring at him, horrified, touched, confused and amazed by how drastically two people can misunderstand each other. Like two rail cars running side by side for miles, heading to the same destination, when suddenly one veers off the tracks and crashes, and all the conductors can think is, "What went wrong? Was there a way I could have stopped this?"

The only answer is an exquisite silence and the smell of smoke haunting the air like a spirit lost in shadows.

***

We talk for hours. I'm afraid to stop, terrified that once we run out of things to say he will be taken from me once again. So I tell him everything: my new job at the hospital, how I've been feeling distant from Charlene and my friends, how Mom went to his funeral even though they'd been divorced for years, even about the new guy I went out with a few weeks ago. I bring up everything in my life with one exception: the shadow people.

I consider taking him on a tour of the house, vaguely interested in what he would think of all his old furniture in my new place, but decide against it. For one thing, the lamp at the end of the hall seems like a safe bubble of yellow light that I'm afraid to leave. For another, these things will no longer be mine when I'm finished visiting with him.

That thought takes me back to my deal, and I look at him. "Dad?"

He can tell by my tone that I'm about to ask something serious. He uncrosses his legs and sits straighter in his chair.

I'm almost too afraid to ask. Too fearful of what the answer might be. But this is the big one, the thing I need to know before I lose my chance. I force the words through cobwebs. "Are you happy now?"

Dad leans back and lets out a big puff of air. I hold my breath. "Happy? No. But I'm not unhappy anymore, either. I'm not anything, really. Content, now that I've seen you once more. But generally now I'm nothing. I am not. I guess, in other words, that I'm at peace. I'm at rest, sweet pea. I'm resting. And that is as it should be."

My eyes flood for the umpteenth time and I smile. "That's good, Dad. I'm glad." Have I disturbed him? Did I make the right choice? There's guilt at every turn, for every answer. I have run out of things to say.

"I'm going to leave now," he tells me. I nod, trying to memorize the wrinkles in his face. Then he adds, very somberly, "Don't take any more deals."

My lips part on unformed questions, but he interrupts.

"Close your eyes, Eva."

I squeeze my eyelids together as tight as I can. I don't want to see him disappear. I don't want to watch him walk into shadows.

I know when he's gone. I feel his absence the way I feel it when my cat used to leave the foot of my bed in the middle of the night. It hurts too much to cry. I slide from my chair to the floor without opening my eyes. I wrap my arms around my legs and fall to my side curled into a little ball of grief.

I can't bear the thought of forgetting him. *Sleep*, I beg myself. *Sleep*. And eventually, I do, as the sobs burrow themselves deeply into my chest and the darkness of the empty house closes in around me.

***

When I wake, the shadow man from the break room at work is in front of me on the carpet. He sits with his legs swept gracefully to the side of his hips, sitting partially on his heels. He blinks his wolfish eyes at me once, then smiles.

"Hello," he says calmly.

I uncurl my body. Judging from the protest of my cold muscles, I've slept a long time. I sit up and push my back against the wall next to the chair, trying to keep as much distance between us as possible. I give him a nod.

"Why you?" I ask, not really interested in the answer. "Why not the old woman or the little boy?" I am suddenly aware that I can still remember my dad. That the chair I inherited from him is still next to the lamp. I haven't lost him yet. Is this man here to take the things away? That's the deal.

"You like me," he says calmly, still smiling. I must look as suspicious as I feel, because he laughs. "You are more comfortable around me than the others, then." That I can agree with, though it's a slim difference.

"Okay…" I struggle to come up with something to say. Why is he stalling? Does he not realize I can still remember my dad? Panic strikes through my chest at the thought, but I calm it with memories of him: the smell of cedar, the color of his eyes, the way he would hum while he cooked dinner. I'm afraid to ask the man why I still know these things. Afraid to bring it to his attention.

He leans forward, and I am again reminded how attractive he is. I press my back further into the wall, fascinated by the movement of his lips as he says, "I am here to offer you an out."

My eyes widen. "An out? What do you mean?"

He waves his hand in the air as if dismissing something. "Another option. An alternative to our previous deal."

I can't breathe. *Don't take any more deals.*

"You do not want to give up everything, now do you?"

"No." The word escapes with no air to hold it.

"And what, of the possessions your father has given you, do you hold most dear? The money? This lovely home? Those antique chairs passed down for generations?" He smiles at me, tilting his head to the side like a curious bird.

He knows the answer; he's toying with me. But I say it anyway. "The memories. I don't want to forget him." I'm too scared to be angry that my voice cracks over the words.

He nods patiently, as if I am a small child. "Yes, of course. You do love him, indeed—a loyal daughter. Now what if I told you that you don't quite yet have to give up *everything*? What if I told you that your memories can remain your own?"

I try to speak, but my mouth has filled with hope that tastes like mud. I swallow it and squeeze out, "Yes. Please. What do you want?" I am thinking of my newfound peace, the knowledge that my dad has given me, the joy I felt in hugging him one last time. I lock eyes with the shadow man. I steel my jaw and say through gritted teeth, "Anything you want."

The gleaming white smile is wiped from his face as if he were a living chalkboard. His nostrils flicker as he scents the air in front of me.

He leans in even further, invading my space, cementing my back against the wall. I clutch my necklace tightly.

"Join us," he hisses.

***

Choices are a funny thing. We can pretend to take the emotion out of them with lists or long discussions, but in the end we realize that we knew our answer all along. Outcomes rarely affect our decisions.

I suppose I could refuse the trade. But then what? End up like Jerry? The image of his loss still haunts me. I think of him and his photograph that reads LOVE ALWAYS. I finally know what Jerry meant by saying he can't regret taking the deal, only not taking the deal. I cannot make the same mistake.

The living are here; we can't forget them. It is the dead who have the potential to slip away. And that is why we cling so desperately to them, why we value them more.

On impulse, I pop off the lid of my necklace vial to shake the contents into my palm, but there aren't any. The necklace is empty, the ashes gone. I stare at the inscription: ALWAYS REMEMBER. I do. I will. I don't need money or possessions for that.

I choose to remember. It is as simple as that. A final trade.

This leaves me stalking hollow alleyways, appearing in empty subway cars, bargaining with people too desperate to live their lives as given. I walk in darkness, offering light in return for shadows.

I cannot regret my choice. I cannot regret anything, anymore. So now I am left with only one question that truly matters:

Who have you lost?

ABOUT ANNIE NEUGEBAUER

ANNIE NEUGEBAUER is a novelist, short story author, and poet. She has work appearing in more than a hundred publications, including magazines such as *Cemetery Dance*, *Apex*, and *Black Static*, as well as anthologies such as Bram Stoker Award® finalist *The Beauty of Death* and #1 Amazon bestseller *Killing It Softly*. Annie's an active member of the Horror Writers Association and a columnist for *Writer Unboxed* and *LitReactor*. She lives in Texas with two crazy cute cats and a husband who's exceptionally well-prepared for the zombie apocalypse. You can find her on Twitter at @AnnieNeugebauer or visit her at annieneugebauer.com for blogs, poems, organizational tools for writers, and more.

ANOTHER WORLD

Ramsey Campbell

W HEN SONNY THOUGHT HIS FATHER HADN'T STIRRED for three days he took the old man's spectacles off. His father was sitting in the chair stuffed with pages from the Bible, facing the cracked window that looked towards the church beyond the shattered targets of the maisonnettes, the church that the women came out of. The black lenses rose from his father's ashen face, and sunlight blazed into the grey eyes, ball-bearings set in webs of blood. They didn't blink. Sonny pulled the wrinkled lids over them and fell to his knees on the knobbly carpet to pray that the Kingdom of God would come to him. He hadn't said a tithe of the prayers he knew when the sunlight crept away towards the church.

He had to keep his promise that he'd made on all the Bibles in the chair—proofs of the Bibles they printed where his father used to work until he'd realised that God's words required no proof—but he shouldn't leave his father where the world might see that he was helpless. He slipped one arm beneath his father's shrivelled thighs and the other around his shoulders, which protruded like the beginnings of wings, and lifted him. His father was almost the shape of the chair, and not at all pliable. His dusty boots kicked the air as Sonny carried him up the narrow walled-in staircase and lowered him onto the bed. He flourished his bent legs until Sonny eased him onto his side, where he lay as if he were trying to shrink, legs pressed together, hands clasped to his chest. The sight was far less dismaying than the thought of going out of the house.

He didn't know how many nights he had kept watch by his father, but he was so tired that he wasn't sure if he'd heard the world scratching at the walls on both sides of him. His father must have suspected that the Kingdom of God wouldn't be here by now, whatever he'd been told the last time he had gone out into the world. Sonny made himself hurry downstairs and take the spectacles from the tiled mantelpiece.

"Eye of the needle, eye of the needle," his father would mutter whenever he put on the spectacles. Sonny had thought they were meant to blind him to the world, the devil's work—that the Almighty had guided his father as he strode to the market beyond the church, striding so fiercely that the world fell back—but now he saw that two holes had been scratched in the thick black paint which coated the lenses. The arms nipped the side of his skull, and two fists seemed to close around his eyes: the hands of God? The little he could see through the two holes was piercingly clear. He gazed at the room that shared the ground floor with the stony kitchen where his father scrubbed the clothes in disinfectant, gazed at the walls his father had scraped bare for humility to help God repossess the house, the Stations of the Cross that led around them to the poster of the Shroud. Blood appeared to start out of the nailed hands, but he mustn't let that detain him. Surely it was a sign that he could stride through hell, as his father used to.

His father had braved the forbidden world out there on his behalf, and Sonny had grown more and more admiring and grateful, but now he wished his father had taken him out just once, so that he would know what to expect. His father had asked them to come from the Kingdom of God to take care of his body, but would they provide for Sonny? If not, where was his food to come from? You weren't supposed to expect miracles, not in this world. He clasped his hands together until the fingers burned red and white and prayed for guidance, his voice ringing like a stone bell between the scraped walls, and then he made himself grasp the latch on the outer door.

As he inched the door open his mouth filled with the taste of the disinfectant his father used to wash their food. A breeze darted through the gap and touched his face. It felt as if the world had given him a large soft kiss that smelled of dust and smoke and the heat of the summer day. He flinched, almost trapping his fingers as he thrust the door away from him, and reminded himself of his promise. Gripping the key in his pocket as if it were a holy relic, he took his first step into the world.

The smell of the world surged at him, heat and fallen houses and charred rubbish, murmuring with voices and machinery. The sunlight lifted his scalp. Even with the spectacles to protect him, the world felt capable of bursting his senses. He pressed himself against the wall of the house, and felt it shiver. He recoiled from the threat of finding it less solid than he prayed it was, and the pavement that met the house flung him to his knees.

The whole pavement was uneven. The few stones that weren't broken had reared up as though the Day of Judgement were at hand. As he rubbed his bare knees, he saw that every house except his father's was derelict, gaping. Behind him the street ended at a wall higher than the other houses, where litter struggled to tear itself loose from coils of barbed wire.

He would never be able to walk on the upheaved pavement unless he could see better. He narrowed his eyes and took off the spectacles, praying breathlessly. The husks of houses surged forward on a wave of sound and smells, but so long as he kept his eyes slitted it seemed he could stave off the world. He strode along the pavement, which flickered like a storm as his eyelids trembled. He had only just passed the house when he staggered and pressed his hands to his scalp. The world had opened around him, and he felt as if his skull had.

The market stretched across waste land scribbled out by tracks of vehicles. There were so many vans and stalls and open suitcases he was afraid to think of counting them. A crowd that seemed trapped within the boundaries of the market trudged the muddy aisles and picked at merchandise. A man was sprinkling petrol on a heap of sprouts to help them burn. Beyond the shouts of traders and the smouldering piles of rubbish, a few blackened trees poked at a sky like luminous chalk. To his left, past several roofless streets, were concrete stacks of fifty floors or more, where the crowd in the market must live. So this was hell, and only the near edge of hell. Sonny retreated towards the church.

Then he caught hold of his mouth to keep in a cry. It wasn't a church any more, it was a GIVEAWAY DISCOUNT WAREHOUSE. All women were prostitutes, and he'd thought the women he'd seen leaving the church every night had been confessing their sins—but they'd been using God's house to sell the devil's wares. The realisation felt as if the world had made a grab at him. He fumbled the spectacles onto his face just as three muddy children sidled towards him.

Their faces crowded into the clear area of the lens. "Are you a singer or something, mister?" a boy whose nostrils were stained brown demanded. "Are you on video?"

"He's that horror writer with them glasses," said a girl with a bruised mouth missing several teeth.

"Thought he was a fucking Boy Scout before," said a girl in a mangy fur coat. A fleshy bubble swelled out of her mouth and popped sharply. "That why you're dressed like that, mister, because you like little boys?"

They were only imps, sent to torment him. If they seemed about to touch him he could lash out at them with his heavy boots. "Where can I find the Kingdom of God?" he said.

"Here it is, mister," the bubbling girl sniggered, lifting the hem of her coat.

"He means the church, the real church," the bruised girl said reprovingly. "You mean the real church, don't you, mister? It's past them hoardings."

Beyond the discount warehouse, at the end of the street that bordered the market, stood three large boards propped with timber. Once the stares and titters were behind him, he took the spectacles off. There was so much smoke and dust on the road ahead that the cars speeding nowhere in both directions appeared to be driverless. The road led under hooked lamps past buildings which he knew instinctively were no longer what they had been created for, lengths of plastic low on the black façades announcing that they were VIDEO UNIVERSE WITH HORROR AND SCI-FI AND WAR, THE SMOKE SHOP, THE DRUGSTORE, MAGAZINES TO SUIT ALL TASTES. There was CLEANORAMA, but he thought it came far too late. He peered narrowly to his left, and the hoardings thrust their temptations at him, a long giant suntanned woman wearing three scraps of cloth, an enormous car made out of sunset, a cigarette several times as long as he was tall. Past them was the church.

It didn't look much like one. It was a wedge that he supposed you'd call a pyramid, almost featureless except for a few slits full of coloured splinters and, at the tip of the wedge, a concrete cross. Feeling as if he were in a parable, though he'd no notion what it meant or if it was intended to convey anything to him, he stalked past the hoardings and a police station like the sheared-off bottom storey of a tower block, and up the gravel path.

The doors of the church seemed less solid than the doors of his father's house. When he closed them behind him, the noise of traffic seeped in. A least the colours draped over the pine pews were peaceful. Kneeling women glanced and then stared at him as he tiptoed towards the altar. The light through a red splinter caught a sign on a door. FATHER PAUL, it said. Daring to open his eyes fully at last, Sonny stepped through the veils of coloured light he couldn't see until they touched him, and pushed the door wide.

A priest was kneeling on a low velvety shelf, the only furniture in the stark room. His broad red face clenched on a pale O of mouth. "That's not the way, my son. Stay on the other side if you're here to confess."

"I'm looking for the Kingdom of God," Sonny pleaded.

"So should we all, and nothing could be simpler. Everything is God's."

"In here, you mean?"

"And outside too."

He was a false prophet, Sonny realised with a shudder that set bright colours dancing on his arms and legs, and this was the devil's mockery of a church. He stepped out of reach of the hairy hands that looked boiled red and collided with a pew, which spilled black books. The priest was rising like smoke and flames when a voice behind Sonny said "Any trouble, Father?"

He might have been another priest, he was dressed blackly enough. The thought of being locked up before he could have his father taken care of made Sonny reckless. "He's not a priest," he blurted.

"I'd like to know what you think you are, coming to church dressed like that," the policeman said, low and leaden. "It may be legal now, but we can do without your sort flaunting yourselves in church. Just give me the word, Father, and I'll teach him to say his prayers."

Sonny backed away and fled as colours snatched at him. Slitting his eyes, he blundered out of the concrete trap. He ought to take refuge at home before the policeman saw where he lived, and then venture out after dark. But he had only reached the elbow upon which the giantess was supporting herself when a car drew up beside him.

He thought he was going to be arrested. He recoiled against the hot giantess, who yielded far too much like flesh, as the driver's square head poked out, a titan's blonde shaving brush. "Are you lost?" the driver said. "Can I help?"

Sonny heaved himself away from the cardboardy flesh and staggered against the car. Not having eaten since before his father had stopped moving was catching up with him. He managed to steady himself as the driver climbed out of the car. "Do you live near here? Can I take you home? Unless you'd like me to find you somewhere else to stay."

He was trying to find out where Sonny lived. "The Kingdom of God," Sonny said deliberately.

"Is that a church organisation? I don't know where it is, but we'll go there if you can tell me."

That took Sonny aback. Surely anyone who meant to tempt him must claim to know where it was. Could this person be as lost and in need of it as Sonny was? "You really look as if you should be with someone," the driver said. "Have you nobody at home?"

Before Sonny could close himself against it, a flood of loss and loneliness passed through him. "Nobody who can help," he croaked.

"Then let's find you where you're looking for. My name's Sam, by the way." Sam held out a hand as if to take Sonny's, but stopped short of doing so. "What's it like, do you know? What kind of building?"

The sensitivity Sam had shown by not touching him won Sonny over. "All I know is it's not far."

"We can still drive if you like."

They would be tooclose in the car, and Sonny would be giving up too much control. He peered back at the church, where the policeman seemed content to glower from the doorway. "I'll walk," he said.

Past the hoardings, the smell of the market pounced on him. The smoke of charred vegetables scraped inside his head as he hurried by, trying to blink his pinched eyes clear. Ahead of him the road of cars flexed like a serpent, like the leg of a giantess. He dug his knuckles into his eyes and told himself that it was only curving past more old buildings claimed by names MACHO MILITARIA, CAPTIVATING TOTS, LUSCIOUS LEGS, SEX AIDS... Some of the strips of plastic embraced two buildings. "It is an actual place we're looking for, is it?" Sam said, trotting beside him.

Sonny hesitated, but how could he save a soul unless he spoke the truth? "That's what my father said."

"He sent you out, did he?"

"Into the world, yes." Both question and answer seemed to suggest more than they said, but what did the parable mean? "I had to come," he said in his father's defence. "There's nobody else."

Now that the market and its stretch were left behind, the houses appeared to be flourishing. The façades ahead were white or newly painted, their front windows swelled importantly. Gleaming plaques beside their doors named doctors and dentists, false healers one must never turn to. Weren't these houses too puffed up to harbour the Kingdom of God? But the people were the same as the lost souls of the waste land: faces stared at him from cars, murmured about him beyond the lacy curtains of a waiting-room; two young women exhaling smoke sidled past him and hooted with laughter. "He'll get no girls if he goes around dressed like that," one spluttered.

"Maybe he's got better things to do," Sam said icily.

Sonny drew in a breath that tasted of disinfectant, which seemed too clear a sign to doubt. As he strode past the dentist's open door he experienced a rush of trust and hope such as he'd never even felt towards his father. There must be others like him or potentially like himself in the world, and surely Sam was one. "It's how my father dressed me," he confided.

"Has it anything to do with what we're looking for?"

"Yes, to remind me I'm a child of God," Sonny said, and was reminded more keenly by a twinge from the marks of the birch.

"Does your father dress like that too, then?"

"Of course not," Sonny giggled. "He was, he's my father."

Sam appeared not to notice his indiscretion. "How old are you anyway? You dress like you're ten years old, but you could be in your early thirties."

"We don't need to know. Years like that don't matter, only the minutes before the fire that consumes the world. If we've spent our time counting our years we'll never be able to prepare ourselves to enter the Kingdom of God. Not the place we're going now, the place of which that's a symbol. Where we're going now is the first and last church, the one that won't be

cast into the fire where all corruption goes. That's because we keep ourselves pure in every way and cast out the women once they've given birth."

Sam's mouth opened, but what it said seemed not to be what it had
opened for. "You mean your mother."

Though it hadn't the tone of a question, Sonny thought it best to make
things clear. "Questions come from the devil. They're how the world tries
to trick the faithful."

"So you have to look after your father all by yourself."

Why should that matter to Sam? Sonny couldn't recall having said his
father needed looking after. He tried to let the truth speak through him as
he searched the curves ahead, where gleaming houses rested their bellies
on mats of grass. Newspapers and boards quoting newspapers hung on
the corner of a side street, and he glanced away from the devil's messages,
perhaps too hastily: the world seemed to pant hotly at him, the houses
swelled with another breath. "Only the pure may touch the pure," he
mumbled.

"That's why I mustn't touch you."

Such a surge of trust passed through Sonny that his body felt unfamil-
iar. "Maybe you'll be able to," he blurted.

"Not if—"

"We can all be saved. We just have to admit we need to be," Sonny
reassured Sam, who agreed so readily that Sonny wondered if he'd missed
the point somehow. Houses white as virgins breathed their stony breaths
and expanded their bellies until every polished name-plaque turned to the
sun and shone. For a moment he thought it was God who was filling the
virgin bellies, and then he recoiled from himself. How could he let the
world think for him? Where had he gone wrong? "Quick," he gasped, and
tottered round, almost touching Sam's bare downy arm.

The world twisted and tried to throw him. The fat houses between him
and the market began to dance, wobbling their whited bellies. He mustn't
think of leaning on Sam, but a distant edge of him wished he could. He
held the spectacles to his eyes as he came abreast of the dangling newspapers, but the darkness of the lenses seemed a pit into which he was close
to falling. As he stepped off the pavement to cross the side street, he felt as
if he were stepping off a cliff.

He faltered in the middle of the side street, though cars snarled beside him. He thought a voice had spoken to him, saying "King God." He snatched off the spectacles so eagerly that one lens shattered between his finger and thumb. Black shards crunched under his feet, the sun went for his eyes, but none of this mattered. He hadn't heard a voice, he'd seen a sign. It hadn't just said King God; only the lens had made it seem to. It said Kingdom of God, and it was in a window.

He ran across the side street, scrambled onto the pavement. How could he have missed the sign before? Surely he needn't blame Sam for distracting him. The Kingdom was here now, that was all that mattered— here beyond the window that blazed like a golden door, like a fire in which only the name of the Kingdom was visible, never to be consumed. He took another pace towards it, and the sunlight drained out of the window, leaving a surface grey with dust and old rain, which he was nevertheless able to see through. Beyond it was ruined emptiness.

He stumbled forward so as not to fall. The sign he'd seen was a faded placard in the window, beside a door whose lock had been gouged out. A rail dragged down by stained curtains leaned diagonally across the window. Several chairs lay on the bare floorboards, their legs broken, their entrails sprung. On a table against the ragged wall, a dead cat glistened restlessly.

Sam pressed his forehead against the window. "This can't be it, can it? Nobody's been here for months."

Sonny's father had been, only days ago: wasn't that what he'd said? He must have meant it as a parable, or meant that he'd met some of the brethren. What could Sonny do now, as the world throbbed with muffled mocking laughter? Go back home in case the Kingdom had come there and if not, stay nearby until they found him? Then Sam said "Don't worry, I'll help you. Shall we see to your father first?"

The window had blackened his forehead as if he'd been branded, and Sonny seemed to perceive him all at once more clearly. "See to him how?"

"Have him taken care of, however he needs to be."

"Who by?"

"I won't know until I've seen him. I promise I'll do whatever's best for both of you."

Sonny swallowed, though it felt like swallowing chunks of the world. "Who are you?"

"Nobody special, but you might say I help save people too. I'm a social worker."

Sonny felt as if he'd been punched in the stomach, the way his father had punched him sometimes to make him remember. He doubled up, but he had nothing to vomit. People who said they were social were socialists, communists, architects of the devil's kingdom, and he'd let one of them entice him, hadn't even realised he was being led. Perhaps the ruined shop had been set up for him to see, to turn him aside from searching further.

Sam had stepped back. He was afraid Sonny would be sick on him, Sonny realised, and flew at him, retching. When Sam retreated, Sonny turned with the whirlpool of sky and bloated buildings and staggered to the corner of the street, almost toppling into the parade of cars. He jammed the one-eyed spectacles onto his face and fled.

His legs were wavering so much that a kind of dance was the only way he could keep on his feet. The houses joined in, sluggishly flirting their bellies at him, growing blacker as he jigged onward. The giantess lazily raised her uppermost leg, the stench of charred rotten vegetables surged at him down the uneven street. Compared with Sam and the virginal buildings, the smell seemed at least honestly corrupt. It made him feel he was going home.

He was appalled by how familiar the world already seemed to him. The children jeering "Pirate" at him, the pinched faces eager for a bargain, a trader kicking a van that wouldn't start, Sonny thought for a moment which felt like the rim of a bottomless pit that he could have been any one of them. As he stumbled past the discount church and down the disused street he wept to realise that he liked the feel of the open sky more than he expected to like the low dimness of the house. Then he wondered if he might have left his father alone for too long, and fell twice in his haste to get home.

He dug his key into the lock, reeled into the house as the door yielded, shouldered it closed behind him. A smell of disinfectant that seemed holier than incense closed around him. He mustn't let it comfort him until he had taken care of his father. Anyone who'd seen his father sitting in the Bible chair might wonder where he was now, might even try to find him.

His father lay as Sonny had left him, straining to touch his clasped hands with his knees. Sonny gathered him up and wavered downstairs, thumping the staircase wall with his father's shrivelled ankles and once with his uncombed head. Would it look more natural to have his father kneeling in the front room? As soon as he tried, his father keeled over. Sonny sat him on the Bibles and stood back. His father looked at peace now, ready for anything. The sight was making Sonny feel that the Kingdom of God was near when he heard the key turn in the front door.

He'd been so anxious to reach his father that he'd left the key in the lock. He knew instinctively that it wasn't the Kingdom of God at the door. He felt the house stiffen against the world that was reaching in for his father and him. He scrabbled the hall door open. Sam was in the hall.

All Sonny could think of was his father, powerless to defend himself or even dodge the grasp of the world. "Get out," he screamed, and when his voice only made Sam flinch he forgot the warning his father had given him, the warning that was so important Sonny's stomach had been bruised for a week. He put his hands on Sam to cast the intruder out of the house.

And then he realised how thoroughly the world had tricked him, for Sam's chest was the memory Sonny had driven so deep in his mind it had been like forgetting: his mother's chest, soft and warm and thrusting. He cried out as loudly and shrilly as Sam did, and flung her backwards onto the broken road. He staggered after her, for he wasn't fit to stay in a house that had been dedicated to God. He hadn't been ready to venture into the world after all, and it had possessed him. In the moment when he'd flung Sam's breasts away from him he'd felt his body reach secretly for her.

He slammed the door and snatched the key and flew at her, driving her towards the waste where the lost souls swarmed under the dead sky. He tore the spectacles off and shied them at her, narrowly missing her face. The lost souls might tear him to pieces when they saw he was routing one of them, but perhaps he could destroy her first—anything to prevent the world from reaching his father ahead of the Kingdom of God. Then he threw up his hands and wailed and gnashed his teeth, for the world had already touched his father. He had been so anxious to take his father to the safety of the Bibles that he'd forgotten to disinfect himself. He'd held his father with hands the world had tainted.

A smell that made him think of disinfectant drifted along the street to mock him. It was of petrol, in a jug that the trader who had kicked the van was carrying. The trader glanced at the spectacle of Sonny lurching at Sam, trying to knock her down as she retreated towards the market with her hands held out to calm him, and then the trader turned away as if he'd seen nothing unusual. He put down the jug in order to unscrew the cap on the side of the van, and at once Sonny knew exactly what to do.

He ran past Sam and grabbed a stick with a peeling red-hot tip from the nearest fire, and darted to the jug of petrol. He had just seized the handle when the trader turned and lunged at him. Sonny would have splashed petrol over him to drive him back, but how could he waste his father's only salvation? He tipped the jug over himself, and the world shrank back from him, unable to stop him. He poured the last inch of petrol into his mouth.

"Don't," Sam cried, and Sonny knew he was doing right at last. The taste like disinfectant stronger than he'd ever drunk confirmed it too. He ran at Sam, and she sprawled backwards, afraid he meant to spew petrol at her or brand her with the stick. Smiling for the first time since he could remember, Sonny strode back into the house.

He was turning the key when Sam and more of the devil's horde came running. Sonny made a red-hot sign of the cross in the air and stepped into the house, and threw the key contemptuously at them. The stick had burned short as he strode, the mouthful of petrol was searing his nostrils, but he had time, he mustn't swallow. The stick scorched his fingers as he took the three strides across the room to his father. Carefully opening his mouth, he anointed his father and the chair, and then he sat on his father's lap for the first time in his life. It was unyielding as iron, yet he had never felt so peaceful. Perhaps this was the Kingdom of God, or was about to be. As he touched the fire to his chest, he knew he had reached the end of the parable. He prayed he was about to learn its meaning.

ABOUT RAMSEY CAMPBELL

The *Oxford Companion to English Literature* describes **RAMSEY CAMPBELL** as "Britain's most respected living horror writer". He has been given more awards than any other writer in the field, including the Grand Master Award of the World Horror Convention, the Lifetime Achievement Award of the Horror Writers Association, the Living Legend Award of the International Horror Guild and the World Fantasy Lifetime Achievement Award. In 2015 he was made an Honorary Fellow of Liverpool John Moores University for outstanding services to literature. Among his novels are *The Face That Must Die, Incarnate, Midnight Sun, The Count of Eleven, Silent Children, The Darkest Part of the Woods, The Overnight, Secret Story, The Grin of the Dark, Thieving Fear, Creatures of the Pool, The Seven Days of Cain, Ghosts Know, The Kind Folk, Think Yourself Lucky* and *Thirteen Days by Sunset Beach*. He is presently working on a trilogy, The Three Births of Daoloth – the first volume, *The Searching Dead*, was published in 2016, followed by *Born to the Dark*, and *The Way of the Worm* is forthcoming. *Needing Ghosts, The Last Revelation of Gla'aki, The Pretence* and *The Booking* are novellas. His collections include *Waking Nightmares, Alone with the Horrors, Ghosts and Grisly Things, Told by the Dead, Just Behind You* and *Holes for Faces*, and his non-fiction is collected as *Ramsey Campbell, Probably. Limericks of the Alarming and Phantasmal* are what they sound like. His novels *The Nameless* and *Pact of the Father*s have been filmed in Spain. He is the President of the Society of Fantastic Films.

Ramsey Campbell lives on Merseyside with his wife Jenny. His pleasures include classical music, good food and wine, and whatever's in that pipe. His web site is at www.ramseycampbell.com.

THE HOPELESS IN THE UNINHABITABLE PLACES

Letitia Trent

D O WE HAVE TO GO THROUGH THERE? Chloe asked. She wore her hair up in a bun created by complex arrangements of pins and had applied red lipstick in anticipation of the performance, to look the way the wife of a near-famous violinist should look. Garrett was expected to arrive at ten for the performance at ten thirty. In truth, it was only thirty miles away, a forty-minute drive on a good night, but there were no more good nights since the space between their town and the city had been officially declared off-limits for habitation, only a through-way with no rest stops. DO NOT LEAVE YOUR CAR, said the messages that lined the road in yellow letters on red, a new signage created specifically for the uninhabited lands, one that echoed equally the blood and alarm of these new no-places. LOCK YOUR DOORS.

If we hadn't had to go back, we could have taken the other way, he said, giving her a quick glance. This is the only way to make it on time now.

Chloe looked down into her lap. She'd made them late by forgetting her medicine. She wasn't even sure if she had to take it anymore, but she was afraid to go without it for one night, particularly on a night when he would need her to be present and awake and not slumped in her chair or in the bathroom.

We have to go through, he said. It's the quickest way. If we don't go through, we have to go all the way around the mountain. Which will take two hours. Which will mean that I'm late to my first major solo performance in two years.

I'm sorry, she said.

No reason to be sorry, he told her, not bothering to give her a glance this time. This is just the way it is.

I know, she said. I know how important it is. But it's dangerous. I'm just—

It's dangerous only if you go outside, he said. The trick is to never go outside, no matter what.

Chloe closed her eyes and shook her head. You couldn't get me outside on this road at night for anything, she said.

They remained silent for a while as the car passed the signs that marked the limits of the safe zone, as they passed the warning lights, and then the enormous wall with armed guards who nodded and opened the gate after examining their trunk and the backseat. A routine search, done with efficiency. She remembered how at first it had seemed so strange, like living in the Gaza Strip, like something you'd see on the news, people waiting in cages while their purses are upturned and swabbed for bomb material. The news, though, explained why it was necessary. Early on, people had gone through with traps in their trunks, false bottoms to hold a Hopeless One. They meant to lure them out and into the cars to bring them home. Early on, some people still hoped. Some succeeded in bringing them back, but it never ended well. Most didn't make it back—their cars were stripped clean by the time the soldiers arrived, the bodies gone.

She watched the two young soldiers, both men, one blond and pale and one dark-skinned with a beard, type into tablets. The blond one waved them on. She waved back. The soldiers identified the license plate, listed it in the database, and if family members complained that they'd lost somebody who had gone through the uninhabitable zones, a government search party would find them and, if necessary, send their remains home. This was rarely necessary. The only people who died in the uninhabitable zone anymore were thrill seekers or parents who didn't realize their children were long gone, not children at all. If you didn't leave the car, for any reason whatsoever, you were safe.

It wasn't hard to keep the Hopeless out, she'd learned. Few tried to come through, and those that did were easy to pick off, despite their size and agility. They were risk-takers, unable to think through a plan past the initial steps. That was part of the illness.

I wonder how Amy and Richard feel, she said aloud. If they still think about her.

Garrett made a sharp sound with his tongue. She thought he would scold her for being sentimental, but he simply replied yes, it must have been hard.

But they had to do it, he said. Don't you remember?

She did. By the end, they'd had to keep their daughter Adrianne in a separate room, she'd become so difficult to handle. She'd bitten a neighbor's ankle, just like a dog. They resorted to sliding food through a makeshift hole in the door, covered by a piece of a plastic tarp, until she'd punched through the door, one bloody fist waving through the hole in the door as they both watched in horror.

Around the car, it was growing dark. Now, on the other side of the gate, there were no streetlights, no government signs, nothing but the remains of houses, wrecked cars pushed to the side of the road, and random detritus: children's shoes, tires, broken sunglasses.

***

It doesn't work, she said, after a long silence.

What?

The isolation policy doesn't work. It doesn't make the children better.

He looked at the road. She was nervous in the dark, without streetlights, watching the trees that surrounded the road brighten in the headlights and then grow dark again as they passed her on the passenger side.

It's not meant to make them better, he said. Nothing makes them better. It's genetic, it can't be fixed yet. The policy is meant to keep us safe from them.

They were silent. By some understanding, neither had tried to turn on the radio. The radio waves were weak through the uninhabitable zones, the stations that happened to be within the zones having been left along with everything else, though she'd heard that some of the Hopeless had set up shop in them, sending messages across the spaces only they controlled. Some had made it to adulthood, she'd heard. *A ticking time bomb,* some television commentator had called them.

You should slow down, she said. I read they try to run into the road, like deer, and if you hit one, the rest will come and drag you out of the car—

That's rare, he interrupted, clearly irritated by her now. It has happened, what, once or twice in five years? And both times, it was parents, stupid parents coming back to get them, thinking they'd made a mistake, slowing down to take pity, to ask if any of these creatures had seen their child. And what happened each time? They were killed. Torn apart by their own children, or things that had been *somebody's* children, before they were the Hopeless. You know they aren't children after they turn, right? You can't call them children anymore.

He was agitated, staring straight forward into the dark.

She nodded. I know, she said. I'm just afraid. She spoke quietly, looking out the window…

…at nothing.

I'm sorry, he said. He breathed slowly through his nose, a technique she knew he'd learned to calm himself down. I didn't mean to shout, he said. I'm just nervous. You know how many people I'm playing for tonight, how nervous I get before a show.

She touched his knee, which she could feel tensed beneath her hand. He was a ball of nerves right now, wound tight, and too much prodding, too much of her own tension wound with his, might ruin his concentration and throw off his performance. The performance was all that mattered to him right now. He would have driven through a sea of Hopeless to get to the performance, would have gotten out of the car, pulled his violin from the back, and run through a pack of them to get to the opera house steps.

Garrett would throw me at them, she thought, just to get to his performance. She removed her hand from his knee.

It's going to be fine, she said. We'll get there. You'll play beautifully, as you always do, and we'll come home tomorrow, take the long way, and there'll be nothing to worry about.

***

They still have a picture of her, she said aloud a half-hour later. She couldn't help it. Her mind wouldn't move beyond it.

Amy keeps a picture of her in the bathroom, she said. In their medicine cabinet, on the very top shelf. I was looking for tampons once, over at their house—she kept speaking, though she knew that he didn't like her to talk about things like tampons, like toilet paper, like razors, anything to do with the refuse of the body—it was a picture from when Adrianne was young, Chloe said. Three years old, remember? She seemed normal, then. We used to hold her, do you remember?

What's the point of this? Garrett asked.

Chloe flinched. He had never hit her, but his disdain was always palpable, like a slap of water against her cheek. Nothing, she said. I'm just talking. I'm nervous.

I'm nervous too, he said. Let's just keep quiet, okay? You can put on the radio, if you can find a station.

She fiddled with the dial, which buzzed faintly, and familiar music weaved in and out of the static. Then, a voice came clearly, if imperfectly, through an old or damaged microphone.

It's one of them, he said. Turn it off.

No, she said, her hand still on the scan button. I want to hear. She turned it up.

The illegal purging of those they call the Hopeless, *those who I prefer to call the* Fully Alive, *is illegal, vicious, and violent—and* it will be paid in—

He reached over and brushed aside her hand, clicking the radio off.

I heard about this on NPR, he said. Gangs who survive. Not many. And they die off eventually. They have a radio station somewhere, and they advertise this terrorist stuff—

Terrorist stuff, she repeated.

Yeah, he said. Burning down buildings. Terrorizing people. He turned to her, briefly, hearing her sharp intake of breath. They threaten it, he clarified. One of us is harmed and the army rolls in and takes care of it. They know that. As addled as their brains are, they know killing us doesn't do any good.

She wondered, silently, how the Hopeless could be both so much like animals and so much like people, aware of cause and effect, smart enough to take over a radio station. She didn't say anything aloud, though. This was the kind of musing that would send Garrett into a rage.

He listened to her sniffle for a few moments. I'm sorry you had to hear that, he said. She looked away. You chose too, though. You chose to listen.

I know, she said. I just wish I hadn't—

The impact threw her head forward, sinking her teeth deep into her tongue and bashing her forehead into the glass of the passenger side window. The jolt caused Garrett to momentarily let go of the steering wheel and they skidded sideways, off into the gravel ditch.

Chloe had been in a car that hit a deer once when she was a teenager. She'd been riding with her first boyfriend, a friendly, corn-fed boy who couldn't seem to stop committing petty crime, no matter how often he got caught, no matter how much it cost him. But he'd been gentle with her, careful even, and he'd driven her home every night from her job at the seasonal ice-cream stand by the deer park. She remembered, in the dusk, how something had flashed in her eyes and, then, the car had lurched, swerved from the road and righted before it hit the ditch. The deer they'd hit was in the middle of the road, kicking its thin legs, trying to get up.

Garrett regained control of the steering wheel and hit the brakes before they went out far into the field beyond the road, rotten remnants of the cornfield it had once been still standing.

Jesus, did we hit something? she asked through bloody teeth. She pressed a tissue against her tongue and tasted the copper in her mouth, a taste she'd always found slightly comforting for no reason she could understand.

I think so, he said. Maybe a small animal. I felt something go under the tires. Our bumper is probably damaged, but the car is fine. You okay?

Yeah, she said. We should see what it is, don't you think? We should see if we hit one.

What? One of *them*? Garrett shook his head. You're trying to get us killed.

We can't leave it in the middle of the road, she said. She recalled the deer, blackish blood flowing from one impaled eye as it kicked against the pavement. Her boyfriend, the good country boy that he was, had kept a rifle in his car just for these purposes. He'd pressed the gun against the deer's head and asked her to turn away. The sound of the gun had been so loud she'd felt the vibrations in her teeth.

She fished a bottle of ibuprofen from the purse at her feet and took out six pills.

Take some, she said, handing him half of the pills. They sipped from a cold cup of coffee. Her heart beat quickly and she thought, for a moment, that her throat might close up. She closed her eyes and breathed through her nose until the feeling passed. In her lap, her hands shook. She tucked them between her knees.

Will you be able to play tonight? she asked.

He nodded. I'll have an egg on my head, he said, probably blue and purple by the time we get there, but I'll be fine. But we have to go now.

Let's just see, she said. We don't have to get out of the car. Let's just turn and let the headlights show us what we hit.

He nodded. Probably a good idea, anyway. If it's an animal, and dead, I'll get out and check the damage.

Don't get out, she said. She was surprised by her own cowardice, though he could not know what she was thinking; she wasn't afraid that he'd be killed as much as she was afraid of being left alone to drive the rest of way herself. The body lay just a few feet from the car as they backed up; a wider turn and they would have hit it again.

The child wore the remnants of a dress. She lay with her back to them, exposing a still-knotted bow at the back of her dress, bare legs, bare feet. Her hair was a tangle. She was still, one arm slung back behind her, the other somewhere before her.

I think she's dead, he said.

Beep the horn, she said, to be sure.

I'm not going to do that out here, he said. Christ, do you want to kill us both?

They watched the child for a few moments, until they were almost satisfied that she was dead. Chloe was almost going to tell him to turn around when the head began to rise, just slightly. Then the child began to push herself up on the opposite arm, haltingly. Her other arm must have been broken, because it dangled behind her as she rose up onto her palm. Her wild hair hung in her face, obscuring it.

She was, miraculously, alive, trying to get to her feet now, stumbling, not able to navigate the broken arm.

She's alive! The woman cried out, almost clapping. She's still alive!

I don't have a gun, he said. I guess we have to let her go. Or run her over again. But it seems cruel to let her go—

Chloe put her hands down. You can't shoot her.

I know, he said. I don't have a gun.

I mean you can't. You can't shoot a person.

He sighed. I don't know how many times you have to—

Shut up, she said. Just shut up.

They watched the child crawl to her knees and, with tenacity that made the woman grit her teeth at the thought of pain, the child sat on her knees on the pavement, grabbed her broken arm and jerked it back down so it hung straight, screaming as she did so, so loudly they could hear her through the car, over the sound of the engine.

Mommy! She screamed over and over again, until the word became a howl.

The child finally noticed the headlights. She'd been so intent on rising, on getting her arm back in place, that the light must have seemed incidental. She stood on her knees, cradling the broken arm, and turned to them, her face half-visible through the tangled veil of her hair. She was dirty, but not so dirty that her face was completely unrecognizable.

It looks like Adrianne, he said. Christ, do you think it's Adrianne?

I don't know, she said. It could be. The child's hair was so stringy, her face so smudged.

The child looked at the car for a long time. She could not see inside, beyond the blinding headlights, but the woman felt exposed anyway. The child began to scream.

Help me! She shouted. Help me! You hurt me. You have to help me!

She began to make her way closer to the car on her knees, half-falling in her haste. She caught herself with her hand, which left her broken arm to fall heavily, dangling by its own weight. She screamed and clutched it against her body.

They both had the same idea at the same time: *She'll call over the others. She'll kill us.*

The woman touched the man's knee. We have to go, she said. Let's go now. Let's go.

Should I hit her again? He asked. Just to be sure she can't hurt us?

No, just go, Jesus Christ. Just go. Maybe one of the others will help her. Maybe another car will come. She can't do anything to us now. Go.

When he turned and drove away, the woman looked behind her, and the child was a small, black figure in the reddish distance, and farther up the road, just five miles from the city, she was gone completely.

Adrianne had known their car well. She'd played in it as a toddler, pushing the automatic door locks over and over again to hear that satisfying click. Chloe had held her in her lap and let her pretend to drive. Chloe and Garrett had once hoped that if they had a child, she or he would be just like Adrianne, all warmth and curiosity.

Adrianne never had a dress like that, Chloe told herself. Surely it was not her.

We'll report her to the guards at the gate, Chloe said, her tears dried, her makeup re-applied to cover the new, red and bluish spot on her forehead where she'd hit the window. She applied makeup to his forehead, too. He'd be under harsh, hot lights, and who knew if somebody was videotaping the performance or not?

We'll tell them that one of the Hopeless are hurt, she said, and they'll help her, right?

He shrugged and said nothing.

She looked into the small mirror underneath her sun visor. She could see a small portion of her face: one eye-shadowed eyelid and the tender skin of her forehead and her hairline. One grey hair blended with the blonde, almost imperceptibly.

She was probably just bait, you know that, right? He said. They probably pushed her out in front of the car. They were probably there in the bushes, just waiting for us to get out of the car. They push the youngest ones out, the cute ones, ones who can pass as real children. And then, when you are out of the car, they beat you over the head with a rock, leave you for dead, and take the car. That's how it's been done every time.

It wasn't Adrianne, she told herself. When they took her away, her clothes were already torn and bloody. This was a new child. A child who looked like Adrianne.

She flipped the sun visor up. She didn't want to look at her own face anymore.

You were very calm there, Garrett said. When you told me to just drive. He laughed. I was the jittery one, he said. I was even willing to run her over again, to make sure she didn't suffer. You had your head screwed on right. I appreciate that.

He reached over and touched her knee, squeezing it.

They approached the city gates, which were lit brightly. Thirty feet from the gates they had to stop at the verification station and provide their papers and open the windows to press their hands against the sensors and make sure that their fingerprints matched the fingerprints kept in the enormous government database.

I was just scared, she said. I wasn't brave. I was scared of that child.

Hopeless One, he said. She's not a child. Language matters.

I was scared of her, she said, and so I wanted to run away. I'm a coward.

They rolled past the security and to the gate where heavily armored soldiers ordered them to open the trunk, to open the doors, to step outside while they inspected the car.

Garrett held Chloe's hand as two soldiers searched the car, two stood between them and the road. This was always the most frightening part, this moment between being secure in your car, despite being beyond the gates, and then being outside your car, trusting only these men with guns and the suddenly delicate-seeming barbed wire that enclosed the entrance.

Sometimes the smartest thing to do is run away, he said. Running away means you live. That's the point of fear. It keeps you alive.

They walked in front of the car, making way for the soldiers, and she saw the enormous dent in the bumper, six inches deep at its center, a handful of knotted hair snagged on a piece of splintered metal and a few splotches of blood.

We hit one of them on the road, she said to the closest soldier. She didn't die. She's hurt, walking on the road on her knees, arm broken. She's very young, six or seven at the most.

The woman swallowed. She thought of Amy and Richard in their two-story family home, the upstairs bedroom still smelling of the white paint they'd had to layer on, over and over, to cover Adrianne's pink walls.

He nodded. Ma'am, we'll go clean up.

She nodded in return. Please go soon, she said. Please make sure she's dead.

The man nodded, as though she'd said nothing particularly extraordinary. And she hadn't. It was like the man had said: these were not children anymore. You had to believe that, or the whole new world became the kind of place you couldn't bear to live in.

It wasn't Adrianne, Chloe was almost absolutely sure. Adrianne had been a smart girl. She never would have been in the road like that to being with.

They made their way through the gate with ease. The performance was waiting for them in the city on the hill. By the time they had reached the hall, the child who wasn't Adrianne didn't matter anymore, the Hopeless One. Whatever happened, she didn't matter anymore—she was dead or taken away by the others of her kind. Garrett's hands moved fluidly, easing into his solo. The sound of percussion echoed in Chloe's teeth, the vibrations opening up the gash on her tongue, returning the taste of blood to her mouth. She watched Garrett's hands. It was almost motherly, how he coaxed the solo out, the delicacy of the start, the ferocity of the finish. She swallowed, her mouth full of salt and copper, and put the Hopeless One from her mind. Here was a place where the world was still as it should be: right and safe and full of beauty.

ABOUT LETITIA TRENT

LETITIA TRENT's books include the novels *Almost Dark* and *Echo Lake* and the poetry collections *One Perfect Bird* and *Match Cut* (available in 2018). Trent's essays, poetry, and fiction have been published widely both online and in print. Her short story, "Wilderness," was featured in *Best Horror of the Year, Volume 8* and was nominated for a Shirley Jackson Award. Trent is an associate poetry editor for *Tupelo Quarterly*. She lives in a haunted Ozark mountain town with her son, husband, and three black cats.

MOTHER OF SHADOWS

Benjamin Knox

L ATE ON THE DAY OF HER GRANDMOTHER IDA'S FUNERAL, Anna went missing.

Kenneth and Shauna had searched the house and the large garden out back that swept down from the house towards the woods.

Nothing.

Then Kenneth called the police. There was no dismissal, no "you need to wait twenty-four hours" that he had expected, but they had been searching for hours and had still discovered no trace.

Kenneth stood in soft mud by the small stream marking the boundary between the garden and woods. The rain made everything swell and drip. It was also destroying any evidence that might yet be lingering. He watched as police dogs splashed through mud, sniffing for any scent of their daughter and caught glimpses of the officers in high-visibility jackets between the lichen-encrusted trees, heard them urging the dogs onward over the hissing deluge.

The little stream was narrow and winding, and Ken made out the camouflaged crabs only when they moved beneath the clear water. With his eyes, he followed its course to a mat of coiled roots amid the soft earth. Hidden within this nest of roots at the base of a small oak stood a small shrine: little more than a few carvings in the bark, a bed of dried herbs with a brass saucer atop it. One of Ida's little traditions.

He wanted to step over the stream and assist the search but the officers had insisted he not interfere. They were the professionals after all. The rain slid off his hooded jacket but managed to find its way inside nonetheless, leaving him shivering and soaked, but he could not bring himself to return inside.

A cry of grief roused him, and he turned to see Shauna in the back garden, the rain turning her nightgown transparent and clingy, matting her hair into twisting snakes plastered to her face. She fell to her knees and an officer and EMT rushed to her side. The lump that had settled in his throat bobbed, and his own cry escaped his lips, ugly and raw. He clapped his hand over his mouth and shut his eyes, but tears managed to squeeze out regardless. He rushed over to the shrieking knot of human misery that was the love of his life.

With Ken's help, a gruff but reassuring officer took her inside.

"Don't give up," the dour-faced officer said. "We still have every hope of finding Anna safe and sound"

Once out of the rain, Ken helped Shauna out of her soaked clothes and into bed. The EMTs checked her over and informed him she was medically fine, it had been the stress of the situation. Ken refused to think about it. Instead, he imposed mental blinkers, focused on small tasks and kept busy.

He needed to hold on as long as he could.

Shauna needed him to be strong.

So did Anna.

***

The police continued searching the grounds into the early night, but called it off due to rain and poor visibility. They would resume in the morning.

"I'll have a pair of officers remain on the premises, just in case," the local sergeant assured him, squeezing Ken's shoulder.

"Thank you, officer," Ken replied. Perhaps it was a token gesture, but it was one Ken appreciated.

Soon the house was empty, except for himself and his grief-stricken wife.

Ken was familiar with the house from when he and Shauna had brought Anna to visit her grandmother, yet he'd never explored it much, staying mainly on the communal areas of the ground floor and in the guest rooms of the floor above. But the house was old and large and there was much more to it than he'd seen. Ida had even press-ganged him with kindness, and food, into wallpapering the top floor corridor in that strange Celtic pattern she liked so much. Still, most of the house remained a mystery to him.

Ken wiped tears from his cheeks as he recalled telling Anna to count the rooms. The rain had kept her inside with nothing to do. Anna was an active girl, with an active imagination. Sticking her in a frilly dress and keeping her indoors was akin to torture.

Ken shook away the thought. He didn't want to get caught in endlessly looping grief. It was an old fashioned instinct—the man must be strong. He wasn't macho or bullish in that way, he had no issues with showing his emotions. It was something Shauna appreciated and told him so. Emotional openness and honesty was the core of their partnership, because that's what they were, not husband and wife, but a team. Together in the world.

Shauna needed him now, and he'd be damned if he wasn't going to be there for her.

***

Shauna had been crying in her sleep, enough to rouse herself. It was the wee hours, and she came to in a slow, penumbral half-dreaming state, where reality was pliable and at the mercy of the subconscious. Exhausted the night before, she had collapsed into a fitful, dreamless sleep, trapped in the endless cycle of not knowing. Of fearing the worst.

Shauna replayed the last few days, looping back to scrutinize her memory and fixate on the tiniest of irrelevancies. She recalled the shock she'd felt when she had received the call that her mother had passed. At first she hadn't believed it, couldn't accept it. But even knowing her mother was elderly, Shauna wasn't sure anyone was ever truly ready to lose family.

They'd had their differences, certainly. Most of all, that silliness with the herbs and charms. Ida's little Celtic traditions, that her mother refused to give up, even after she'd married Duncan Harris and began going to church regularly.

When Shauna was a child it had all been enchanting and fun. She'd give anything now to have her mum ring a silver bell in the corners of her room to chase away bad spirits, or burn some sage to release its cleansing smoke. Her mother loved sage, she used to tie dried bunches and place them under Shauna's pillow. She even left a saucer of milk out for the fairies.

As she grew into adulthood it became...silly and embarrassing. Yet her mother had kept it up over the years, the little traditions and superstitions. And her death had been no different. Her wishes had been very clear. She was to be cremated with a bough of oak, a bough of birch, another of ash and, of course, sage. Her ashes would then be placed within a coffin and interred beside her husband in the graveyard plot he'd purchased for them.

Ida might have had her own beliefs but she also respected her husband's as well. This seemed like a fair compromise.

When Shauna first arrived back in the old house, she found little twists of rough paper bound with twine by the window sills and under the furniture. Everywhere. Shauna cleaned them up and gave the place a once-over with the vacuum in preparation for the extended family ready to descend upon the house to pay their respects.

There had been so much to do and Shauna could see how listless Anna was. She didn't even have cousins to play with. Nothing to keep her busy.

Shauna wasn't quite sure how her daughter was taking the passing of her grandmother. Anna seemed fine, but Shauna worried that the full impact of death was a little beyond her.

Then just after the funeral, as they were listening to the solicitor read Ida's will—Mother's parting bit of oddness for the rest of the family— Anna disappeared.

Oh, my sweet girl. Where are you?

She looked over at her sleeping husband. He'd been so brave for them both. She hadn't meant to, but she'd left Ken to deal with it all. She leaned in, careful not to wake him, and kissed him on the cheek. Then she shifted carefully to the side of the bed and padded away towards the hallway, in search of the bathroom.

Shauna eased the bedroom door open but it still creaked. Outside, the hallway had a carpet runner that warmed her bare feet as she wandered through the gloom of the house. Her eyes were sore from crying and heavy from restless sleep, and in her periphery the shadows shifted and coiled like ink in water.

At the bathroom, she glanced back down the long empty hallway and a chill caught her. She rubbed her arms and entered the bathroom. Hours of weeping had left her eyes raw, so she refrained from switching the light on, to spare herself the wince-inducing glare. By touch, she ran the water and soothed her eyes with a damp cloth.

Only then did she brave a glance up; her reflection a grim silhouette in the mirror—hair messy, shoulders slouched, wearing only the gossamer of her nightgown. It was a withered spectral version of herself, and it made her uneasy.

On her way back to the bedroom something caught her attention. Shauna turned to look down the adjacent hallway and found the attic hatch yawning open and the stairs unfolded. It hadn't been like that earlier had it?

Her eyes had grown accustomed to the dark yet still the blackness of the attic hatch was impenetrable.

Had Kenneth gone up there? Or the police? It didn't matter—right now she needed sleep. Shauna had her hand on the bedroom doorknob when the sound of something falling softly onto carpet made her stop. Off in the darkness, where the attic stairs met the carpeted floor, was a shoe, small, shiny and black.

The hair on Shauna's neck stood on end and her arm erupted in goose-flesh.

One of Anna's shoes. Part of the pair she'd bought her for the funeral. Anna had hated them, called them—what was it?—shiny black beetle shoes.

Shauna shook her head; she must be imagining it. Surely Ken or the police would have found the shoe, yet reason fled as her heart welled up with hope.

She strode towards the attic stairs, eyes fixed on the shoe. She leaned down hesitantly, terrified it was merely a figment ready to evaporate at her touch.

A few days before, Anna had been helping Shauna dish out the serving trays of food for the guests at her mother's wake, when she snuck off. Shauna had found her a little while later, right here in this hallway.

"You weren't trying to get into the attic were you?"

"No," Anna replied quickly, "I was just bored, so I decided to explore Grandma's house."

"Oh," Shauna said, relieved. She didn't want Anna up there with all that junk, especially since it was where they'd found her own mother, collapsed and unmoving. "Good, I wouldn't want you going up there anyway. It's so old I don't know when someone last went up there. It's probably not safe, and all that dust besides."

Shauna touched the beetle-like shoe and found it very real. The polish was hard and glossy and cold. Could she hope? Was it so simple? Was Anna merely hiding because she didn't want to leave her grandmother's house?

Hiding could be Anna's way of dealing with the loss. She could imagine how strange and confusing death must seem to a child.

Shauna held the shoe to her chest—a talisman of hope. She stood and put a hand on the cold rail of the folding stairs, then stopped.

For a brief moment, the stairs seemed a metallic tongue lapping her up into the open mouth of the hatch.

Shrugging the image away, Shauna climbed into the black.

***

Ken stretched out his fingers to discover the absence of his wife. He forced his heavy lids open and blinked away his malaise. The sheets were cold. She'd gotten up some time ago.

He sat up in bed, swung his legs out the side, and found his slippers by questing touch alone.

He stood and let his eyes slowly adjust to the ambient light, dragged his feet out to the staircase, and used the ornate banister to guide him down to the ground floor.

He hurried across the black-and-white tiles into the kitchen and opened the fridge and fetched out the milk, noticing as he did so the expanse of night through the rippled glass of the windows. Beyond them was the back garden and then the woods themselves. Ken couldn't see the trees, yet he knew they were there, waiting in the dark.

He took a glass and poured himself some milk, using the light from the fridge to perform what felt like brain surgery to his sleep-addled fingers.

A single sip and he spat it into the sink where the sour clots clung. He checked the expiration date and it was still good for another four days. He sniffed, winced, emptied the sour liquid down the drain, then fixed himself a glass of water instead. A glass he almost dropped when he saw the distorted silhouette reflected in the kitchen window.

"Anna?" It escaped his lips before he could think to stop himself.

There was nothing and no one there.

A trick of shadows and imagination.

The girl in the window had been the same height as Anna.

Ken took himself into the parlour and switched on a small lamp by the side of an old armchair. On the tableside sat an old leather-bound book and a letter, both of which had been left to Shauna by her mother in her will. With all the worry of Anna disappearing, Shauna hadn't yet opened the letter.

He left the letter sealed, but he took the book and opened it to find page upon page of old Ida's careful calligraphy. Her penmanship was immaculate, and there were sketches and drawings scattered throughout.

Ken let the book fall open randomly and began to read.

***

Shauna reached for the lip of the hatch. As she found it, her fingers pressed into a thin layer of dust. It wasn't just the dark that set her at unease, but the fact that Shauna's mother had passed away in the attic, and the position she'd been found in suggested that Ida Harris's end had not been a peaceful one. That knowledge stuck in her mind like a glass splinter, tormenting her.

Not an easy end for her, no last moments surrounded by loved ones, as she'd no doubt always hoped. Instead, she had been frail, alone and in the dark of her own attic.

Shauna had to use her hands to climb the steep steps, and as she did so she traced an indentation in the wood by the front of the hatch entrance. It, too, was covered in dust and discoverable only by touch. Continuing to trace the shape she recognised it instantly: a Celtic knot.

These ancient symbols were part of her heritage and were Ida's particular obsession, amongst all the superstition and Druidic traditions. As a girl, Shauna had seen such knot-like symbols often: etched on books her mother owned, woven into jumpers her mother had knitted for her and her sisters. It even featured on much of the woodwork in this old house, in one fashion or another: sometimes it was the whirl of a banister head, or the pattern along the wainscoting or doorframe, and frequently along the window sills throughout the house. It gave the old house an eccentric yet still homely feel, blending into the background and adding a subtle charm.

Is this what her mother had been doing up here when she died, carving more Celtic knots?

She reached up knowing there would be a pull cord for a bulb. She found it and tugged lightly. The weak bulb stuttered to life. Yet after the deep gloom, Shauna winced at the sudden sharp contrast of the electric light.

Shauna raised her hand to shield her eyes from the harsh glow. As she did, she found her hands were caked in grey, not dust as she'd first thought. She rubbed her fingers together and felt a cool, velvety smoothness.

"It's ash," she said aloud.

She looked about the tight confines of the attic. The light from the bulb didn't reach far and the support beams above her threw angular shadows across the sloped ceiling. She was at the apex of the house, yet she had the claustrophobic sensation of being underground. The attic was full of strange shapes covered in once-white dust cloths. They reminded Shauna a little of cubist ghosts. The ash was everywhere, forming a thin layer over everything, yet in the glare of the naked bulb Shauna could see little dashes in the grey: footsteps. She placed her own naked foot next to one of them. Small feet made these. Recently too, from the looks of the marks.

"Anna?" she called, her voice a hoarse whisper.

She was about to call out again when something moved in one of the passages between the clutter of the attic. Her heart jumped in her chest. "Anna!" she cried out, already moving before she had even willed herself to do so.

She turned a corner, following the shape. The light barely reached this far, only slips and flickers made it, highlighting the ghostly objects draped around her. The items under the sheets were piled high, and atop each cluster sat an offering. On some it was a bundle of dried sage bound in twine. On another, several cloves of garlic. There was even an old loaf of bread that looked so stale it would crumble at the touch. Then she saw the coil of old hemp rope woven into a simple Celtic knot. Each of these things were placed high up off the floor. Someone Anna's height would not have been able to see them.

Why had her mother done this? Had she gone a little loopy before she passed? She'd seemed perfectly lucid on the phone when Shauna had last spoken to her. Was this just another one of her little rituals, like the tiny shrine down by the stream? Her mother had taken the equinoxes and major Celtic festivals seriously, in particular the autumnal festival of Samhain. Did all this have something to do with that?

"Anna?" Shauna called again softly. Her voice loud even at a whisper in this solitary place. There was a sense of trespass that kept the hairs on her neck stanidng on end. It wasn't just the cold air; she couldn't escape the sensation of being watched. "Anna, sweetie, it's mummy, we've been so worried about you. Please come out. You're not in any trouble, I promise."

"Promise?" A chorus of voices whispered from off to her side, deeper in the attic. In her periphery, the darkness seethed like a living thing. Cold sweat broke out across Shauna's brow.

The bulb by the entrance flared then burst. In the tinkling music of broken glass and the silence that followed, Shauna's mind burned with the after-image the flare had revealed: a small, pale face peering from between the clusters of sheets. A girl's face. The deep shadows made the child's eyes look black.

Shauna wanted to turn and bolt, sprint back to the steps, climb down and nail the hatch shut. She couldn't though, for the pale face that frightened her so badly was familiar: the slope of the cheeks, full bowed lips and big eyes. It was Anna.

"Anna, baby, it's me," she said, her voice trembling. She'd found her, she'd found her Anna. When all else had failed, *she* had found her.

Shauna moved carefully, pressing forward towards the far end of the space where she had seen the face. She squeezed by an old globe and a tailor's dummy with a bonnet where its head should have been. Finally the narrow confines opened up and she was at the farthest end of the attic, where a large trunk was pushed up against the wall and a girl sat atop it.

This girl was not Anna. And yet there was a similarity, something almost familial. The girl was pale, in fact it was part of the reason Shauna could see her now the attic light was out. The girl's dress was an indistinct blur of utter night, more void than the surrounding darkness. Shauna wanted to believe her mind was playing tricks, searching out patterns in the dark. She'd had the same phenomena as a child, where she would see terrifying shapes moving in her room at night, and shadowy figures standing by her bedside. When her mother had found out, she rang a silver bell in each corner and burned some sage. Childish foolishness.

Yet...

That same deep-seated fear bubbled up to the surface again, all the way from those dark, childhood nights to engulf her now.

"Y-You're...not Anna," she spoke softly.

The little girl cocked her head to one side, a smile spreading across her dainty bowed lips, then shook her head like this was a game. Like she was having fun.

This is some twisted dream?

The girl stood, and Shauna flinched back a step.

"Where's my daughter?"

The only reply was a tittering little laugh that was all the more terrifying because it held a malicious, childish cruelty.

"What have you done with my Anna?" she said, her voice growing in strength as her fear boiled into anger.

The girl tittered as she approached, and Shauna could see that it was not a trick of the gloom, this girl's eyes were black like pools of ink. There was a sinister, calculating intelligence in her eyes.

"I'll never tell," the girl whispered. When she spoke she had a lilting accent, a hint of that old delicateness of Gaelic. But her voice was not one voice but many whispering in unison.

Shauna kept distance between herself and the girl, this spectre from her own broken subconscious. Her animal brain shrieked at her to take flight, her motherly instinct kept her feet rooted in place.

When she spoke this time, it was not in the whisperings, but in Anna's voice, clear as day, "Mummy, I want to go home," she said, holding out her arms.

Shauna collapsed to her knees, sobbing.

The shadows that danced about the girl spread outward from her dress and along the floorboards towards Shauna. The streams of darkness were hands, dozens of them, reaching out for her. They slithered around her calves, and then her thighs. Where they touched she felt a deep cold, deeper than a mere physical chill. The shadowy tendrils were spiritually void, feeding on her despair. The girl was a parasite, a living black hole.

More of the two-dimensional hands roiled up her arms, held her fast in their glacial grip.

"Tell me, Mummy," the girl continued in Anna's voice, "how you punished Anna when she was six for breaking a vase that the family tabby had knocked over. Tell me of how you wish secretly that your daughter wasn't so imaginative because there's no future is silly imaginings, that life is ever so hard for a sensitive and creative soul like little Anna."

The girl was standing in front of her. With Shauna on her knees they two were eye-to-eye. She stared into those twin pools of utter blackness and saw the void stretch out infinitely within them.

"Tell me," the girl spoke again, an eerie chorus of whispers cascading over one another in a bid for ascendancy, "how you sometimes text that old flame of yours on those lonely nights when there is no magic left with Kenneth. Tell me how you tell yourself you still love him because he is known and comfortable. Tell me how you lust, what you look at when your fingers delve your warmth, to push back the aching sense that you've wasted your life. Tell me of the dreams you had when you were twenty and in art school; how you posed for life drawing class in the nude and still have one of the pictures, and take it out to gaze upon how beautiful, young and full of promise you were. Tell me how your heart aches at your misspent life. How you spoke to your mother that last time on the phone. How you never had the time to talk. She was old and you knew deep down that you didn't have much time left, yet still you never gave the time. She was just a silly, superstitious old woman. Tell me how you snubbed her that day on the phone, made up an excuse—'*Sorry Mum, can't talk, Anna's late for dance class*'—and hung up on her. Tell me how you feel like a disappointment."

With each secret fear, the shadow hands inched further along her skin, up her body, while the girl's gaze held Shauna locked in their abyss.

None of it was silly superstition: the dried herbs, the fresh bread, the sage, even the Celtic knots she found everywhere in the house. They were to bind this thing to the attic. To trap it here. Had her mother been doing that all this time? Supplying these offerings, letting this little parasite sap the goodness from things like bread and fresh cut herbs, the same cleansing herbs that kept her at bay. And the ash—no doubt birch wood and oak—that lay like a carpet over everything. Shauna touched the floor with the flat of her hand, then slapped her ash-covered palm across the girls face.

The shriek of pain and rage was deafening, more psychic than sound, and made the darkness itself vibrate.

The shadow tendrils tightened, pinning Shauna down. The girl's porcelain visage—that eerie, almost doll-like death mask—now had cracks and flaking fragments where the ash had touched her.

Her black eyes burned with cold hatred, but she smiled and leaned in close to Shauna's ear and whispered, "I'm going to tell you a secret."

As she did, the frigid shadow-hands covered Shauna's entire skin, reaching up to her upturned face. As she opened her mouth to scream, they slipped over her lips and tumbled in.

***

Kenneth closed the old book with an exasperated sigh. His mother-in-law hadn't merely been quirky, she'd actually believed in spirits and herbs and magic. Ken was starting to understand why Shauna had distanced herself over the years and why she'd always been careful about how much time Anna spent with her grandma.

He chuckled in the empty parlour, his voice eerily loud in the silent small hours.

As stark as the contrast was, he needed the sound of a human voice to dispel the things he'd just read. Spirits of the dead. Changelings. Living shadows.

It was all foolishness and folklore, but old Ida was starting to make sense to him now. He traced the three-sided Celtic knot on the leather cover of the book and then the weaving patterns along the edges and spine. These were the knot-like patterns that could confuse or even ward off evil spirits. And they weren't just on the book.

Ken realised the pattern was everywhere in the old house: woven into the carpets; carved into the skirting boards, banisters and door frames. It could even be found on the upper floor's hallway, in the very wallpaper Ida had had him put up one summer when Anna was an infant.

Shauna had complained of finding her mother's little charms and dried sage twists throughout the house. It was now obvious to Ken what Ida had done. She'd turned the entire place into a spirit trap. Wards, sigils and protection spells were everywhere, so numerous as to be invisible—the forest for the trees.

Ken sighed and placed the old book on a side table then pulled himself up out of the armchair. He rubbed the bridge of his nose, clearing his mind of the spooks and fairies he'd been reading about. It was too late to be creeping himself out with Ida's hocus pocus. He needed sleep. He needed to check on his wife. Tomorrow would be another long and trying day searching for their lost daughter.

He left his glass by the book, promising himself he'd tidy it all up in the morning, and padded quietly back upstairs.

Yet he couldn't shake it. His feet slipped across Celtic patterns on the carpet; his hand traced them as he held the banister as he ascended the stairs. A glimpse of moonlight through a high ornate window above the stairwell had the triple curve of a knot etched in it. How many times had he been to this house and never noticed?

Pale streaks running the length of the hallway seized Ken's attention. He turned about on the spot following their trail. He lifted a foot and found a pale, dry substance clinging to it.

Ash?

The trail led down the hall to the unfolded steps and black yawning maw of the attic hatch.

As he took a step towards it a scraping noise came from one of the rooms behind him.

"Shauna?" he called. It must be all that malarkey in Ida's book giving him the heebie-jeebies. "Shauna," he said again, louder, as he followed the ash trail along back towards their bedroom. There were gouges in the hardwood and the runner carpet had been pushed aside, evidence that something heavy had been dragged across the floor.

Something from the attic.

The sound of metal sliding across metal made his hair stand on end. The door to their room was ajar, and he pushed it open just enough to peer inside. He could make out the wan form of his wife slouched over something large on the bed with her.

Ken pushed the door the rest of the way and stepped inside. He could hear more metallic scraping and the creak of old leather.

"Shauna… Honey, what are you—" The words died in his throat.

Shauna was hunched over a large trunk that she must have hauled down from the attic. In her hand she held a long, shining pair of tailor's scissors that she used to slash at the straps and dig at the locks.

"Honey?" he said.

Shauna raised her hand and snapped the scissor blades together twice in quick succession.

In slow, jerky motions, she turned her head. Her hair hid most of her face, save for the inky void in her eyes and a manic grin that went a little too wide.

The trunk was positioned at an angle, partly resting against the headboard. The sheets were a mess, smeared with the ashes from the hallway.

She eyed him from behind a fringe of tangled hair, grinning all the while. She licked the scissor blades in an obscene mockery of lust, and moved like a spider changing position on its web.

"Shauna…" He didn't know what he could say.

With a tittering giggle that was not one manic voice but thousands, Shauna snipped at the final straps keeping the trunk shut.

He didn't want to see what was inside the trunk, he didn't want to know.

"Come," Shauna moved her lips, but the voices were a multitude coming from all about him, surrounding him, invisible in the ether. "Let's be a family again." Once more that too-wide grin spread beneath twin pools of night.

The *thing* held out her arms, the gleaming blades of the scissors forgotten among the sheets.

"Come," the chorus beckoned again, and Ken found himself moving towards her. Not like a puppet on strings, but of his own volition, of his own broken will. He knew it was wrong, this creature was not the woman he had married, was not the woman he loved. But he believed her when she spoke of family, and ached for it. Ached to recapture even a fleeting illusion of that time, so recently gone, when there were three of them.

He joined her on the bed, fearful and wary. She wrapped him in icy limbs and purred terrible secrets into his ear.

The trunk creaked open of its own accord, spilling dried sage and bound charms onto the bed with them, but something larger came free as well. A body, dressed in black, a shiny black shoe on one foot, eyes glassy and vacant.

Now they could be a family again.

Forever.

ABOUT BENJAMIN KNOX

Rogue author and Scotsman **BENJAMIN KNOX** is best known for his *Dead of Winter* novellas, the *Dream-Shock Cthulhu* collection, and the cyberpunk-action-horror epic, *VIRAL*, written with Toby Bennett.

His work has appeared in numerous anthologies, most recently *The Lovecraft eZine #38*, *Elements: A Dragon Writers Anthology* and *Bloody Parchment: Blue Honey and the Valley of Shadows* of which his story "Blue Honey" is one of title tales.

The events of "Mother of Shadows" follow on from "A Keeper of Secrets" (originally published in *Suspended in Dusk: Volume One*) and will continue in "House of Night."

For further info and oddities visit his website: benjaminknox.net

THE MOURNFUL CRY OF OWLS
CHRISTOPHER GOLDEN

O N A WARM, LATE SUMMER'S NIGHT, Donika Ristani sat on the roof outside her open window—fat-bellied acoustic guitar in her hands—and searched for the chords that would bring life to the music she knew lay within her. The shingles were warm from the sun, though an hour had passed since dusk, and the smell of tar and cut grass filled her with a pleasant summery feeling that kept her normally flighty spirit from drifting into fancy.

The radio played in her room, competing with the music of the woods around the house—the crickets and owls and rustling things—which grew to a crescendo as though attempting to draw her down amongst the trees. Her fingers plucked and strummed, for she despised the use of a pick, and she created a third melody that created a kind of balance between the radio and the woods, the inside and outside.

Joe Jackson sang "Is She Really Going Out With Him?" Donika liked the song well enough, but her thoughts were elsewhere, thinking about inside and outside—about the person she was for her mother's sake, and the person that all of her instincts told her she ought to be. She found herself strumming Harry Chapin's "Taxi," lost in her head, and singing along to the weird bridge in the middle of the tune, the one about wasting your days being the person you wanted others to see, instead of who you really were.

The truth frustrated the hell out of her and she brought her right hand down on the strings to stop herself playing another note of that song. Her gaze drifted down her driveway to the darkened ribbon of Blackberry

Lane, searching for headlights, for some sign of her mother's return. Without so much as a glimmer from the road, she looked out across the dark, thick woods north of the house, impatient to be down there, following the path to Josh Orton's house. He'd be waiting already, and she could practically feel his arms around her, his face nuzzling her throat.

Donika laughed softly at herself; or perhaps she sighed. She couldn't tell the difference sometimes.

The DJ did his cool voice and introduced the next tune. Donika smiled and started playing the first notes on her acoustic before it even started on the radio. Bad Company. "Rock and Roll Fantasy." Good song. Her bedroom walls were covered with posters for Pink Floyd, Zeppelin, and Sabbath, but she liked a little bit of everything. Most of her girlfriends would have laughed at some of the stuff she sang along to on the radio. Or maybe not. Hell, most of them thought Donna Summer the pinnacle of musical achievement.

Now she wished she'd listened more closely to the Joe Jackson tune. She might have to break into her babysitting stash to buy that album.

Her fingers moved up and down the frets, playing Bad Company by ear. She'd never played the song before, but the guitar was like an extension of herself and picking out the notes presented no greater difficulty than singing along. The crickets had gotten louder, but she managed not to hear them. The radio crackled a bit; some kind of interference, maybe the weather or a passing jet. She didn't understand such things very well. Turn on the box, the music came out. What else did she need to know?

The heat of the day still lingered in her skin the same way it did in the shingles. No more sticky humidity, so that was nice. She felt comfortably warm up there in her spaghetti strap tank top and cutoff jeans, as if the sun had gotten down inside her instead of setting over the horizon, and it would hide there until morning.

Owls cried out in the woods, and Donika glanced up, searching the trees as though she might spot one, the strings of her guitar momentarily forgotten. Other people thought they were funny birds, but she had always heard something else in their hooting, a terrible sadness that she always wanted to answer with her own frustrations.

A flash of light came from the road. She watched the headlights move along Blackberry Lane and her breath caught as she thought of Josh again.

When the car drove by without slowing down, she sighed and lay back against the slanted roof, the shingles rough and hot against her back. She hugged the guitar and wondered if Josh was sitting outside, waiting for her, or if he was up in his room listening to music on his bed. Both images had their appeal.

Somehow she missed the sound of an approaching engine, and looked up only as light washed across the trees and she heard tires rolling up the driveway. Donika sat forward as her mother's ancient Dodge Dart putted up to the house. When she turned off the engine, it ticked and popped, and then the door creaked open.

"Get off that roof, 'Nika!"

The girl laughed. The woman had eyes like a hawk, even in the dark.

She slipped in through her bedroom window and put away her guitar before going downstairs. Her mother stood in the kitchen, looking through the day's mail. Qendressa Ristani had lush black hair like her daughter, but streaked with gray. She wore it pulled back tightly. Though her mother was nearly fifty, Donika thought her hairstyle too severe, more appropriate for a grandmother. Her clothes reflected the same sensibility, which probably explained why she never dated. Though she'd given up wearing black a decade or so back, Donika's mother still saw herself as a widow. Men might flirt with her—she was prettier than most women her age—but Qendressa would not encourage them. She'd been widowed young, and had no desire to replace the only man she had ever loved.

Her life was the seamstress shop where she worked in downtown Jameson, and the home she'd made for herself and her daughter upon coming to America a dozen years before. But her old world upbringing still persisted in many ways, not the least of which was her insistence on using herbs and oils as homegrown remedies for all sorts of ills, both physical and spiritual.

"How was your day, Mom?"

"Eh," the woman said, "is the same."

Donika grabbed her sandals and sat down at the table, slipping one on. Her mother dropped the mail on the table. As she fastened the straps on her sandals, she looked up to find her mother staring at her.

"Where you going?"

"Josh's. Sue and Carrie and a couple of Josh's friends are there already, waiting for me. We're going to walk into town for pizza."

"You going to hang around those boys dressed like that?"

Donika flushed with anger and stood up, the chair scraping backward on the floor.

"Look, Ma, you need to get off this stuff. This is 1979, not 1950, and we're in Massachusetts, not Albania. You want me to be home when you get back from work so you won't worry about me? Okay, I sort of understand that. I don't like it, but I get it. But look around. I don't dress differently from other girls. Turn on the TV once in a while—"

"TV," her mother muttered in disgust, averting her eyes.

"I'm going to be sixteen tomorrow," Donika protested.

Qendressa Ristani sniffed. "This is supposed to make me less worried? This is *why* I worry!"

"Well don't! I'm fine. Just let me enjoy being sixteen, okay?"

The woman hesitated, taking a long breath, and then she nodded slowly and waved her daughter away. "Go. Be a good girl, 'Nika. Don't make me shamed."

"Have I ever?"

Finally, her mother smiled. "No. Never." Her expression turned serious. "Tomorrow, we celebrate, though. Yes? Just the two of us, all the things you love for dinner. You can have your friends over on Friday and we have a cake. But, tomorrow, just us girls."

Donika smiled. "Just us girls."

***

The path emerged from the woods in the backyard of an older couple who were known to shout at trespassers from their screened-in back porch. Donika had never experienced their wrath and wondered if they didn't mind so much when a girl crossed their yard—maybe thinking girls didn't cause as much trouble as boys—or if they simply didn't see her. As she left the comfortable quiet of the woods and strolled across the back lawn and then alongside the house, she watched the windows, wondering if either of the old folks were looking out. Nothing stirred inside there. It hadn't been dark for long, but she wondered if they were already asleep, and thought how sad it must be to get old.

When she reached the street, she saw Josh sitting on the granite curb at the corner, smoking a cigarette. Her sandals slapped the pavement as she walked and he looked up at the sound. One corner of his mouth lifted in a little smile that made her heart flutter. He flicked his cigarette away and stood to meet her, cool as hell in his faded jeans and Jimi Hendrix t-shirt.

"Hey," he said.

Donika smiled, feeling strangely shy. "Hey."

Josh pushed his shoulder-length blond hair away from his eyes. "Your mom kept you waiting."

"Sorry. Sometimes I think she stays late on purpose. Maybe she figures if she keeps me waiting long enough, I won't go out."

"So much for that plan."

"I'm glad you didn't give up on me," Donika said.

They'd been standing a couple of feet apart, just feeling the static energy of the distance between them. Now Josh reached out and touched her face.

"Never happen."

A shiver went through her. Josh did that to her, just by standing there, and the way he looked at her.

His hand slipped around to the back of her neck and he bent to kiss her. Donika tilted her head back and closed her eyes, letting the details of the moment wash over her, the feel of him so near, the softness of his lips, the strange, burnt taste of nicotine as his tongue sought hers.

Only when they broke apart, a giddy little thrill rushing through her, did she look around and remember where they were. Lights were on in some of the houses along Rolling Lane, and anyone could be watching them.

She felt pleasantly buzzed, as though she'd had a few beers, but she slid her hand along his arm and tangled her fingers in his.

"We shouldn't be doing this out here. I told my mother Sue and Carrie and those guys were gonna be here and we were going to get pizza. If anyone ever saw us and told her, she'd have a fit."

"She doesn't think you've ever kissed me?"

"I don't know, and I don't plan to ask," Donika said. "God, she already thinks I'm slutty just for wearing cutoffs and hanging around with boys."

Josh arched an eyebrow and took out another cigarette. "Boys? Are there others?"

She hit him. "You know what I mean."

"Your mom's pretty old world."

Donika rolled her eyes. "You have *no* idea. She burns candles for me and puts little bunches of dried herbs and stuff under my bed, tied in little ribbons. Pretty sure they're supposed to ward off boys."

"How's that going?"

Donika only smiled.

Josh kissed her forehead. "So, do you want to go get pizza?"

"Only if you're hungry."

Josh laughed softly, unlit cigarette in his hand. His blue eyes were almost gray in the night time. "I could eat. I could always eat. But I'm good. We could just hang out. Why don't we walk downtown, get an ice cream or something."

"Or we could just go for a walk in the woods. I love those paths. Especially at night."

"You're not afraid?" Josh asked as he thumbed his lighter, the little flame igniting the tip of his cigarette. He drew a lungful of smoke and stared at her.

"Why would I be?" Donika said. "I've got you with me."

She led him by the hand back across the street and through the yard of the belligerent old couple. Josh's cigarette glowed orange in the dark. The moon and stars were bright, but as they passed alongside the house and into the back yard of that old split-level house, with the canopy of the woods reaching out above them, the darkness thickened and little of the celestial light filtered through.

"Goddamn you kids!" a screechy voice shouted from the porch. "You're gonna burn the whole damn forest down with those cigarettes!"

Donika started and looked at the darkened porch anxiously. Josh put a hand up to try to keep himself from laughing, and that started Donika grinning as well. The voice was faintly ridiculous, like something out of a cartoon or a movie. On the porch, in the dark, another pinprick of burning orange glowed. The old man was smoking, too.

Josh paused to drop the butt and grind it out with his heel. Then, laughing, they ran into the trees, following the path that had been worn there by generations.

Hand in hand, they followed the gently curving path through the woods and talked about their friends and families, and about music.

"I love talking about music with you," Josh told her. "The way your eyes light up...I don't know, it's like you feel it inside you more than most people because you can make music with your guitar."

Donika shuddered at that. No one had ever understood that part of her the way that Josh did. He liked the sad songs best, the tragic ones, just as she did. Their conversation meandered, but she didn't mind. All she wanted was his company.

Mostly, they just walked.

The paths had been there forever, or so it seemed. There were low stone walls, centuries-old property markers that had been built up by hand and ran for miles. Old, thick roots crossed the path and small animals rustled in the branches above them and in the underbrush on either side. An entire system of paths ran through the woods. They reached a fork and followed the right-hand path. The left would have taken them up the hill toward her house, and that was the last place she wanted to go.

"You seem far away," Josh said as they passed through a small clearing where someone had built a firepit. Charred logs lay in the pit and the stones around it had been blackened by flames.

Donika squeezed his hand and looked up at him. "Nope. Just happy. I love the woods. Being out here... it's so peaceful. So far away from other people. I walk through here all the time, but having you here with me makes it so much better."

Josh stopped walking and gazed down at her. The moon and stars illuminated the clearing, and she saw the mischief in his eyes.

"Better how?" he asked.

She gave him a shy little shrug. "Just feels right."

He kissed her again and she could hear music in her head. Or maybe it was her heart. His hands slid down her back, pulling her close, so that their bodies pressed together. She liked the feel of him against her, his strong arms wrapped around her. Through his jeans she could feel his hardness pressing into her, and she liked that very much. Just knowing that she had that effect on him made her catch her breath.

His hands roamed, fingers tracing along her arms, and then he stepped back just slightly so that he could reach up and touch her breasts through the thin cotton of her tank top.

"Josh," she rasped, enjoying it far too much.

"Yeah."

Donika took his hands in hers and kissed him quickly. "I think maybe I want ice cream after all."

"But it's beautiful right here."

He grinned and ducked his head, kissing her again. Their fingers were still intertwined and he made no attempt to pull his hands away, to touch her again. Donika felt her body yearning toward him, missing the weight and warmth of him.

This is it, she thought. *This is what frightens Ma so much.*

Donika pulled her hands from his and slid her arms around him, breaking off the kiss. She lay her head on his chest and just held herself against him, nuzzling there. Josh stroked her hair.

Deep in the woods, she heard an owl hoot sadly, and then another joined in. A chorus.

"I *am* far away," she confessed. "But you're with me. I wish we could be even further away, together. I love feeling lost in the woods, like something wild. When I'm out here alone, I like to just run. You'll laugh, but sometimes I imagine I'm running naked through the forest, like I'm some kind of fairy queen or something."

Josh didn't laugh. "Hmm. I like the sound of that," he said. "What's stopping you?"

She blushed deeply and stepped back, trying not to smile. One hip outthrust, she pointed at him.

"You are bad."

"Only in good ways. Seriously, I dare you."

Donika's breath came in shallow sips as she regarded him, lips pressed together, corners of her mouth upturned. The mischief in his eyes seemed to have gotten inside of her somehow. Her skin tingled all over. Nodding her head, she crossed her arms.

"You first."

Without hesitation, he stripped off his t-shirt and dropped it at the edge of the path. He arched an eyebrow and looked at her expectantly.

A rush went through her, a kind of freedom she'd never felt before. It was as though she had just woken from some strange slumber. She grabbed the bottom hem of her tank top and slid it up over her head, then unhooked her bra and let it drop to the ground. The night breeze brushed warmly against her, but she shivered.

Josh stared at her, all the mischief and archness gone from his face, replaced by sheer wonderment. He'd never seen her breasts before—Donika didn't know if he'd ever seen this much of *any* girl.

She didn't wait for him to make the next move. Their gazes locked as she kicked her sandals off and then moved her hand down, unbuttoning her cutoffs. She slid them and her panties down together and stepped out of them, tossing them on top of her tank.

"Jesus, you're beautiful," he whispered.

The breeze picked up, rustling leaves. Somewhere close by, the owls cried again. For once, the sound did not seem sad. Josh stepped toward her and she knew how badly he wanted to touch her. She could already imagine his hands on her, the way she had so many times at home in her bed.

She shook her head, smiling, and stepped backward. "Uh uh. Not so fast, mister. We're going to run, remember. And you're not quite ready."

For a moment he only stared at her, his mouth hanging open. Donika laughed at how silly he looked, but thrilled to know that she'd beguiled him so completely.

Staggering around, hopping on one foot, Josh pulled off one sneaker and then the other. He shucked his jeans and then paused for a second before slipping off his underwear.

Donika trembled at the sight of him. She'd seen an older boy from the neighborhood skinny-dipping in Bowditch Pond one time, but this was something else entirely.

"Oh," she said.

Josh walked toward her. Donika backed up and then turned, giggling, and began to run as swiftly as she dared, watching the roots and rocks and fallen branches in her path. Josh pursued her, laughing even as he called for her to wait for him. As she ran the thrill of it all rushed through her—her nakedness, his nakedness and nearness, and the forest around them. In her whole life, she had never felt as wonderful as she did there in the woods, running wild, full of passion and laughter.

The heat rose from deep inside her, desire unlike anything she'd ever known. Flush with abandon, she slowed her pace, and let Josh catch up.

He nearly crashed into her and they slid together on the path. His lips were on hers and their tongues met. His hands were rough and caressing in equal turns, touching her everywhere, and she let him.

A small part of her—the part that remained her mother's daughter—knew that she would not let him make love to her. But, oh, how she wanted to. Anything else he wished would be his, only not that.

In the branches above them, the owls sighed.

***

Tangled in her sheets, drifting in that limbo between sleep and wakefulness, Donika knew morning had come. She loved how long the summer days lasted; she just wished they didn't start so damned early. Dimly aware of the bedroom around her, she squeezed her eyes tightly closed and admonished herself for not having drawn the shades the night before. She rolled over to face the other direction, twisting the sheets even more. For a moment she remembered her walk in the woods with Josh the night before and the way his hands had felt on her. A contented moan escaped her lips as she slipped back into blissful oblivion.

Drifting.

Somewhere, lost in sleep, she sensed a presence enter the room and began to stir. Then someone started to sing, loudly and horribly, and Donika sat up in bed, drawing a sharp breath, eyes wide.

Her mother sang "Happy Birthday" in a silly, overly dramatic fashion, gesturing with her hands as though on stage. She wore an enormous grin and Donika couldn't help laughing. Her mother always seemed so grim, and seeing her like this gave the girl such pleasure.

When the song finished, Qendressa bowed deeply. Donika applauded, shaking her head. During her childhood, it had not been quite so uncommon for her mother to clown around for Donika's amusement. They'd shared so many wonderful times together. Now that she was older and their desires and morals clashed so often, it had become hard for Donika to remember those times.

Not this morning, however. This morning, all the laughter came back to her. Her mother would be off to work in moments, decked out in her usual sensible skirt and blouse and dark shoes, and her hair was tied back severely, but for a few minutes, it felt like Donika was a little girl again.

"Thank you, thank you," Qendressa said, her accent almost unnoticeable as she mimicked performers she had seen on television. "And for my next trick, I leave work early to come home and make all your favorites."

She ticked the parts of the birthday meal off on her fingers. "Tavë kosi, Tirana furghes with peppers, and kadaif for dessert. With candles and more bad singing."

Donika's stomach rumbled just thinking about dinner. The main course was baked lamb and yogurt, which she'd always loved. But the dessert—she could practically taste the walnuts and cinnamon of the kadaif now.

"Can we have dinner for breakfast instead?" she asked, stretching, extricating herself from her sheets.

Her mother shook a finger at her. "The birthday girl gets what she wants, but not until tonight. Breakfast, you make your own. Toast, I bet. You going out today?"

"Maybe to the mall, if Gina can borrow her mom's car."

"All right. Back by three o'clock, please. We'll cook together?" Donika smiled. "Wouldn't miss it."

That was the truth, too. There were times her mother drove her crazy with all her old world stodginess, but on her birthday and on holidays, she loved nothing better than to spend hours in the kitchen, cooking with her mom. She could practically smell all the wonderful aromas that would fill the house later.

"What about the girls? You talk to them?" Qendressa asked.

"Tomorrow night. They're going to come by to celebrate. We can just have pizza, though."

"Pizza, again?" her mother said. "You going to turn into pizza."

Donika didn't argue. She wasn't about to confess that she and Josh had never gotten around to having pizza last night. Maybe that was the reason she felt so hungry this morning. Her belly growled and she felt a gnawing there, as if she hadn't eaten in weeks instead of half a day.

"We love pizza," she said, shrugging.

"I promised birthday cake tomorrow night, too. And if you are lucky, maybe some good singing."

"Chocolate cake?" Donika asked, propping herself up on one arm, head still muzzy with sleep.

"Of course," her mother replied, as though any other kind would be unthinkable.

"Excellent!"

A flutter of wings came from the open window and a scratching upon the screen. Mother and daughter turned together to see a dark-eyed owl perched on the ledge outside the window, imperious and wise. Brown and white feathers cloaked the owl and it tucked its wings behind it.

"What the...? That's freaky," Donika said, sitting up in bed. "I hear them in the woods all the time, but I've never seen one during the day. Do you think it's sick or some—"

"Away!" her mother shouted. She rushed at the window and banged her open palm against the screen. A string of curses in her native tongue followed.

The owl cocked its head as if to let them know it wasn't troubled by Qendressa's attack, then spread its wings and took flight again. Through the window, Donika caught a glimpse of it gliding back toward the woods.

She stared at her mother. The woman had completely wigged out and now she stood by the window, arms around herself as though a frigid wind had just blown through the room. She had her back to her daughter.

"Ma?"

Qendressa turned, a wan smile on her face. Donika studied her mother and realized that the birthday morning silliness was over. A strange sadness had come over her, as though the bird's arrival had forced her to drop some happy mask she'd been wearing.

"I should go to work," she said, but she seemed torn.

"What is it, Ma?"

"Nothing," she said with a wave of her hand, averting her gaze. "Just... sixteen. You're not a girl anymore, 'Nika. Soon, you leave me."

Donika kicked aside the sheet that still covered the bottom of her legs and climbed out of bed. She went to her mother. Even with no shoes on, she was the taller of the Ristani women.

"I'm not going anywhere, Ma."

It didn't sound true, even when she said it. There had been many days when Donika had dreamed of nothing but leaving Jameson, finding a life of her own, making her own decisions and not having to live in the shadow of the old country anymore. Her body still weighted down by some secret sadness, Qendressa reached out and brushed Donika's unruly hair away from her eyes.

"Tonight, we talk about the future. And the past."

Donika blinked. What did that mean? She would have asked but saw her mother stiffen. The woman's eyes narrowed as she stared at her daughter's bed.

"What is that?"

The girl turned. Specks of dirt, a small leaf, and a few pine needles were scattered at the foot of the bed, revealed when Donika had whipped the sheet off of her. A shiver went through her, some terrible combination of elation and guilt. She tried to stifle it as best she could.

"We cut through the woods to get downtown. I always go that way. I took off my sandals. I like going barefoot out there. It's nice. It's all… it's wild."

Donika couldn't read the look on her mother's face. If the woman suspected anything, she would have been angry or disappointed. Maybe those emotions were there—maybe Donika read her expression wrong— but the look in her eyes and the way she took a harsh little breath seemed like something else. Weird as it was, in that moment, Donika thought her mother seemed afraid.

The woman turned, all grim seriousness now. At Donika's bedroom door she paused and looked back at her daughter, taking in the whole room—the guitar, the stereo, the records and posters, and the clothes she would never approve of that were hung from the back of her chair and over the end of her bed.

"No boys here while I'm gone. No boys, 'Nika."

"I know, Ma. You think I'm stupid?"

"No," her mother said, shaking her head, the sadness returning to her gaze. "No, you my baby girl, 'Nika. I don't think you are stupid."

With that, Qendressa left. Donika stood and listened to her go down the stairs and out the door. She heard the car start up outside and the sound of tires on the driveway, and then all was silent again except for the birds singing outside the window and the drone of a plane flying somewhere high above the house.

She wasn't sure what her mother suspected or feared, didn't know what had caused her to behave so oddly or why she'd freaked out so completely at the sight of the owl. But Donika had the feeling it was going to be a very weird birthday.

***

Gina couldn't get the car, so the trip to the mall was off. Donika knew that she ought to have been bummed out, but she couldn't muster up much disappointment. She'd be seeing her friends tomorrow night, and today she wasn't in the mood to window shop at the mall. The idea of wandering around Jordan Marsh or going to Orange Julius for a nasty cheese dog for lunch didn't have much appeal. If it had been raining, maybe she would have felt differently. But the day was beautiful, and in truth, she wanted to be on her own for a while.

All kinds of different thoughts were swirling in her head, and she wanted to make sense of them, if she could. Her mother's strange behavior that morning troubled her, but she was still looking forward to the afternoon of them cooking together. The lamb in the fridge was fresh, not frozen. It had come from the butcher the day before. They'd put some music on—something her mother liked, the Carpenters, maybe, or Neil Diamond—and work side by side at the counter. Normally, that kind of music made Donika want to stick pencils in her eyes, but somehow with her mother whipping up the yogurt sauce for the lamb or slicing peppers as she hummed along, it seemed perfect.

At lunch time she sat on the front porch with a glass of iced tea and a salami sandwich. A fly buzzed around the plate and then sat on the lip of her glass. Donika ignored it, more interested in the droplets of moisture that slid down the sides of the cup. She stared at them as she strummed her acoustic, singing another Harry Chapin song. Harry was one of the only musicians she and her mother could agree on.

Her fingers kept playing, but she faltered with the words and then stopped singing altogether. Despite her concerns about her mother, she could not focus on anything for very long without her thoughts returning to the previous night.

Pausing for a moment in the song, she leaned over to pick up the iced tea, pressing the glass against the back of her neck. The icy condensation felt wonderful on her skin. Donika took a long sip, liking the sound the melting ice made as it clinked together. Then she set the glass down and grabbed half of the salami sandwich. All morning she had been ravenously hungry, yet when she'd eaten breakfast—Trix cereal, an indulgence left over from when she'd been very small—it hadn't filled her at all. Later in the morning she'd had a nectarine and some grapes, and that hadn't done anything for her either.

Now, even though she still felt as hungry as before—hungrier, in fact, if that was possible—the idea of eating her sandwich held very little appeal. She took an experimental bite, and then another. The salami tasted just as good as it always did, salty and a little spicy. But for some reason she simply did not want it.

She set the sandwich down and took another swig of iced tea to wash away the salt. Her fingers returned to the guitar and started playing chords she wasn't even paying attention to. Whatever song she might be drawing from her instrument, it came from her subconscious. Her conscious mind was otherwise occupied.

"You're a crazy girl," she said aloud, and then she smiled. Talking to herself sort of proved the point, didn't it? Her mother had always been a little crazy, and now Donika knew she shared the trait.

Her hunger didn't come only from her stomach. Her whole body felt ravenous. Her skin tingled with the memory of Josh's hands—on her belly, her breasts, the small of her back, the soft insides of her thighs—and of his kisses, which touched nearly all of the places his hands had gone.

She squeezed her legs together and trembled at the thought of stripping off her clothes, of running through the woods, and then Josh, his body outlined in moonlight, catching up to her. She'd felt, in those moments when she raced along the rutted path and he pursued her, as though she could spread her arms and take wing… as though she could have flown, and taken Josh with her.

Touching him, kissing him, that had been a little like flying.

"God," she whispered to herself. "What's wrong with you?"

Her fingers fumbled on the strings and she stopped playing, a sly smile touching her lips. Nothing was wrong with her. It all felt so amazingly good. How could anything be wrong with that?

But that was a lie. There was one thing wrong.

Her hunger. She yearned for Josh so badly that it gnawed at her insides. She wondered if her mother had seen it in her eyes this morning, had sensed it, had *smelled* it on her.

Donika needed to have his hands on her again, to taste his lips and the salty sweat on his fingers and his neck. She felt as though she couldn't get enough of him. She wanted him completely, yearned to consume him, and the only way to do that was to do the one thing she promised herself she would not do.

She had to have him inside her.

Only that could satisfy her hunger.

Her certainty thrilled and terrified her all at once.

***

With the smell of cinnamon filling the kitchen, her mother leaned back in her chair, hands over her stomach as though she had some voluminous belly.

"I don't think I ever eat again."

Donika smiled, but it felt forced. They had followed the same recipes they had always used, brought over from Albania with her mother years ago, passed down for generations. Somehow, though, the food had tasted bland. Even the cinnamon had seemed stale in her mouth. The smell of dessert had been tantalizing, but its taste had not delivered on that promise. She had eaten as much as she did mainly because she hadn't wanted to hurt her mother's feelings. And the hunger remained.

How she could still feel hungry after such a meal—particularly when nothing seemed to taste good to her—Donika didn't know. She chalked it up to hormones. Today was her sixteenth birthday. According to her mother, she had become a woman all of sudden, like flipping a switch. She had never believed it really worked that way, but given the way she felt, maybe it did. Maybe that was exactly how it worked. She always craved chocolate right before she got her period—could have eaten gallons of ice cream if she'd given in—so this might be similar.

Or maybe it's love. The thought skittered across her mind. She'd heard of people not being able to eat when they were in love. It occurred to her that this could be another symptom.

She tasted the idea on the back of her tongue. Did she love Josh? Maybe.

She hungered for him, certainly. Longed for him. Could that be love? No. Donika had seen enough movies and read enough books to know that desire and love might not be mutually exclusive, but they weren't the same thing either.

But desire like this? It hurts. It burns.

"—you listening to me, 'Nika?"

"What?" she asked, blinking.

Her mother studied her, concern etched upon her face. "You okay? You feel sick?"

"No. Sorry, Ma. Just tired, I guess."

A lame excuse. She expected her mother to call her on it, maybe to make some insinuating comment about her walk in the woods the night before, about how maybe if she wasn't always out talking to boys and running around with her friends, she wouldn't be so tired. Her mother didn't let her do very much, and she'd been hanging around the house all day playing guitar, and then cooking, but logic never stopped her mother from suspicion or judgment.

But Qendressa didn't say anything like that.

"You like dinner, though, right?" she asked, and just then it seemed the most important question in the world to her. "Your sixteenth birthday the sweetest. You should be happy today. Celebrate."

Donika felt such love for her mother, then. Sometimes she became so angry and frustrated with the woman's old world traditions, but always she knew that beneath all of that lay nothing but adoration and worry, a mother's constant companions. She thought she understood fairly well for a fifteen year old girl.

Sixteen, she reminded herself. *Sixteen, today.*

"I love you, Ma."

They both seemed surprised she'd said it out loud. It had never been common to speak of love, though they both felt it all the time.

Her mother smiled, took a long, shuddering breath, and then began to cry. Donika stared at her in confusion. Qendressa turned her face away to hide her tears and raised a hand to forestall any questions.

After a moment, she wiped her eyes. "You all grown, now, 'Nika. Walk with me. Tonight, I tell you the story of how you were born."

"What do you mean, how I was born?"

Her mother smiled and slid her chair back. It squeaked on the kitchen floor. "Walk with me," she said as she stood. "In the woods. How you like. And maybe you learn why you like it so much."

Donika got up, dropping her napkin on the table. Bewildered, she tried to make sense of her mother's words and behavior, doing her best to push away the hunger inside her and to not think about the fact that Josh had said he'd be out on the corner later, waiting for her if she could manage to get out tonight.

Her mother took her hand. "Come."

Together they left the house. The screen door slammed shut behind them as if in emphasis, the house happy to have them gone. The porch steps creaked underfoot. When her mother led her across the driveway toward the path, Donika hesitated a moment. The woods were hers. She might see other people in there, but something about going into the forest with her mother troubled her. Much as Donika loved her, she didn't want to share.

"Ma," she said, hesitating.

"It won't take long," Qendressa said. "But you need to know the story. Should have told you long time ago. I am selfish."

Donika shook her head. What the hell was her mother talking about?

They walked into the trees. The summer sun had fallen low on the horizon. Soon dusk would arrive. For now, wan daylight still filtered through the thick trees, slanted and pale, shadows long.

"My mother, she knew things," Qendressa began. Her grip on Donika's hand tightened. "How to make two people love. How to heal sickness in body and heart. How to keep spirits away."

Donika tried not to smile. This was what their big talk was about? Old World superstition?

"She was a witch?"

Her mother scowled. "Witch. Stupid word. She was smart. Clever woman. She used herbs and oils—"

"So she was the village wise woman, or whatever," Donika said, and it wasn't a question this time. She thought it was kind of adorable the way her mother said herbs—with a hard 'H,' like the man's name. But this talk of potions and evil spirits made her impatient, too. "I get that she taught you all of that stuff, but how can you still believe it after living in America so long?"

Her mother stopped and pulled her hand away. "Will you be quiet and listen?"

The anguish in her mother's voice stopped her cold. Donika had never heard her mother speak that way. The daylight had waned further and now the slices of sky that could be seen through the thatch of branches had grown a deeper blue. Not dusk yet, but soon. It seemed to be coming on fast.

"I'll listen," she said.

Her mother nodded, then turned and continued along the path. Donika watched the ground, stepped over roots and rocks. The woods were strangely quiet as the dusk approached, with the night birds and nocturnal animals not yet active and the other beasts of the forest already making their beds for the evening.

"She knew things, my mother. And so she taught me these things, just as I teach you to cook the old way. When I married, I made a good wife. Even then, I made money as a seamstress, just like now. But always my husband knew that one day the people in our town would start to come to me with their troubles the way they came to my mother. The ones who believed in superstitions."

Donika couldn't help but hear the admonishment in those words. Her mother wanted her to know she wasn't the only one who still believed in such things.

"There were spirits there, in the hills and the forest. Always, there were spirits, some of them good and some terrible. Other things, too. Believe if you want, or don't believe. But still I will tell you.

"I loved my husband. He had strong hands, but always gentle with me. Some people, they acted strange around my mother and me, but not him. He was so kind, and smiled always, and when he laughed, all the women in our town wanted to take him home. But it was me he loved. We talked all the time about babies, about having a little boy look just like him, or a little girl with my eyes.

"And then he dies. Such a stupid death. Fixing the roof, he slips and falls and breaks his neck. No herbs or oils could raise the dead. He was gone, Donika. Always his face lit up when he talked of babies and now he was dead and the worst part was there wouldn't be any babies."

The patches of sky visible up through the branches had turned indigo. The dusk had come on, and full darkness was only a heartbeat away. It had happened almost without Donika realizing, and now she heard rustling in the underbrush and in the branches above. A light breeze caressed her bare arms and legs and only then did she realize how warm she'd been.

She halted on the path and stared at her mother, eyes narrowed. "What are you talking about, Ma? What the hell are you... you had *me*."

Qendressa slid her hands into the pockets of her skirt as though fighting the urge to reach out and take her daughter's hand. Her features were lost in the gathering darkness.

"No, 'Nika. You came later."

"How could I—"

"Hush now," her mother said. "Just hush. You want to know. You need to know. So hush."

Something shifted in the branches right above them and an owl hooted softly, sadly. Her mother glanced up sharply and scanned the trees as though the mournful cry of that nightbird presented some threat.

Donika shook her head, more confused than ever. "Ma?"

Qendressa narrowed her eyes and took a step away from her daughter, casting herself in shadows again. "You know the word *shtriga*?"

"No."

"No." Her mother sighed, and the sound was enough to break Donika's heart. "I was so much like you, 'Nika. Still very young, though already I was a widow. So many questions in my head. I walked in the forest always, cold and grieving and alone. I knew I had to have a baby, to be a mother. I would never love another, but a child I could love. I could have what my husband and I dreamed of...even if part of it is *only* a dream.

"One night I am in the forest, walking and dreaming, and I hear voices. Some men and some women. I hear a laugh, and I do not like the way it sounds, that laugh. So I walk quietly, slowly, and go through the trees, following the voices. I walked in the forest so much that I learned to make almost no noise at all. From the trees, I see them, two women and three men, all with no clothes. I felt ashamed to spy on them like that. I would have gone, but could not look away.

"They looked up at the sky and reached up to their mouths and they slipped off their skins, like they were only jackets. Inside were shtriga. They looked like owls, but they were not. I could not breathe and just watched, praying not to be seen. They flew away. I stood there until I could not hear the wings anymore and then I could breathe again."

Qendressa paused. Donika realized that she had been holding her breath, just the way her mother had described. As the story unfolded, she had pictured it all in her mind, so simple to imagine because of all of the hours she had spent walking these woods by herself and because, just last night, she and Josh had been naked beneath the trees and the night sky. But this…her imagination could only go so far.

"Ma, you must have been dreaming. You said you were dreaming, right? You fell asleep. That couldn't have been real."

Her mother approached her, stepping into the moonlight, and Donika saw the tears streaking her face. Sorrow weighed on her and made her look like an old woman.

"No?" Qendressa said.

Somewhere in the trees, an owl hooted. Donika flinched and looked up, searching the branches, just as her mother had done. A second owl replied, sharing the sad song.

"Even when they were gone, I could not go away. I should have run. I did not know when they would be back for their skins, the shtriga, but I knew that they *would* be back. The shtriga went 'round the town and through the forest and they hunted the lustful and licentious. They had the scent of those whose lust was strongest, and the shtriga drank their blood to sate their own hungers."

"Sounds like a vampire," Donika said.

Qendressa frowned, shaking her head. "No, 'Nika. Vampires are make-believe. The shtriga are real. But the power they have, it has rules. The shtriga must come back to its skin by morning.

"My mother had told me many stories of them. How they grow. How to stop them. And I dreamed of a baby, 'Nika. It hurt my heart, I wanted it so much.

"I knew I only had till morning, and maybe not even that long. I ran into the clearing and I took the skin of one of the women, with her beautiful black hair. I carried it home, hurrying and falling, and I locked the door behind me. I took my scissors and sat at my work table and I cut the skin of the shtriga. I cut away large pieces and later I burned them.

"And then I started to sew. With the shtriga's black hair for my thread, I patched the skin back together, only now it was not the skin of a grown woman, but the skin of a baby girl."

Donika shivered and hugged herself, staring at her mother's eyes shining in the moonlight, tears glistening on her face.

"No," the girl said.

When her mother spoke again, her voice had fallen to the whisper of confession.

"I sat and waited in the corner of the room, in a chair that my husband had loved so much. A little before dawn, the shtriga comes looking for her skin. I left the window open and the owl flew in and landed on my work table. It spread its wings and ducked its head down to pick at the skin it had left behind. The owl pushed itself into the skin.

"When the sun rose, a baby girl lay on my work table and she cried, so sad, so lonely. I took her in my arms and rocked her and I sang to her an old song that my mother loved, and my baby loved it, too. She didn't cry anymore."

Qendressa bit her and gazed forlornly at her daughter. Through her tears, she began to sing that same old song, a lullaby that Donika knew so well. Her mother had been singing it to her all her life.

"I don't believe you."

But then the owls began to cry their mournful song again, hooting softly, not only one or two but four or five of them now. Donika saw the fear in her mother's eyes as the woman searched the trees. Qendressa put out a hand to her.

"Come, 'Nika. We go home."

Donika stared at her.

"I don't believe you," she said again.

But she could taste the salt of her own tears and feel them warm upon her cheeks. She backed away from her mother's outstretched hand, shaking her head. Denials rose up in her heart and mind but somehow would not reach her lips.

She knew. The hunger churned in her gut, gnawing at her, and she knew.

"Why did you tell me?"

Qendressa sobbed. "Because you are not my baby anymore, 'Nika. You sixteen. Sixteen years since that night. I know the stories. You are shtriga now."

Donika felt something break inside her. She spun on one heel and ran. Low branches whipped at her face and she raised her arms to protect herself. She stumbled over roots and rocks that she'd always avoided before. The owls hooted above her and now she could hear their wings flapping as they moved through the trees, keeping pace.

In her life, she had never felt so cold. No matter how fast she ran, no matter how her pulse quickened, she could not get warm. Her sobs were words, denials that felt as hollow as her own stomach. The hunger clutched at her belly and a yearning burned in her. Desire.

Josh. She summoned an image of him in her mind and focused on it. They could run together. He would hold her. He could touch her, and maybe, for a little while, the madness and hunger would fade.

A numbness came over her, but Donika began to get control of herself. She still wept, but silently now. Her feet were surer on the path. She saw the stone wall to one side and the firepit ahead and the memory of last night gave her something to hold on to.

Soon, she found herself at the end of the path, stepping out into the backyard of the bitter old couple. An owl hooted, back in the woods, and she hurried away from the trees, wanting to leave the forest behind for the first time in her life.

She strode across the back lawn unnoticed. A dog barked nearby, the angry yip of a canine scenting the presence of an enemy. Donika made her way between houses, but as she came in sight of the corner where Josh would be waiting, she paused.

Hidden in the night-black shadows of those homes, she watched him. Josh sat on the curb, smoking a cigarette, content to be by himself. He waited for her, and didn't mind. In the golden glow of a nearby streetlamp, he was beautiful to her. They would run through the dark woods together once again, but this time she would give herself to him.

Desire clawed at her insides. She ran her tongue out to wet her lips. She could almost taste the salt of his skin, and the urge to do so, to taste him, tugged at her.

A smile touched her lips and she almost called out.

Donika's smile faded.

No, she thought. *It isn't love. Desire isn't love. Hunger isn't.*

She understood hunger now. Donika fled silently back into the woods, where she belonged. The owls cried and flew with her. Loneliness clutched at her until she realized that she wasn't alone at all. She had never been alone.

The woods received her with love. She could never go back to her mother's house. Not now.

She hurtled along the path and then left the trail, breaking off into rough terrain. She raced through the woods, leaped fallen branches, and exulted in the night wind whispering around her. Her tears continued to fall but they were no longer merely tears of sorrow. Her mind whirled in a storm of emotions, but beneath them all, the hunger remained.

Surrendering to the forest and the night, she stripped her clothes off as she ran, paying no attention to where she left them. The moonlight and the breeze caressed her naked flesh and now the warmth returned to her at last. She felt herself burning with want. With need. And then she could feel her skin hanging on her the same way that clothes did and she reached up to the edges of her mouth and pulled it wide like a hood, slipping it back over her head.

Donika slid from her skin and, at last, took flight, returning to the night sky after sixteen very long years. Reborn.

She flew through the trees, thinking again of the boy she desired, thinking that maybe he would be inside her tonight after all, and they would both get what they wanted.

Her mouth opened in a low, mournful cry. It was a tune she'd always known, a night song that had been in her heart all along.

ABOUT CHRISTOPHER GOLDEN

CHRISTOPHER GOLDEN is the *New York Times* bestselling, Bram Stoker Award-winning author of such novels as *Ararat, Snowblind, Of Saints and Shadows,* and *Strangewood.* With Mike Mignola, he is the co-creator of two cult favorite comic book series, *Baltimore* and *Joe Golem: Occult Detective.* As an editor, he has worked on the short story anthologies *Seize the Night, Dark Cities,* and *The New Dead,* among others, and he has also written and co-written comic books, video games, screenplays, and a network television pilot. Golden co-hosts the podcasts *Three Guys with Beards* and *Defenders Dialogue.* In 2015 he founded the popular Merrimack Valley Halloween Book Festival. He was born and raised in Massachusetts, where he still lives with his family. His work has been nominated for the British Fantasy Award, the Eisner Award, and multiple Shirley Jackson Awards. For the Bram Stoker Awards, Golden has been nominated eight times in eight different categories. His original novels have been published in more than fifteen languages in countries around the world. Please visit him at christophergolden.com.

WANTS AND NEEDS

Paul Michael Anderson

FOOTFALLS ACROSS THE KITCHEN LINOLEUM, the *shup* of the refrigerator door opening and the dry rattle of the pages hanging from magnets when it closed, the *creak* of cabinet doors opening and the *clack* of them closing, the *thrum* of the baseboard heaters kicking; Emily moved from one side of the kitchen to the other, putting away groceries.

The answering machine's red light blinked silently on the counter.

She paused as she collapsed the cloth grocery bags, staring at it. Holding them in a wad, she hit PLAY and went to the pantry, shoving the bags onto the bottom shelf.

The machine clicked and the hollow sound of an open line filled the kitchen, faintly punctuated by what seemed like the air passage of highway traffic. Then a sigh, thick and watery, and the *click* of the caller hanging up.

She froze, hand still on the pantry door. "Shaun?" she said aloud, her voice almost a croak. The echoes of their last argument bounced around her brain.

—*you're keeping this place like a fucking museum*—

—*are you trying to forget our son*—

She went to her smartphone, next to the answering machine and cordless. Two bars out of a possible five. No missed calls or messages.

She closed her eyes. The heater cut out and the clock above the microwave ticked off the seconds. Everything else was silent and silent and silent.

"Fuck it." She reached into the kitchen cabinet, pulling the pack of Newports from the top shelf where they couldn't be reached by little fingers.

She went to the patio door and slid it open, a blast of winter wind punching her in the face, snow crunching beneath her boots as she went to the railing. Their property was built on a slope, their backyard descending a good fifty yards into the forest, and the winter-denuded trees looked like the broken bones of a dead monster. Snow coated everything, making it easier to look at the vague humps that were the wooden swing set and plastic jungle gym.

Above the neighboring Shenandoah Mountains, a rolling line of fat, coal-colored clouds approached. It was late in the season, but the news said they were due for another storm.

The menthol burned a trail down her throat. Interior voices tried to encroach, tested the weaknesses in her defensive wall. There were a lot of voices—voices of reason, voices of bargaining, voices of grief, voices of rage. Sometimes articulate, more often just roars of emotion. It'd been like this since before Shaun left. He'd said at one point it was like they'd lost one person only to gain all the people now living in Emily's head. She'd screamed at him until he left the room.

Emily exhaled smoke like a dragon warming up a burst of fire. She looked down to tap ash over the railing and saw the footprints. It was a single line, cutting across her yard, right in front of the swing set.

Too large to be anything but human.

A shiver zipped up her back. People were few on this mountain, which was what had drawn her and Shaun ten years ago. The homes around her were shut down, their owners spending winter in warmer climes. The only other resident was the caretaker, Al, near the top of the mountain.

Those prints shouldn't be there.

An interior voice snuck into the center of her brain: *poachers*. Echoes filled her head again—Shaun's this time—as she'd heard them from the woods, screaming Ethan's name, screaming her name, screaming for help.

Her view crystalized as her eyes watered. The unwanted memory followed the unwanted voice of Shaun running out of the woods, carrying Ethan's small body, blood falling in a rain behind him onto the ground, and her *screaming*—

The phone rang inside, and she yelped. Her cigarette—forgotten, burnt down to the filter—fell over the side of the patio.

She took a deep breath and started to turn away when she thought she saw the flicker of something black at the tree line. She paused and the landline trilled again, insistent.

—*Shaun*—

She rushed back inside, dragging snow across the linoleum, and snatched up the cordless. "Hello?"

"Emily?" her sister asked, her voice crisp and urgent. "Emily, are you okay?"

Emily leaned against the counter, lowering her head. "I was just outside."

Lauren pressed, "But are you *okay*?"

She rubbed her forehead with the heel of her hand. "I'm fine. Thought you were Shaun."

"Have you talked to him recently? Seen him?"

She hissed silently, regretted saying anything. "Not for a few weeks."

Technically true; they'd spoken the week after he left, back in January. She could still count that in weeks.

A beat of silence from Lauren's end.

"What's up?" Emily asked.

Lauren cleared her throat. "I just wanted to make sure you were okay."

"I'm *fine*. As fine as can be expected. As fine as I was last week and the week before that."

"Don't say it like that, kiddo. I'm not trying to bug you and you know it. I hate the idea of you up in that house. It must be like a museum of horrors."

Emily gritted her teeth. That was the second person to call it a museum.

"You're rattling around up there," Lauren went on, "refusing to see anyone, surrounded by the past—"

"It's my home, Lauren," she said, an edge creeping into her voice.

"A home that you're all alone in, trying to deal with—with *this*. You *need* more than that. Jesus, if a storm came along and knocked everything out, what would you do?"

"Rely on my generator and four-wheel drive," Emily said. "Like I have for years. Nothing's changed, Lauren."

"*Everything's* changed, Emily!" Lauren burst out. "You keep acting like everything's the way it was and it *isn't!*"

Emily closed her eyes. "Don't you think I know that?" she asked softly. Silence.

"I don't wanna fight with you," Lauren said finally.

"Then don't." She cleared her throat. "Listen, I have groceries that need put away."

A loud exhale on the phone line. "Okay, but call me if you need to talk, okay? *Okay*, Emily?"

"Fine," Emily said, and hit the POWER button. She gave herself points for not jabbing it over and over again, or hurling the fucking thing across the room. No one would call her or bother her then.

Instead, she dropped it back into the charger and focused on breathing, hands clenching and unclenching at her sides. She glanced over at the fridge; a sheet of construction paper with ETHAN written in large, shaky capitals hung askew from its magnet.

The muscles of Emily's face rippled, and she lunged off the counter, going through the archway and into the main room. The house was an A-frame with a main room and second-floor loft. She took to the stairs, her winter boots knocking against the risers. The door at the top was closed like the other two along the gallery, but this door had a wooden oval sign with ETHAN burned into it in a rustic style. A baby gift from his Aunt Lauren.

Emily stared at it, teeth grinding together, and then she opened the door and stepped inside.

The bedroom was gloomy, the sun on the other side of the house. The left wall had been built out with a tall window in the center casting a rectangle of cold silver light onto the carpet.

Emily breathed in the lingering smell of boy and ignored how faded it seemed. Her eyes ticked over the toys littering the front of a shelf in typical "boy neat" manner, the tousled sheets on the bed in the corner, waiting for the boy that slept there to climb back in.

Her gaze fell on the two Xerox paper boxes in the center like invaders that didn't know they'd been outnumbered, their lids off and insides empty.

Shaun's first and last attempt. A week after she'd discovered him with the boxes he was gone.

—everything's changed...you keep acting like everything's the way it was and it isn't—

"I want it to be," she said through gritted teeth. She didn't feel the hot tears coursing down her face. "I just *want* it to be. It was *mine*."

***

A truck engine roared, and Emily looked up from the communal mailboxes to see a '70s-era Ford pickup with a plow-mount on the front coming down the lane from the highway. The pickup slowed as it approached, parking behind her Bronco. The engine cut off and an older man climbed out of the cab. "Emily!" he called. "I was just thinking of dropping by."

"Hey, Al," she said, inserting a key into the mailbox. "Stopping by? Why?"

He unlocked his own box. "Checking in ahead of the storm. Was gonna make it a part of my rounds. It's just you and me, with all the snow-bunnies now in Florida or whatever."

"Thanks, Al," she said, pulling out a rubber-banded wad of junk mail.

Al shrugged. "Nothing to it. Neighbors look out for each other."

"I'm set," she said, relocking the mailbox. "Went to Walmart this morning."

He pulled his mail out. "Good, good," he said, nodding. As he relocked his box he said, softer than before, "Have you spoken with Shaun recently?"

She lowered her head so he wouldn't see her lips thin. This was her thing, now, it seemed—the woman who lost her child, then her husband. All conversations for the foreseeable future would have to circle this at least once. "No, I haven't." She looked up. "Why?"

Al glanced around. "The other reason I was gonna stop by. I wanted to know if you were going to be alone in this storm."

She held her mail to her chest, eyes narrowing. "Why?" she repeated.

Al wouldn't look at her. "There've been some break-ins in the other houses."

The footprints she'd seen flashed through her mind. "Really?"

He exhaled, exasperated. "Happens every once in a while with property's empty half a year. Helluva thing to have to call in. Makes it look like

I'm sleeping on the job." He shot her a look, as if trying to determine if she thought the same. "A bunch of kids get their asses ripped and then dare each other to do it. Easy vandalism—too cold and too far out in the boonies for more, usually. But there's been four or five of them since December."

"Damage?"

"Minor—broken windows, jimmied locks. Kitchens are trashed. Think it's someone homeless, looking for a roof and some food. Whoever it is, he's avoiding the houses with people in them." He fixed her with a firm gaze. "You seen anything?"

"Some footprints across my yard this morning."

"Shit." He looked down at his boots. "I was hoping whoever it was had moved on." When he looked up, he said, "Make sure you lock it down tight tonight. This storm might make him crazy and take a risk. He's in a blizzard and sees light and warmth? Might get a touch of the wendigo in him."

She blinked. "What?"

He grinned ruefully. "Touch of the wendigo. My pa's from Minnesota and it's a mix of old Indian stuff. One version has a guy who covets so much, and gets so territorial over what he does have, that he kills and loses his soul and becomes a monster, starts feasting on human flesh. Whenever my pa thought me and my brother were getting greedy, he'd say we got some wendigo in us." His grin widened at the memory.

She didn't know how to respond to that.

Slowly, Al's grin faded. "But, seriously, anyone out in this storm to-night's gonna be a little cuckoo for Cocoa Puffs, y'know? Batten down the hatches."

She thought of the flicker she *thought* she'd seen. "Thanks, Al. I will."

He nodded. "You call if you need anything, okay? Anything goes on the fritz, or if you think you see something, I can get *down* faster with my truck than the county cops can get *up*, y'know?"

"I will," she repeated, although something inside clenched at the idea of calling him to her house.

An interior voice snuck in: *touch of the wendigo?*

Al sketched a salute and walked to his truck. Before he climbed in he turned back. He looked, she thought, like a textbook example of a Dutch

Uncle. "Not trying to tell you your business, but I am gonna say that sometimes the best way to heal is with loved ones."

—are you trying to forget our son?—

Al shook his head—she thought, at himself. "Never mind me, I'm a fool. I just like you and Shaun."

Emily didn't respond.

He climbed in and shouted, "Call me!" as he fired up the engine.

She raised a hand as the truck went up around the curve. Something cold touched her fingertips.

She lowered her hand and saw a snowflake melting on the pad.

*** *

The snow came down light and easy as she shut the door to the generator's shelter—a squat wooden structure next to the house's fuel tank—and straightened. The gennie was wired into the house, fueled by the tank. When the power went, the gennie would automatically switch on.

She glanced at the darkening sky, then looked down the yard at the footprints she'd spied earlier. Al's voice filled her head:

—whoever it is, he's avoiding the houses with people in them—

She made her way down the hill, the thin crust breaking under her boots, then sinking her leg almost past her knees. She stopped near the tracks and glanced back at the house. It loomed over her. What would it look like at night if you were hungry, cold, and half-crazed enough you'd break into empty homes hoping for food?

"Knock that shit off," she told herself. Poachers had been bad enough, but that was just horrifically-timed speculation. If these prints matched who Al was talking about, then that gave these prints an owner and her a knowledge of what the owner had done.

She looked at the prints again. Someone trying to clear the yard as quickly as possible to get to the trees where the snow wasn't as bad. She followed the prints to the tree line and saw a roughly circle of stamped-down snow with glimpses of last season's leaves beneath. The kind of thing an animal would do when clearing a space.

Why not just skirt the yard completely and go through the trees at the end?

Al's voice in her head again:

—*we got some wendigo in us*—

—*batten down the hatches*—

She started to turn away when she thought she saw a flicker of black amongst the trees at the far end of her yard.

She turned back, but nothing moved except the falling snow, the soft *paf* of the flakes hitting the icy crust.

But she was filled with that crinkly feeling of being watched.

—*you call if you need anything, okay?*—

"Don't come here," she said, watching the trees. Nothing moved, of course—no animal, person, or mythological monster. "Not here. This is mine."

She trudged back to the patio stairs, cutting a sluggish trail across the snow. That staticky, hairs-standing-on-the-back-of-her-neck feeling of being watched clung to her the entire time.

***

She knows it's a dream, but that doesn't change the heft of Ethan's weight in her arms, the heat of blood on her clothes, how ragged her throat is from screaming. She's not grieving now; she is enraged that someone would do this to her son, her family. The echo of a poacher's rifle shot is fading and she's tracking it.

She hears screaming, not hers, fading with distance. It sounds like Lauren and Shaun.

—*a fucking museum*—

—*a museum of horrors*—

It's not a museum, it's their home, and if she can only catch the motherfucker who did this, find out once and for all who did this, it'll be all right again, they'll be whole again, Ethan will be fine again. This isn't about what she wants; this is about what needs to happen.

She can smell him now—the sharp tang of gun smoke, the acidic tang of fear. She'll catch him. She'll know who did this to her son.

And she'll tear out his throat with her teeth.

She roars, and it doesn't sound human to her ears—

—*the wendigo!*—

—but that doesn't matter. It'll all be all right soon. It'll all be over soon.

***

Emily awoke with a jerk. She blinked owlishly at the lights of the main room, then pulled herself higher in the leather chair.

"Shit," she muttered. The dream—so vivid her muscles thrummed with the exertion of holding Ethan's body—pulled apart like cobwebs in her head.

She glanced at the television mounted on the wall. The DirecTV logo bounced like a 1990s computer screensaver. Satellite knocked out. Not the first time. The Blu-ray player on the table beneath told her it was after eleven.

And then the lights went out.

She sat there for a full minute in a darkness punctuated only by the squares of soft bluish light in the windows, waiting for the generator to kick everything back on. When it didn't, she grunted and pawed for the long-barreled flashlight on the table. This meant the generator had already *been* on and the power had tripped the breakers. Also not the first time.

She clicked the flashlight on and a long spear of white light shot across the room, highlighting the staircase. She stood, swinging the light briefly towards the front door—deadbolted and chain-locked—and moved towards the kitchen, unplugging things as she went. The generator tended to kick over because of too many things running at once for it to handle from a dead stop. Probably had just clicked on, took one look at the needed wattage, and went "Fuck this!" Stupid of her not to pull this stuff already.

She reached the pantry and opened it, revealing two circuit breakers, one on top of the other. The bottom was the generator.

Emily opened the hatch door. The breakers were still on. She stared at them for a moment. That meant the problem lay with the actual generator outside. In the blizzard.

"Fuck," she said.

She went to the kitchen table where she'd left her jacket and gloves, her snow boots on a thick towel by the door, and glanced outside. Visibility was for shit, anything beyond the patio railing lost in the flickering static of heavy falling snow.

She caught her reflection in the glass. The overhead light above the table turned her eyes into sockets from which the whites flickered in the glow, made her face longer and more angular, her features thin and blade-like. An inhuman face. A monster's face.

—*wendigo*—

Emily turned away and bundled up. She could hear the wind screaming through the angles and corners of the house as she unlocked and opened the door. An icy gust knocked her head back, froze her cheeks. No one would be out in this.

Unless they have a touch of wendigo in them.

Then they would freeze out here, crazy and wanting.

The trek to the side of the house left her neck sweaty, her leg muscles twanging, and a yellow stitch in her side. The snow was already waist-high. The generator box was becoming a vague hump under the drifts, the back end already buried, but the hobbit door was still clear, helped by the angle of the snowfall.

She grabbed the handle, yanked hard, and the door flew open. She staggered back, then trained the light on the inside. The generator hulked in its tight confines, ticking to itself. No snow had gotten in. It didn't reek of fuel or ozone. Nothing smoked.

The manual switch along the side was flipped to OFF.

She stared at it for a long moment, forgetting the storm and the snow and the wind. She swallowed. That tingly, being-watched feeling surged, localizing on a spot in the center of her back.

She spun, sure that whoever had turned the generator off would be leaping at her. She raised the flashlight high to bring it down—

—there was no one there.

Still, someone had turned her generator off.

Turn it on and get your goddamned ass inside, that interior voice said, and she listened. Immediately the big blocky machine fired up, engine catching speed. She began the awkward journey back to the patio. She pulled herself up the steps, feeling nothing but the burning cold, the heat of her neck, the stitch in her side.

Reaching the top stair of the patio, she saw light spilling out through the glass doors. In spite of her fear, she exhaled with relief—at least she'd be warm while terrified—and thought about Al. He'd said to call. He was right about the cops; he'd get to her before they would. But short of an emergency, she couldn't leave the gritty feeling of allowing someone into *her* home, *her* space. With Shaun gone—for good or not, who knew—it was all she had.

Her home.

Her museum.

Her territory.

She stepped onto the patio, looked through the glass, and saw melting clumps of snow on the linoleum floor.

Everything switched off except her sight and her heart. One tall clump fell over in the warm air of her kitchen.

Disarmed, the voices surged into her head, cluttering her thoughts.

Run, one said.

Run where? another challenged. *Into the fucking storm?*

We can't stay out here, a third explained. *We'll die.*

Slowly, the shock melted, replaced by something she couldn't immediately identify. Her mind turned over like an old car engine, and then revved, circling through options. She thought of her smartphone on the counter, the cordless next to it.

The knives in the block near the stove.

Someone was in her house, in her *museum*, with her—

—*Ethan's*—

—things.

Emily opened the patio door slowly to minimize sound, then stepped inside, making sure to plant both feet on the towel and close the door silently behind her.

Keeping an eye on the archway, she hunkered down and did a quick dry of her boots with the towel. When they were as dry as they were going to get, she straightened, reached out, and snagged the cordless off the charger.

Call! one of the voices yelled. *Call for help! Call Now!*

And then what? Police wouldn't arrive for at least three days. It would take an hour for Al to get here, and that was being generous.

An hour—or more—alone with whoever was in her house.

She dropped the phone into her coat pocket and sidestepped to the left, towards the stove. She side-eyed the floor, avoiding the spots that tended to creak.

She reached the oven and waited, listening. The baseboard heaters thrummed, a backbeat to the guitar-solo howling of the wind outside. She took off her gloves, set them on the counter behind her, then pulled the butcher's knife from the block. Its blade slid along the edges of its wooden sheaf with a silver whisper.

Emily took a step towards the archway, then another, walking on the balls of her feet. The pounding of her heartbeat jumped up a notch. Two blind spots on either side of the archway. She tried to see around each of them, sidled up along the wall, checking one, then moved to the other wall to check the other.

Clear.

She let out a breath she hadn't been aware of holding as she looked around the room. Everything seemed alien—the chair she'd napped on, the triple-locked front door which seemed like a cruel joke.

She heard a creak upstairs. A footstep.

She backed slowly out into the main room, looking up as the second-floor loft revealed itself, tensing to reveal the stranger in her home.

The loft was empty.

But Ethan's door was open.

Watching it, she tightened her grip on the knife and made her way to the staircase. She took the first step, keeping to the wall to avoid creaks, and climbed.

She waited at the landing, then flicked a glance at the other two doors. Bathroom, master bedroom. Both closed. The stranger could be in either of them—but then why leave her son's door open?

Shouldn't be in there, she thought. Beneath that, though, was a more primal voice, a more primal emotion.

—mine—

No one could come and take what was hers, not when she had so little left. The world had taken Ethan; it couldn't take the home she'd had with him.

Knife raised to chest-level, Emily stepped into her son's doorway.

The man stood in the center with his back to her, a tall and lanky black silhouette outlined by the snow-light of the window.

Her voice was a shaking growl. "Get. Out."

The man turned. His milk-pale face was blade-thin, shadowed by the hoodie he wore, revealing just the pointed chin, knife-nose, hollowed cheeks.

"I needed warmth," he said and his voice was as thin and reedy as he was. "I didn't know you had a son."

"Out," she hissed.

The man rushed her and she recoiled. They collided, him tucking his shoulder to catch her dead-center, her knife coming down on nothing but air. Momentum picked her off her feet, drove her against the gallery railing and then over.

She hit the floor, the knife clattering away. Her thick coat saved her from any broken bones, but the force wailed on her like a punch from God. She felt more than heard the cordless crunch beneath her.

Pounding footsteps and then the tiny sip of air she'd managed to take in was knocked out as the man jumped her, reaching for her throat. He thrummed, thin limbs ropy with shaky muscle.

She fought his grip, her hands hooked into claws, digging into his face. He cried out and swung at her. A bomb exploded against the side of her face and they rolled on the floor. He grabbed at the collar of her coat, and she went with the movement, her face darting forward to bite down on whatever she could reach—his nose. The dirty slickness of sweaty flesh touched her tongue, and then hot copper flooded her mouth.

A hateful triumph filled her and she bore down. She worked her teeth, crunching cartilage, and he screamed, shoving her away.

Emily spun, scrambling for the knife. She turned and the man was hunched over, hands cupping his face, blood falling between the fingers. "Bitch!" he screamed, a bad Foghorn Leghorn impersonation. "Fuckin' bitch!"

She bared her teeth at him, hot blood coating her chin, and went for him. She brought the knife down, got him in the shoulder—

—*MINE*—

—and then he drove her into the kitchen. They squeaked over the linoleum, grabbing and pulling, screaming into each other's faces. She hefted a knee into his crotch. He shuddered, loosening his grip on her, and she shoved him, yanking the knife from his shoulder with blood trailing.

He stumbled against the kitchen table and she spun, hitting the patio door. She threw it open and leaped outside. In the snow, they were equal. In the snow, she was bruised while he was stabbed and kicked and bit.

One of the voices spoke up:

—*why would he follow?*—

But he immediately answered that: *"GET BACK HERE!"*

She skidded across the frozen patio boards and hit the railing. Her weight shifted up and her center of gravity danced just in front of her. For the second time, she went over a railing.

Her fall this time was softer thanks to the snow, but it still stunned her, going down the back of her jacket, into her mouth, burning her flesh. She fought against it, kicking and punching her way through.

Still holding onto the knife, she plunged down the hill. She heard him grunt as he hit the snow, and then the race was on. She had no plan, nothing but the raging hatred of someone trying to come and take—

—*Ethan*—

—what little she had left. The smart thing for him to do would be to stay inside. The smart thing for her to do would be to lose him, then circle back.

Neither would. That took logic, and primal hatred had no time for it.

Her head rang with adrenaline and effort and damage. The humps of Ethan's jungle gym blipped by and then she reached the tree line and glanced behind her. He was barely a dozen yards away, holding his wounded shoulder and cutting through the path she'd cleared. He had it easier; she'd already done the work for him.

She dived into the woods. Because of the overlapping branches above, the snow wasn't as deep, but her boots fetched up against deadfalls and exposed roots. She had no sense of direction, no idea where she was. A clear space. She needed a clear space to turn on this fucker, plunge the knife into his heart—

—*make him pay*—

—*tear out his throat with her teeth*—

He grunted and she could smell him—dirt, sweat, the acidic tang not of fear but of hatred. Altogether, it smelled like dead meat.

She snatched a look back, and her boot plunged into empty air. She fell, twisting, and suddenly she was rolling. Roots and sticks and rocks and trunks came up to smash her. Every muscle cried out.

She fetched up against a rock and shrieked. She made herself stand, even though it was like wide-tooth saws worked on her joints. The trees were jagged black crayons around her, the ground a perfect white. A small hollow in the hillside. A clearing.

She heard him grunting and she turned towards him. The movement made the world tilt crazily. Black stars arced across her vision.

"Come," she said. She opened her mouth to scream it and a roar—

—*not human*—

—cracked the sky. She turned and the world tilted again, but not before she saw the giant emaciated figure behind her, obscured by the snow. The wind carried its stench of decay and corruption in sheets. It looked down at her with eyes that capered with a familiar, mad, amber light. I know you, those eyes said. We know each other.

Its face was the face she'd seen reflected in her patio door.

—*the wendigo!*—

She tried turning back to the man, but the world kept tilting, and the black stars in front of her eyes coalesced, became a spiral that pulled her into itself as she heard someone scream.

***

The first thing she realized, waking up to gray daylight, was that she was cold. Colder than she'd ever been. The kind of cold you read about.

She forced herself to sit up and found herself in her own yard, half-buried by snow near Ethan's jungle gym. It'd acted as an imperfect shield through the night.

She got slowly to her feet. The knife, gore-streaked and frozen, was still in her hand, but she couldn't move her fingers to let go. Her entire body was sheathed in blood, making her coat stiff. Her head was addled, but not too much so. The voices had fallen silent.

Her eyes fell on the lump of snow-covered red in the center of the yard. Uncomfortable snatches—

—*the wendigo!*—

—flash-popped into the center of her head—

—*tearing his throat out*—

—the images searing then fading—

—the blade coming down and down and down—

—too quickly for her to parse which were real and which were imagined.

—the screech of the man dying, her own enraged bellows—

Staring at the body, all the blood on her clothing seemed to gain weight.

She glanced at the trees as if to see the giant monster staring down at her, and a coyote emerged from the forest instead, eyeing her and the lump. It sat down, keeping a fair distance away.

Something growled across from her, and two more coyotes approached and sat.

Emily looked from them to the house. It looked a million miles away.

She glanced at the body, then the coyotes. The coyotes lowered their heads, looked up at her from under their brows, avoided direct contact. They didn't move.

Emily started walking, slowly, towards the house. One of the coyotes howled.

—a roar cracks the sky—

When she heard the sounds of animals fighting for food, she didn't look back. She already knew what that sounded like.

***

The patio door was still open, the heater going full blast to combat the wafting cold. She forced the door closed, fighting the ice that had built into the track, then locked it. Immediately, the heat of the house made her skin tingle unpleasantly.

—my house—

No. This felt like a stranger's now. These things belonged to different people.

She couldn't think any deeper than that, so she stripped naked at the patio door, then went upstairs to stand under the shower until the hot water ran out. It took thirty minutes. For the first ten, she screamed. For the next, she scrubbed the feeling back into her body. For the final, she just stood there.

When she came out of the bathroom she closed Ethan's door, but didn't look in.

Downstairs she told herself she should eat something, get some nourishment, but she wasn't hungry.

How can I after what happened? a part of her thought, but the rest of her mind skittered away from that.

She felt hollow, at a dead end. Not hungry, not...anything.

She took a cigarette, leaving the pack on the counter, and stepped outside. The coyotes and the lump were gone, the snow on her yard much more trampled now. Aside from a busted cordless and the ruined clothes, there was no evidence that anyone had been here.

She tried to recollect last night, but couldn't. Everything was a blur. The head-quivering rage. The taste of blood on her tongue and how *right* it felt.

She flicked her cigarette away half-smoked and went back inside.

Her smartphone had a full battery. Two bars out of five possible. Enough to make a call on. If she wanted.

Did she want to?

Lauren: *Call me if you need to talk okay?*

Al: *You call if you need anything okay?*

She remembered Al's advice—*the best way to heal is with loved ones*—embarrassed that he'd spoken at all, and thought of the voicemail that contained nothing but the sound of traffic and ended with a watery sigh.

She picked up her phone and looked around at everything but the pile of damning clothes on the floor. Maybe it was the man, or the storm, or the conversations with Al and Lauren, or all three, or none of them—this wasn't *her* house, anymore. The one thing she'd fought for, driven people away for—

—*killed for*—

—wasn't hers.

Ethan wasn't running down those steps. Aside from some aging pictures on the refrigerator, this house didn't recognize a child had ever lived here. The air smelled stale and unused, even with the patio door open half the night. There was no *life* here.

It wasn't her territory. She'd wanted it to be something more, wanted it to be what it once had been—a home for her family and not just a place where things she couldn't let go of were stored.

But it was just a hollow structure she happened to be in.

The heater cut out and the clock above the microwave ticked off the seconds. Everything else was silent and silent and silent.

What did she need, then? What came after letting go?

She looked down at her phone, swiped her thumb across the screen.

Taking a deep breath, Emily dialed.

ABOUT PAUL MICHAEL ANDERSON

PAUL MICHAEL ANDERSON is the author of *Bones Are Made to be Broken* (Written Backwards/Dark Regions Press, 2016), and has appeared in dozens of anthologies and magazines, including *Chiral Mad 3*, *Space and Time*, and *Lost Signals*. A sometime editor and occasional journalist, his articles have appeared on sites such as *Bloody Disgusting* and *LitReactor*. He lives in Northern Virginia with his wife and daughter.

AN ELEGY FOR CHILDHOOD MONSTERS

GWENDOLYN KISTE

UNTIL I WAS TWELVE YEARS OLD, my sister Cecilia read me bedtime stories about monsters.

I sat up on the stained mattress next to her, my eyes wide and waiting. We were alone in the house, our father long gone and our mother at her midnight job or her midnight bar.

"And what then?" I asked, as Cecilia turned the page. "Does the maiden defeat the beast?"

She smiled. "Of course, Annie. The maiden always wins."

Cecilia was two years older than me, so I believed her. I didn't realize then she only chose the stories with the happy endings.

Once the dragons and witches and beasts were vanquished, we flipped off the Hello Kitty lamp on the nightstand and waited until dusk.

Until our own monster arrived.

It crawled on its belly, writhing and scratching at the floor. It was smaller than we were, no more than a shadow, but it was strong. And smart. We could hide in light or dark, but it would come for us wherever we went—the bedroom, the rec room, the alcoves of the backyard we thought were ours alone.

It would come, and it would always choose Cecilia.

The first time, we fought it together. She swatted, and I kicked, but it didn't help. The monster was wild and cruel and patient. It simply waited until we tired ourselves out. Then it crawled up the length of my sister's body, its forked tongue in the soft flesh of her ear.

"You're too old for monsters," Mama said when we tried to tell her, as if there was an age limit, the inverse of those colorful yardsticks at the mouth of a carnival attraction. Instead of You Must be This Tall to Ride, it was You Must be Under This Age for Monsters.

But like the bedtime stories that lulled us in the dark, monsters were made for the young. They belonged to us.

And we belonged to them.

***

"I'm pregnant." On the other end of the phone, my sister's voice is thin and strange.

It takes me a moment to recognize her, and a deep shame settles in my guts. I don't know my own sister. I've become that person I always loathed, the city transplant, cold and removed from what came before. Cecilia's practically a stranger to me now. It's been ten years since I was home, since I saw her face in the doorway the day I left at eighteen. I begged her to come with me, but she shook her head.

"Someone needs to stay and take care of Mama."

"Let her fix up herself," I said and squeezed Cecilia's hand. But it wasn't enough. Our Mama, grinning through ruined teeth, her skin bile-yellow with gin and regret, had won. I hated Cecilia for that, for choosing her over me, but I didn't argue. It was her choice.

"Goodbye," I said, and meant it. I didn't come home—*wouldn't* come home—not when Mama went into renal failure, or into hospice, or into the ground. I never planned to come home again.

But with Cecilia's quiet tears salting the line, all my lingering resentment melts away, and I just want to hold my sister.

"Are you keeping it?" I ask at last.

Cecilia sucks in a heavy breath. "Yes."

"Do you want me there?"

"Yes."

I hang up the phone and take the next plane back to Indiana.

The cloudless sky rises to meet me, and I stare out my Plexiglas window, thinking how I shouldn't be surprised. With our parents sick and dying, we're becoming parents of our own. This is the cycle, how it always goes.

On the way home from the airport, I smoke my last Marlboro Light and slip the Uber driver an extra twenty to detour past the old factory outside of town. Even the off-the-book tip almost isn't enough to convince him.

"Nobody goes there," he says, and shudders a little.

I know why. We all know why. The ground there is bitter, the gray weeds twisted with a sickly sheen of rot and secrets.

Our secrets. The ones we could never bury deep enough.

***

Not every kid had a monster. We learned this early. Cecilia and I became good at picking out the ones like us. On Sunday mornings, we would sit cross-legged on the lawn of the church, and whisper to each other.

"The Rigsby twins," I said. You could tell from how their collars were pulled up to their chins, hiding their pink welts. Dressed in too-long skirts, they shuffled everywhere they went, heads tipped to the ground, murmuring to themselves as if they were praying. Maybe they were. Prayers against monsters were as good as any other wards. As in, no good at all.

"Bobby Miller," Cecilia whispered. He was a high school freshman like her, and his marks were the color of storm clouds, speckling his arms and throat. He could see it in us too, what we were hiding. He flashed a grin at Cecilia, and we clambered to our feet to outpace him as the church bells clanged.

"What's with the blotches, Cecilia?" He followed close behind, his breath hot and sticky on the backs of our necks. "You know, if you're ever interested, I'd like to give you some marks of my own."

I whirled around to face him, my hands wadded into aching fists. "Leave her alone."

He guffawed. "Or what?" he asked, and flicked my nose hard.

In a flurry of thrashing arms, I launched at him and scratched his too-close eyes, and we tumbled in a ball of spit and rage on the churchyard, until the pastor came and plucked us apart like flies on yellowed paper.

"That'll be enough," he said and left us heaving and sneering in the grass.

During the sermon that Sunday, the pastor preached forgiveness, and I about puked on the pew. It was always the same shtick. Pardon this. Absolve that. Surrender your wrath because it only hurts you. The way the congregation talked, forgiveness sounded the same as an apology. But why forgive something that hurt you, and would keep on hurting you if it had the chance? Something that probably only stopped when you gave it no other choice.

"What does that old pastor know about forgiveness anyhow?" I asked on the ride home. "What's the worst thing anybody's done to him?"

"You hush, girl," Mama said, her fingers tightening white on the steering wheel. "That pastor is ten times wiser than you'll ever be."

"I doubt that," I murmured, and gazed out the backseat window at the empty sky.

We turned down our street, and our next-door neighbor Maribelle was loitering on her porch. She was a permanent fixture on the block, her figure as lithe as a lamppost, lips the color of the rusted-out stop sign at the corner. At fifteen, she'd dropped out of high school and assumed a full-time profession of lounging. She did a passable job at it, draped across the front steps, her body dripping down the concrete like the head of an ice cream cone melting in the lazy July sun.

She smiled at us in our itchy Sunday best. "How was church?"

"Better without you there," Mama said, trudging up our driveway. "The whole steeple would probably go up in flames if you crossed the threshold."

"Now that would be a good time." Maribelle laughed before slipping back inside through her sagging screen door.

Mama didn't stay for lunch. She'd done her good Christian duty—crooning the right lyrics to all the hymns, tithing in that little golden dish—and now she could go as she pleased.

In the hallway, she shed her ivory cotton dress for a pair of blue jeans. "Take care of your sister," she said to Cecilia, and locked the front door behind her.

After Mama's beat-up Pinto vanished around the corner, Cecilia and I bounded to our bedroom and swapped our church dresses for shorts and tank tops, the last remnants of a summer slipping away too soon.

For hours, we played Twister in the rec room. Cecilia always won.

"It's not fair," I said, scowling. "Your legs are longer."

She grinned and pulled me into her and hugged me until I couldn't breathe.

I scrambled to break free. "I'll grow tall as a redwood someday," I said. "And just as strong too. Then I'll beat you. I'll beat anyone I choose."

She ruffled my hair. "I bet you will."

When we got hungry, Cecilia boiled us hot dogs in an old pan and cut the mold off the week-old buns. The meal tasted like mush, but I never complained. We were together, and that was all that mattered.

"I wish it was just you and me," I said, as we cleared the table. "That everybody else was gone but us."

Cecilia hunched over the sink, our dirty plates clutched in her hands. "How about Mama? Do you want her gone too?"

Especially Mama, I wanted to say. Mama and the pastor and all the other adults who moralized and yelled and didn't ever listen to what we said. They pretended to be strong, but when it really mattered, they turned away and let the monsters come. They couldn't see because they didn't want to.

Cecilia poured me a tumbler of neon green juice and set it on the table.

"Drink up," she said, as if that was an answer.

I stared at the round juice can on the kitchen counter. The label featured a slobbering green beastie, his arms flailing and eyes wild. He looked nothing like our monster.

Nothing looked like our monster.

After the dishes were done, we curled up in front of the television on the brown shag carpet and watched reruns of *Looney Tunes*. Cecilia painted her nails, each toe a different color, while I scarfed down cheeseballs from a shiny silver can, my fingers sticky with orange fuzz.

We pretended we weren't waiting until night. Until it came for us.

"Why does it hate us so much?" The question escaped my lips before I could subdue it.

"I don't know," Cecilia said, her eyes downcast, studying the curves of her feet. "Maybe hate's the only thing a monster can feel."

A twinge of pity tightened in my chest. How lonely a monster's life must be. In that way, it wasn't so different from us.

But then Cecilia rolled onto her belly, and under her waist-high shorts, her bare thighs gleamed in the yellowed incandescent glow of the rec room. There they were, those marks in the shape of wilted carnations. The marks of a monster.

I turned back to the television set, and inside me, something cracked in two. In the flicker of the screen, I promised myself I would never again feel pity.

Not for monsters. And not for us.

***

Cecilia embraces me at the front door. "I've missed you," she whispers, and her belly presses into mine, the three of us entwined as one. "Your room's ready for you."

I shiver against her. My old life, just waiting for me to slide back into it.

All night, I dream of suffocating, of earth packed solid and deep in my lungs.

The next day, on our way to the grocery store, we drive by the old factory. It looks the same as last night—cold and strange and terribly familiar.

The industry here long ago abandoned us, but even back when the whole town paid union dues, this ground was already ruined. That was why the owners never built here, why they left this field fallow. The derelict factory with its heavy metals and hopelessness was only the excuse our parents used to explain why the grass would never blossom.

But we know why, even if we wish we didn't.

In her second trimester, Cecilia develops morning sickness, and we stay in most days, the two of us twisted up together on that old shag carpet, watching *Gilligan's Island* and *The Price is Right*.

"If you need to go home," she says to me, but I shake my head.

"I am home." I smile and squeeze her hand.

On one of her better afternoons, we drive downtown and have lunch at the diner. Bobby Miller is slinging milkshakes and fries at the counter. When we come in, he smiles at Cecilia, and she smiles back, and the way they look at each other makes me seasick sitting still.

In a corner booth, I flick my lighter and let it fizzle, not looking at her.

"How's he been?" I ask, but she pretends not to know. Cecilia was always such a terrible liar.

Before we head home, she and I take our usual detour. But this time, it's not the same. When the factory comes into view, all the breath leaves my chest.

The ground is disturbed. Like something's burrowing up from the dark.

Cecilia's skin turns pale as the dead. "They're returning," she says.

That night, she crawls into bed with me, and we coil together like children.

"What if we're like Mama? What if we can't see them?" She cradles her belly in both hands. "What if I can't protect her?"

"You protected me," I say.

But she shakes her head and turns away. "I'm not sure if I can do it again."

In January, Cecilia's morning sickness worsens, and I take trips to the grocery store alone. In the canned soup aisle, I pass the Rigsby twins in their same faded skirts. They smile at me, ask about my sister, and tell me—without my asking—that they've forgiven their monster.

"It's the right thing to do," they say, as I struggle to pick out the beef barley from the chicken noodle, my gaze wet and bleary with panic.

I fill my cart with an armful of random cans and shove past the twins, but they follow me into the deli.

"It's not fair to leave them alone out there," they say, and talk about digging up what's in the field.

I order a pound of ground chuck and pretend not to hear them, but my chest burns with hatred, not just for monsters, but for those who protect monsters, who proffer them all the power they need. Because monsters can't exist without us, without our denial and our forgiveness.

But I don't soften, and I don't forgive. Day after day I sit across the table from Cecilia, watching her belly swell, holding her hand, protecting her the best I can.

And I try not to scream.

***

It was September, a month before my thirteenth birthday, when the monster turned away from Cecilia and lapped at my ear instead. We never knew why. We didn't know if the monster knew why either.

"Don't worry." I tugged my sister's hand in the dark after it had gone. "If it has me, it won't bother you so much. Maybe it'll be better this way."

"No," she said, and the edge in her voice chilled me. "This is worse, Annie. So much worse."

We no longer read bedtime stories. Now all she could talk about was how to distract the monster—to use herself as bait, to lead it out of town like she was a Pied Piper.

"It'll be okay," she said, her voice quivering over a bowl of stale corn-flakes. She was always a terrible liar.

Maribelle was the one who suggested the field near the old factory.

"That's where everyone goes," she said with a languid wave of one hand. Then she sighed and went back to sunning herself on her over-grown front lawn, as though she gave directions for dispelling monsters every day and it was all so terribly pedestrian.

We believed her, of course. Maribelle knew about the world. She'd seen things, done things—"Too many things," Mama always said—and when personal experience failed her, she'd *heard* about things. And sometimes that was enough. Having an answer, even the wrong one, was comforting in those days.

"Go at sunset and leave it there," she said.

I raised one eyebrow. "Why?"

She shielded her eyes from the sun and frowned at me. "I don't make the rules, pipsqueak," she said. "Just bury it deep. Deep as you can."

"How do we get it into the ground?" Cecilia asked, fidgeting barefoot on the sidewalk.

Maribelle scoffed. "You'll figure it out."

In the late afternoon, I retrieved a shovel from the shed, and Cecilia and I dressed in ratty clothes. Except for our Sunday gowns, most of our clothes were in tatters, which made it easy to choose what to wear, what outfits we would ruin.

The factory was a ten-minute walk from our neighborhood, at once too close and too far away. Ten minutes to leave home. Ten minutes to find where all the monsters had gone.

There was a whole graveyard of them, more mounds than there were kids in this town. The plots were marked off with clumsy symbols—a mishmash of flat stones gathered up from the river and graying limbs broken off once-beloved dolls. I didn't know if these were commemora-tives like gravestones or if they were warnings, tiny portends cautioning others to stay away, to not dig here. Monsters lived in this earth.

We weren't alone. Along one edge of the field, Bobby Miller hunched over a grave, perhaps paying his respects or only checking to make sure what was there had stayed buried. He kicked a stone and wept under his breath.

"I never knew he was afraid of anything," I whispered.

Cecilia sniffled in the gathering cold of the evening. "Everyone's afraid of something, Annie."

We waited to the side and pretended not to see him. When he was done, he slouched past us, his head down.

"Good luck," he said and disappeared into the dusk.

We picked a spot in the middle that bore no marker. The earth was soft, and Cecilia moved a shovelful without strain. But the silver blade hit something small and gray. We squinted in the waning light. A creature writhed beneath the soil.

I heaved out a wheeze, but Cecilia shook her head.

"It won't hurt us," she said.

I inched backwards, the soles of my worn-out Keds making squeak-squawk noises on a slick of dead weeds. "How do you know?"

She shrugged, and a shiver like a death throe ran straight through her. "It doesn't belong to us. Maribelle says other people's monsters rarely turn against you."

Rarely. Not never. This was hardly comforting.

I said nothing as Cecilia heaved the restless dirt back into the grave. When she was done, she patted it in place with both hands, as though she were comforting the earth. Or comforting the monster.

I tipped my head back to the sky. The light was leaving us. Our nightmare was on its way.

Cecilia led me to the far corner of the field. "How's this spot?" she asked, and I nodded.

With a steady hand, my sister plunged the shovel into the earth and started to dig.

***

In the checkout line, the Rigsby twins invite Cecilia and me over to their house that night.

"To discuss our *problem*," they say, as if everyone is overreacting but them.

I agree, only because I want to convince them not to dig up our past. It's coming back on its own. It doesn't need any help.

We're a half hour late—Cecilia is kneeled over the toilet most of the evening—and the Rigsby twins scowl at us for our tardiness as they usher us into the living room. Thanks to that Sunday preacher, they found Jesus, though judging from the crowded walls and curio cabinets, they didn't find him just once. They've unearthed their Savior in every thrift store and yard sale, along with a dizzying array of cats. I count seventeen, a yowling clowder of tabbies, calicos, and Manx with their stubby little tales.

Slung over a winged-back chair, Maribelle is already here. It's the first time I've seen her in ten years. She has a few sprouts of gray hair, but otherwise, she's the same old Maribelle, lounging in the corner with her red lipstick and her ennui.

"Hey, pipsqueak," she says to me, and smiles.

Bobby joins us last, still stinking of hamburger grease from the diner. On the couch, he sits next to Cecilia, careful never to look at her swollen belly, as though regret lives there.

I stand alone against the wall as we decide what to do.

"This is what's meant to be," the Rigsby twins say. "If they want to come back to us, we should accept that."

But Bobby shakes his head. "My cousin has a construction company," he says, his words careful, as though he's practiced this speech a hundred times. "We could dump a truckload of fill on that field."

Maribelle tosses her hair out of her eyes. "I don't know if that would be enough."

"Ten truckloads then," he says. "We could bury them as deep as we always wanted to."

Cecilia crosses her arms over her belly. "I don't think it matters what we do," she says. "They'll still find us."

This goes on for hours, the back and forth, the this-not-that. My hands tighten into fists, and I bite down to keep from shrieking. We can argue or plead or try to reason, but there's no answer that'll satisfy. Not why the monsters chose us or why they're coming back or what we should do.

We were always so afraid of being devoured whole, of the monsters biting deep and not letting go. Instead, they devoured us slowly, one aching piece at a time.

Never again.

Before Cecilia and I leave, Maribelle pulls me aside.

"I was wrong back then," she says. "Burying them didn't help. It only incubated them. Kept them close."

"And if you could do it all over?" I stare at her. "What then?"

"Run," she says. "I'd run and never look back and hope they didn't catch me."

I smile and say goodbye, but I already know she's wrong. Monsters have all the time in the world. That's what makes them so dangerous.

And besides, you can't run forever.

***

The monster found us in the field at dusk. It came like it always did, discovering us wherever we were.

Cecilia kneeled in the dirt, in the grave that she'd hollowed out for the monster. It went for her again, like a goodbye, gliding up her thighs and suckling at her throat.

"One last time to placate it," she whispered.

When it had finished, the monster slid down her body, its belly distended and eyes glazed in the dirt. It was pliable now, and we were ready. Her gaze set skyward, Cecilia crawled from the grave, and I shoveled earth over the creature. It writhed and mewled as the dirt filled its lungs, but it didn't lunge at us or lap at our flesh with its long, thin tongue. Instead, it fell back into the soil. As I heaved the last mound of earth over its hideous face, it flashed us what looked like a smile, as though this were all part of the plan.

Like it had done this before.

We left no stone or trinket to mark the resting place of our monster. We didn't have to. Our feet could have found that place on a moonless night.

In the dark, Cecilia and I shambled home, our shoes caked thick with bitter earth and shame.

That should have been the end of it. The happily-ever-after. Our monster was buried, wasn't it? We'd won, right?

The next morning, Cecilia slept in, her knees tucked tight into her chest, and I was sipping the last of the neon green juice at the table when Mama stumbled in.

"Who tracked dirt into my kitchen?" Her eyes stained red in the corners, she glared at me and pointed to the floor, like I didn't know which mess she meant.

Then with the gray earth at her feet, her face twisted for a moment, as though remembering something.

"You've been in that field outside of town, haven't you?" Her voice was garbled and strange like someone speaking through tin cans tethered together with limp string.

I gripped my juice glass tighter, my words globs of glue in my throat. When I said nothing, Mama grunted and leaned into the refrigerator for the last slice of leftover pizza. I didn't move. I didn't breathe. How could she recognize what came from that field?

Unless she knew. Unless she'd always known. Maybe those stone markers were older than we thought. Maybe they all left something behind in that ground, even that useless preacher lecturing us on forgiveness, as though he had any right.

I moved toward Mama, grasping at her arm like an infant.

"You too?" I asked.

But she yanked away and pretended not to understand.

"You're not the only one with pain, Annie," was all she would say.

I never told Cecilia. I might have been wrong anyhow. I hoped I was wrong.

But that didn't stop Cecilia and me from talking about that field, and what we'd left there.

"What if it digs its way out?"

"What if it comes back for us?"

"Won't it hate us even more for what we've done to it?"

These questions squeezed the air out of our lungs and roped barbed wire around our hearts. In the days before we condemned the monster to its grave, at least we'd memorized its patterns. We knew when it would come and what it would do. Now we could be sure of nothing.

If it would stay buried.

If we'd done the right thing.

If we were even the same girls after everything we'd seen and done and felt.

If we were anyone at all.

***

It's past midnight when Cecilia and I return home from the Rigsby twins', the stench of old cat litter and zealotry clinging to our clothes like a disease.

The rec room is dark, and neither one of us turns on the light, half-afraid of what could be waiting for us in the gloom.

My fingers fumbling, I strike my lighter, and we sigh. The room is empty.

"It'll be here soon, though," Cecilia says.

"No," I say. "It won't."

I take her hand and lead her upstairs where I tuck her into bed and kiss her forehead. Beneath the comforter, the baby kicks.

"Good night," I say, and close the door behind me.

Out back in the shed, I find the old rusted-out shovel, and with my lighter in my pocket, I take the long walk out of town.

I can't heal my sister's scars. I can't wipe them away like tears and pretend they didn't happen. Not even time can do that. But I can do something else.

I can stop hiding. We can all stop hiding.

The field waits for me. Nothing's buried deep here. We were so young, so small, our arms soft and weak. We couldn't delve deep enough to bury these things in the hopeless dark where they belong.

But now I don't want them buried. I want them gone. All of them gone, enough nightmares to last a thousand lifetimes.

In the icy air, the shovel struggling against the frozen earth, I dig up the plots, both marked and unmarked, a hundred or more tiny sepulchers. Cecilia's words from that long-ago night echo in my head.

Other people's monsters rarely turn against you.

Rarely. Not never.

But these things aren't as we left them. Like our parents, the monsters are old now, their bodies shriveled and weak, mouths expanding and contracting like a dying snapper beached on a shore. They're burrowing their way out, only because they need the cycle to continue. Without our children, they're weak and restless and wanting.

But I won't let it continue. Not this time.

In the corner of the field, I save the worst for last. The shovel moves the heavy earth, and I find it there, waiting for me.

With my breath knotted in my chest, I pluck it from its grave, and I cradle our monster. It's smaller now, so small and strange and nothing.

There's no violence in my hand. I won't become a monster, too. I won't do to them what they did to us.

But I won't close my eyes and run either.

This is my choice, even if it's my final one. These things can turn me to cinders if they'd like, but I won't fear them, not anymore.

My fingers quake, and fury burns inside me, brighter than the torches of a pitchfork mob. And it's enough. All around, the earth rumbles with a choir of restless, cowering beasts. Now they fear me, what I've become, the strength I hold inside me. Our monster gazes at me, its eyes gray and empty. It mewls once before folding up in my palm, its body curling into itself, useless and thin as a paper fortune-telling fish.

When we were young, we learned there was power in forgiveness. But there's power in grudges too, in rage that never abates, that never wanes like the moon. Rage that warms you from the inside out and destroys all the bad in this world—or at least all the bad that lives in this earth beneath our feet.

But I'm not done, not yet. One by one, I reach into the open graves and lift out the monsters. I hold them close, a last embrace that stills their hearts. Their chests no longer rising and falling like the tides, they're tranquil and right and resting at last. This wasn't just a gift for us, after all. It was a gift to the monsters too.

When I'm done, there's nothing left to burn.

I strike my lighter and burn it anyway. I burn the ash and the poisoned earth that incubated these nightmares. I burn the past, and I revel in it too. With childish whoops to the sky, I revel in the good and the clean and the parts of us that were never defined by these things that did everything they could to destroy us. They lost. Of course, they did. That's one thing the old bedtime stories got right: the monsters always lose.

When the last flames wink out, I turn toward the dawn, leaving behind the stones and scorched toys as reminders of who we were. Sometimes, remembering isn't so terrible. Sometimes, there's strength in it, in not forgetting, in not forgiving.

In the spring, when the ground thaws and the sun shines lemon-yellow in the sky, the grass will return, green and gleaming. I'll return too. I'll tow barrows of fresh earth and sprinkle pressed packets of wildflowers across the field.

And when she's ready, I'll bring Cecilia. I'll bring her children and maybe someday mine as well. We'll bring all the children here, and we'll tell them about the monsters, about the things that suckled at our skin and siphoned the joy from our hearts. Our children will listen, patient and wide-eyed, but they won't believe a word of it. As though it's a most delightful yarn, they'll just laugh.

We'll laugh too.

ABOUT GWENDOLYN KISTE

GWENDOLYN KISTE is a speculative fiction author based in Pennsylvania. Her work has appeared in *Nightmare Magazine, Shimmer, Interzone, LampLight, Flash Fiction Online*, and *Three-Lobed Burning Eye;* as well as Flame Tree Publishing's *Chilling Horror Short Stories* anthology, among others. Her debut collection, *And Her Smile Will Untether the Universe*, is available now from JournalStone.

A native of Ohio, she currently resides on an abandoned horse farm outside of Pittsburgh with her husband, two cats, and not nearly enough ghosts. You can also find her online on Facebook (www.facebook.com/gwendolynkiste) and Twitter (twitter.com/GwendolynKiste).

LYING IN THE SUN ON A FAIRY TALE DAY

BRACKEN MACLEOD

ONCE UPON A TIME, the sun, high in the afternoon sky, shone down on a mountainside waking from a long, cold slumber. The snow had melted and new grass, straining to grow long, reached up for the shafts of light shining through the evergreens above. Early wildflowers bloomed in a paint stroke of color that shivered in the crisp breeze, and ferns unfurled their fiddleheads like tiny fingers opening to catch the light that had traveled through space to give its nourishment just to them. Green had returned after a long season under frozen white, and the woods were stirring to a bright, renewed cycle of burgeoning life. It was an afternoon so striking, he could have described it as a fairy tale day. If he weren't lying broken in the runoff gap in the middle of a glacier rock.

The sun was not as kind to him as it was to the green things. Though it was warm, he shivered with shock under it. His skin was hot to the touch and red from a blistering sunburn. Those blisters burst and wept tears that congealed and stuck in the hair on his arms and cheeks. His teeth chattered as another breeze swept down the mountain, carrying the scents of pine and pasqueflower. If blue had a scent, he'd once thought, it was the aroma of pasqueflowers. Under that, was the coppery smell of the blood stiffening his sock.

The sight of his shinbone sticking out through his skin seemed unreal, not only because he couldn't feel his left leg below the knee, but also because it was such an alien view of himself. His forearm on the same side was unmistakably broken as well, but that bone remained unseen. Until that morning, what was within his own body had never confronted him openly. Those internal parts had a hidden life of invisibility, and received only occasional conscious acknowledgement. He thought of his stomach when it growled, and his heart when it beat hard. But he never considered his pancreas or bile duct at all. And he only thought of his bones when they broke, which was a rare thing. Even then, he'd never seen one of them—not with an X-ray, *actually seen* one. They say there's a first time for everything, but really, you hope not. Everyone honestly hopes there's no first time for being pulled out to sea by the undertow, or waking up in a house on fire, or…taking a bad spill down a slick glacial rock slope while hiking up before breakfast to watch the sunrise. Everyone hopes that their lives will continue apace without those firsts, because they are sometimes also lasts.

He called out for help, coughing as he tried to raise his voice, but he'd come to the woods alone. There was no one to hear. It was chilly at night still, and his girlfriend didn't like cold weather camping. His oldest outdoors buddy moved to Vail the year before to be a rich people's bartender, and no one else he knew was willing to pack in as far off the trails as he was. But, spring was his favorite season and he loved to sleep outdoors when the night air was crisp and the days weren't buggy and hot. So, he packed his gear and set out for a long weekend by himself. He told Shonna that he was going, but not *where*, specifically. She didn't ask for details, not because she didn't care, but because everyone knew this was a thing he did, and they all trusted that he would be fine, including her. He went deep into the woods by himself from time to time to recover from what he called "city poisoning". He had wilderness experience and didn't take stupid chances, so everyone assumed they'd see him on Tuesday or Wednesday, because they always had before. But it was only Saturday, and he didn't know how he'd make it back to the car to get help. It was parked at the trailhead, miles away, over a rough country hike. And that goddamned bone sticking out of his leg was telling him that even if he dragged his ass out of the rut, he wasn't getting any farther than where he'd made camp at the bottom of the slope. Not without help. And the only way to summon help was to use the cellphone he'd powered down and stuck in the jockey box of the fucking car.

With his good hand, he unclipped his daypack and tried to pull it out from under the small of his back. He could use the 550 Paracord and pocket knife inside to make a tourniquet for his leg. His signal mirror, whistle, matches, solar blanket, and sunscreen were all in there too. Tugging at it was painful and he couldn't arch his back enough to slide it out. His head ached and vision swam, and he gave up trying for a moment. More important to stay awake.

The sun shone in his eyes, so he closed them.

Just for a minute. It's so bright.

When he awoke, the sun had tracked more than a little farther along in the sky. He realized that he'd probably hit his head in the fall and was concussed. He tried to say something aloud, break the silence and provide a comfort to himself where no other was coming, but his throat was dry and it hurt to speak. He longed for a drink of water, but didn't know where his bottle had gone. He figured it must've fallen out of the side pouch of the pack when he slipped and bounced off somewhere he couldn't see, even though it was fluorescent green plastic. It was lost. Like him.

He was sunburnt and growing ever more dehydrated. He knew he'd die of thirst faster than starvation would take him. The reality of it was, though, that neither starvation nor thirst were his most pressing concerns. Exposure would kill him before anything else could even get started. Anything else except blood loss. Or shock. Exposure, he decided, was most likely.

He could spend what was left of his life contemplating all the ways to die.

The breeze blew again, raising prickly gooseflesh on his body. He'd set out from camp wearing a thick flannel shirt, but ended up tying it around his waist halfway up the climb. It too was gone. Lost in the fall. He was left wearing a thin, sweat wicking tee-shirt and shorts, because he *always* wore shorts. It was a joke among his friends. He could be stomping through snow in a parka and boots, but he'd still be wearing pants that stopped above the knee. "I just run hot," he'd tell them. Shonna would snuggle up into his shoulder and smile, nodding. "Better than an electric blanket," she'd agree. That was at home in bed. Not so much here. Here, he was freezing.

He tried to push himself up out of the cleft worn in the rock by tens of thousands of years of trickling water wearing it away, but the pain of moving his broken arm lanced up into his shoulder and he pulled the limb in close to his body to protect it, slumping back down in the crevice. He cried, because everything was suddenly so in focus.

No amount of white pebbles or breadcrumbs would get him home.

He was going to die.

Just like firsts, no one ever thinks about lasts. Unless they're already sick or have a plan to kill themselves, no one wakes up thinking today will be the end of their story.

Once, a friend had shown him a video of some guy walking along the edge of a high building. The guy's foot slipped and he dropped straight down onto the ledge. He expected the man to catch on and the people with him to pull him back up and have a laugh at close calls and luck, but the ledge was narrow and offered nothing to grab on to. The guy's backpack pulled him over into open space right away, where he disappeared into the distance below. His friend showed him that ten-second video loop on his cellphone and, laughing, said, "Natural selection." But it wasn't funny. That person got up in the morning and put on his clothes and ate breakfast and met his friends for their adventure at the top of wherever that was, and not once did he likely imagine that there were only hours left in his life, because of one miscalculated step he had yet to take. That was the furthest distance between any person on Earth and dying. One step. A single second in time. The interval that launched your car through the guardrail, your skis toward the tree line, your foot off the edge of the building, or down a steep rock slope on a lovely spring morning, the sound of your breaking bones startling the birds.

"Up there! What's that up there?"

He raised his head at the sound of footsteps scrambling up the hillside toward him. It was hard to focus through his tears and disorientation, but he recognized Shonna's voice as she cried, "It's him!" He tried to sit up, but couldn't find the leverage, so he held his good arm up in the air for as long as he could. Which wasn't long at all, though it was long enough. Shonna settled onto her knees beside him, leaning close. "Shit! What happened?"

He coughed and tried to tell her that he slipped, but couldn't manage to find his voice. The dreamy shape of someone else, backlit by the bright blue of the late day moved behind her, but he couldn't make them out. "I've been trying to call you," she said. "You have to come home. We have to get you home right now."

"I'm…st-stuck," he managed. The figure behind her stepped around to the other side of him and he felt a tug at his wounded leg. The pain was unbearable and the world swam and his vision blurred again.

"Stay with me," Shonna said. "Don't pass out."

"Stop…pulling. It…hurts."

Shonna snapped at the other person, but he couldn't make out what she said. His head was fuzzy. But the one clear thought that resolved in the fog of it was, he wasn't going to die after all. Shonna and…whoever it was with her, were there to get him off the fucking mountain. He pictured himself hobbling between them, an arm over her shoulders, while the other one held him at the waist. He knew he couldn't make the whole hike like that, but they just had to get to camp, and then he could tell them how to make a travois out of long sticks and his tent fabric. He knew how to get wounded people out of the woods. He could talk them through it. But first, he needed water.

He tried to ask Shonna to find his bottle. She didn't move. He tried to say it again. "Water…bottle."

She cocked her head and just looked at him. "Come on. Get up. We have to go, *now*," she whispered. He didn't know why she was whispering. And then she pulled at his broken arm.

He screamed. She let go and backed away. Daylight dimmed, but it felt like it was him that had moved behind a cloud, not the sun. He clutched his wounded arm and tried to keep from passing out. But willpower never kept anyone from losing too much blood. No amount of intention was sufficient to overcome shock. Shonna leaned forward hesitantly. He wanted her to come close. He wanted—no, needed—her help. But, she was hurting him. He felt like a cornered animal. It was clear what had to be done to save his life. The problem was letting her do that. He wasn't getting out of this fissure without some measure of discomfort. In fact, *considerable pain* was a guarantee. He couldn't put it off forever.

He tried to sit up again, but his arm wouldn't cooperate, and the effort made him see stars in the daylight. He tried to tell Shonna to push him up from behind. Help him get into a seated position, so he could use his good arm and leg to stand. But he choked again. She leaned in and sniffed at him. He felt her breath on his face. Hot and moist. It was disorienting and it made him afraid.

Then, the other figure pulled at his leg again and a fresh jolt of pain brought him back into his body. He craned his neck around to tell them to quit pulling at his leg. "Fu…cking stop…it," he choked.

Another tug. He kicked weakly at the person with his good leg, and they let go.

He looked down his body at Shonna's companion. Who'd she brought with her anyway? Who would make the two-hour drive and then another hour-long hike to come get him, all on a hunch that he'd be at this spot and not some other? Not Dave. He worked the Co-Op on weekends. It had to be Kory. *She* would. Kory was kind and friendly, though not at all outdoorsy. She teased them about going to pretend they were homeless in the woods. But her heart was in the right place and Shonna could convince her to come along if something was really wrong. She'd make the drive, but she definitely wouldn't know what to do with a wounded person. He could tell her, if they'd give him a drink.

He blinked the sun out of his eyes, trying to force himself to see straight. The person crouched at his feet came into focus. Not Kory.

Dad?

He coughed again. "How'd…how'd you find…me?"

His father looked up with furrowed brow and the judgmental expression he wore more often than not when looking at his son. "Find you? You're not found, boy. What makes you say that?" His father licked at his lips.

"You're not…"

His father opened his jacket, showing his red heart hanging in the black cavity the chainsaw had ripped open when it kicked back into his chest decades ago. The heart snarled at him with long, yellow teeth. He tried to kick at it. The woodsman with the hungry heart shimmered and faded and whatever it was that had taken its first tentative tugs at him backed away, along with the ghost of his father, into the shade of the trees.

He turned back in the direction where Shonna was kneeling and saw only the rocks beside him and the low sun setting over the horizon. She'd retreated back to the shadows to wait as well.

Reality dawned on him. No one was coming to his rescue, because no one missed him, and they wouldn't until he was long dead, and maybe they wouldn't even find him until next spring when he'd be a collection of bones and some tattered cloth. Less than a memory, like the fading light of the sun on the spring mountainside. He stared at the line of jagged mountains along the horizon, lit the length of it all in a fire burst of yellow turned to red and then purple until the sky turned black and the wide band of the Milky Way arm replaced the single star of day with cool, diamond light.

And the dark things breathing in the woods waited for him to sleep.

He wished Shonna, or whatever she really was, would come back. He didn't want to die. But if he had to, he didn't want to die *alone*. Even if his only company was a dream of a wild girl who couldn't help but bite at him. He could die with a wolf by his side. As long as it breathed its warm breath on him so he knew he didn't have to do this all by himself. He wanted the company just so he didn't feel so lonely.

When he'd woken up that morning he'd never thought that this was the end of his story. But it was. Like a fairy tale written in reverse.

Once upon a time, there was a boy who had everything he ever wanted, but he left it all to go into the woods alone one beautiful day. There, he met a girl who was a wolf. And he loved her. He loved her hot breath on his neck and her sharp kisses that made new stars shine in his eyes. And there he lived with her, ever after, until the end of his life.

ABOUT BRACKEN MACLEOD

BRACKEN MACLEOD is the author of the novels, *Mountain Home*, *Stranded*, and *Come to Dust*. His short fiction has appeared in several magazines and anthologies including *LampLight*, *ThugLit*, and *Splatterpunk* and has been collected in *13 Views of the Suicide Woods* by ChiZine Publications. He lives outside of Boston with his wife and son, where he is at work on his next novel.

COPYRIGHT DECLARATIONS

MORE DARK FICTION FROM
GREY MATTER PRESS

"Grey Matter Press has managed to establish itself as one of the premiere purveyors of horror fiction currently in existence."

- FANGORIA Magazine

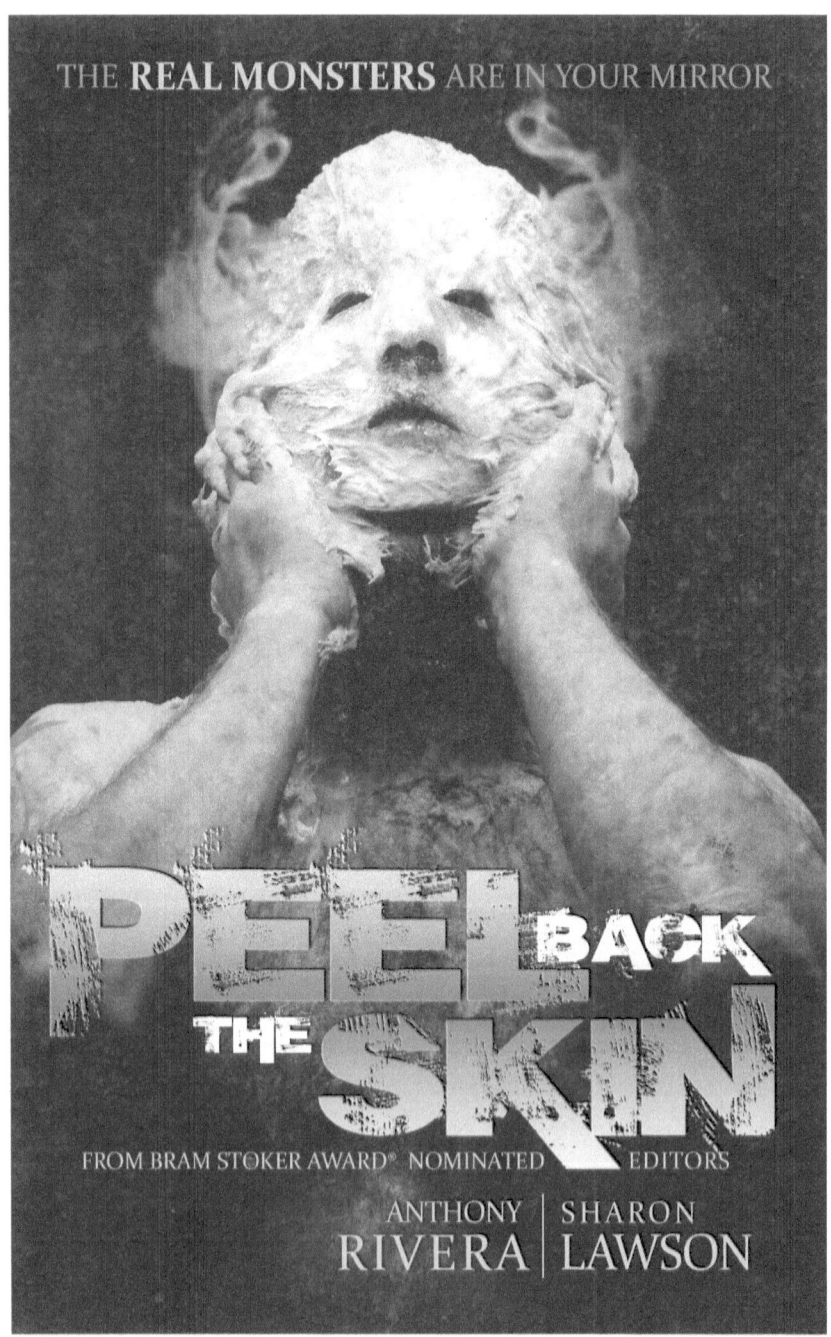

PEEL BACK THE SKIN
THE ANTHOLOGY OF HORROR

#1 Bestselling Amazon Horror Anthology

They are among us.

They live down the street. In the apartment next door. And even in our own homes.

They're the real monsters. And they stare back at us from our bathroom mirrors.

Peel Back the Skin is a powerhouse new anthology of terror that strips away the mask from the real monsters of our time – mankind.

Featuring all-new fiction from a star-studded cast of award-winning authors from the horror, dark fantasy, speculative, transgressive, extreme horror and thriller genres, *Peel Back the Skin* is the next game-changing release from Bram Stoker Award-nominated editors Anthony Rivera and Sharon Lawson.

FEATURING:

Jonathan Maberry	James Lowder
Ray Garton	Lucy Taylor
Tim Lebbon	Joe McKinney
Ed Kurtz	Erik Williams
William Meikle	Charles Austin Muir
Yvonne Navarro	John McCallum Swain
Durand Sheng Welsh	Nancy A. Collins

Graham Masterton

GREY MATTER
PRESS

greymatterpress.com

DREAD

a head full of bad dreams

JONATHAN MABERRY
BRACKEN MACLEOD
WILLIAM MEIKLE
JOHN C. FOSTER
JOHN F.D. TAFF
MICHAEL LAIMO
TIM WAGGONER
RAY GARTON
JG FAHERTY
JOHN EVERSON
TRENT ZELAZNY
AND MANY MORE

from editors
ANTHONY RIVERA
SHARON LAWSON

THE BEST OF GREY MATTER PRESS VOLUME ONE

DREAD
A HEAD FULL OF BAD DREAMS

There are some nightmares from which you can never wake.

Dread: A Head Full of Bad Dreams is a terrifying volume of the darkest hallucinatory revelations from the minds of some of the most accomplished award-winning authors of our time. Travel dark passageways and experience the alarming visions of twenty masters from the horror, fantasy, science fiction, thriller, transgressive and speculative fiction genres as they bare their souls and fill your head with a lifetime of bad dreams.

Dread is the first-ever reader curated volume of horror from Grey Matter Press. The twenty short stories in this book were chosen solely by fans of dark fiction. *Dread* includes a special Introduction from editor Anthony Rivera:

"Readers who embrace darkness are souls of conscience with hearts of passion and voices that deserve to be heard. It's from this group of passionate voices that the nightmares in *Dread: A Head Full of Bad Dreams* were born.

"Turning over the reins of editorial curation for this volume to the readers who matter most may well have been the best decision I've ever made. This book that you've created embodies your passion for dark fiction and serves as your own head of bad dreams come to life." - **Bram Stoker Award-nominated editor Anthony Rivera**

FEATURING:

Ray Garton	Tim Waggoner	Jonathan Maberry	Jane Brooks
John F.D. Taff	Chad McKee	JG Faherty	Peter Whitley
William Meikle	T. Fox Dunham	John Everson	J. Daniel Stone
Rose Blackthorn	Edward Morris	Michael Laimo	Jonathan Balog
Bracken MacLeod	Trent Zelazny	John C. Foster	Martin Rose

GREY MATTER
P R E S S

greymatterpress.com

BRAM STOKER AWARD-NOMINATED

JOHN F.D. TAFF

MODERN HORROR'S KING OF PAIN

"The dazzling array of themes...
has something for everyone."
— GABINO IGLESIAS

LITTLE
DEATHS

THE DEFINITIVE COLLECTION

INTRODUCTION BY JOSH MALERMAN

AUTHOR OF BIRD BOX AND MAD BLACK WHEEL

LITTLE DEATHS
BY JOHN F.D. TAFF

#1 Bestselling Amazon Horror Collection

Step into new rooms of absolute terror.

Five years ago, Bram Stoker Award-nominated author John F.D. Taff welcomed you into the darkest recesses of his mind. Today, he returns to where it all began…opening doors to new rooms of abject horror. Disturbing rooms. Darker rooms.

Rooms where a farmer awakens to find a gigantic tentacle writhing in his fields. Where the desiccated mummy of a young girl wants nothing more than something warm to drink. Where a memorabilia collector resurrects his dead girlfriend with the prop neck bolts from the 1931 movie Frankenstein. And where the sweetest candy of all is a dead man's flesh.

Little Deaths: The Definitive Collection features 24 stories, five of them new to this edition, plus expanded notes for each tale, a new afterword by the author and a new foreword by Josh Malerman, author of *Bird Box* and *Black Mad Wheel.*

"*Little Deaths* is dark magic! Taff's incredible talent washes over you and you know you're in masterful hands and have a book that can reach that spot: the reason we all love reading to begin with." — **Josh Malerman, author of *Bird Box* and *Unbury Carol***

GREY MATTER
P R E S S

greymatterpress.com

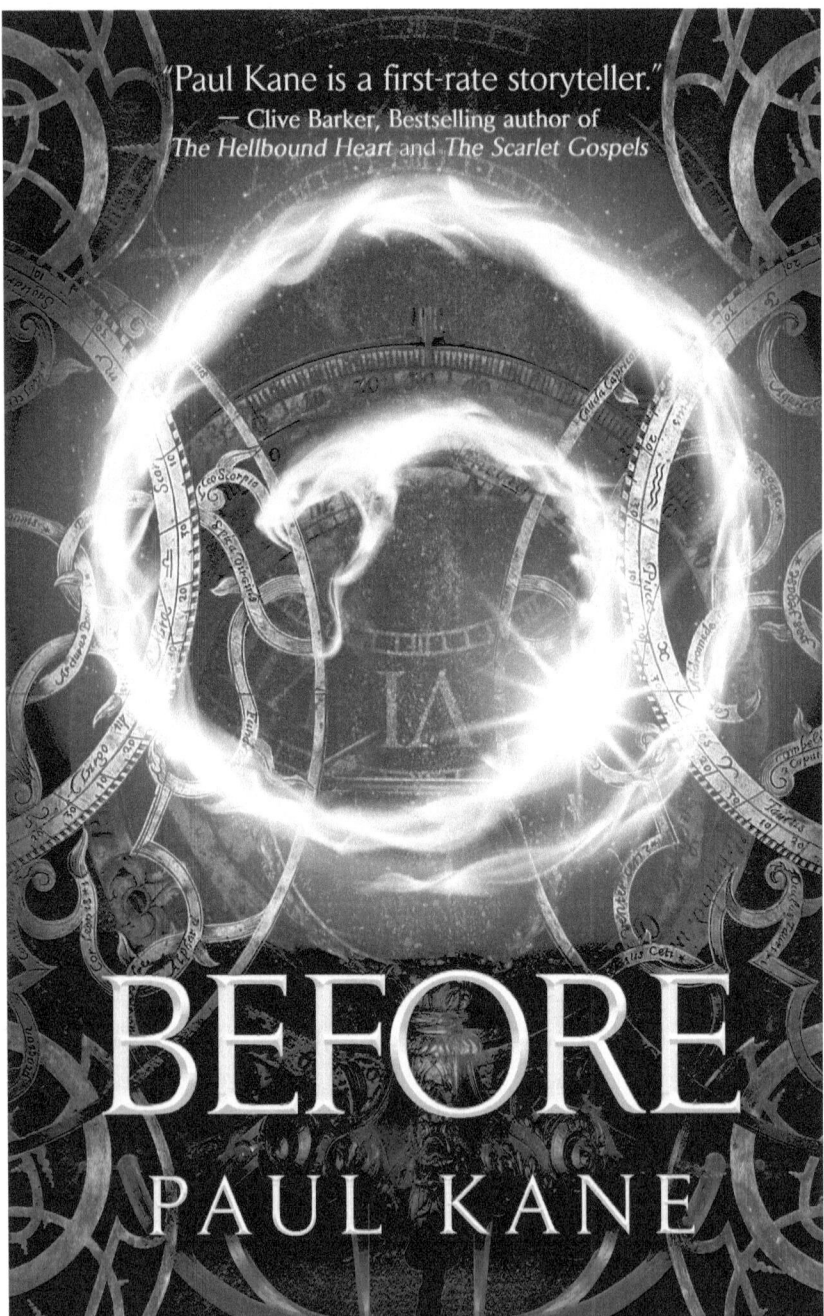

"Paul Kane is a first-rate storyteller."
— Clive Barker, Bestselling author of
The Hellbound Heart and *The Scarlet Gospels*

BEFORE

PAUL KANE

BEFORE
BY PAUL KANE

#1 Bestselling Amazon Dark Fantasy Novel

In 1970s Germany, a mental patient at the end of his life suddenly speaks for the first time in years. A year later in Vietnam, a mission to rescue a group of American POWs becomes a military disaster.

In present day England, the birthday of college lecturer Alex Webber sends his life spiralling out of control as a series of disturbing hallucinations lead him to the office of Dr. Ellen Hayward. And things will never be the same again for either of them. Hunted by an immortal being known only as The Infinity, their capture could mean the end of humanity itself…

Part horror story, part thrilling road adventure, part historical drama, Kane's *Before* is as wide in scope as it is in imagination as it tackles the greatest questions haunting mankind—Who are we? Why are we here? And where are we going?

The author and editor of more than sixty books, Kane's work includes *Sherlock Holmes and the Servants of Hell, Lunar, The Rainbow Man*, the Arrowhead trilogy (later released as the *Hooded Man* omnibus), *The Butterfly Man and Other Stories, Hellbound Hearts, The Mammoth Book of Body Horror, The Hellraiser Films and Their Legacy* and more.

"Paul Kane is a first-rate storyteller, never failing to marry his insights into the world and its anguish with the pleasures of phrases eloquently turned." — Clive Barker, author of *The Hellbound Heart* and *The Scarlet Gospels*

"I'm impressed by the range of Paul Kane's imagination. It seems there is no risk, no high-stakes gamble, he fears to take… Kane's foot never gets even close to the brake pedal." — Peter Straub, author of *Ghost Story*

GREY MATTER
P R E S S

greymatterpress.com

COMING SOON
FROM GREY MATTER PRESS

Little Black Spots — John F.D. Taff

The Madness of Crowds: The Ladies Bristol Occult Adventures #2 — Rhoads Brazos

Suspended in Dusk II: Anthology of Horror — ed. Simon Dewar

The Isle — John C. Foster

AVAILABLE NOW
FROM GREY MATTER PRESS

Before — Paul Kane

The Bell Witch — John F.D. Taff

The Devil's Trill: The Ladies Bristol Occult Adventures #1 — Rhoads Brazos

Dark Visions I — eds. Anthony Rivera & Sharon Lawson

Dark Visions II — eds. Anthony Rivera & Sharon Lawson

Death's Realm — eds. Anthony Rivera & Sharon Lawson

Dread — eds. Anthony Rivera & Sharon Lawson

The End in All Beginnings — John F.D. Taff

Equilibrium Overturned — eds. Anthony Rivera & Sharon Lawson

I Can Taste the Blood — eds. John F.D. Taff & Anthony Rivera

Kill-Off — John F.D. Taff

Little Deaths: 5th Anniversary Edition — John F.D. Taff

Mister White: The Novel — John C. Foster

The Night Marchers and Other Strange Tales — Daniel Braum

Ominous Realities — eds. Anthony Rivera & Sharon Lawson

Peel Back the Skin — eds. Anthony Rivera & Sharon Lawson

Savage Beasts — eds. Anthony Rivera & Sharon Lawson

Secrets of the Weird — Chad Stroup

Seeing Double — Karen Runge

Splatterlands — eds. Anthony Rivera & Sharon Lawson